Mr

a MISTER STANDALONE

ROMANTIC

New York Times Bestselling Author

HUSS

Mr ROMANTIC

New York Times Bestselling Author

JA HUSS

DEDICATION

For everyone who ever got blamed for something they didn't do. It sucks.

CHAPTER ONE

IVY

The whole thing is like a dream, something surreal and inexplicable. A long dark car pulls up in front of the townhouse. A man in a black suit gets out, buttons his suit coat as he walks up towards my front patio where I am reading a book in the late afternoon sun, and stops, staring down at me from behind a decorative iron gate that has no security purpose whatsoever.

"Miss Ivy Rockwell?" the man asks, tilting his head down at me, looking past the sunglasses.

"That's me," I say, nervously putting my book down and getting to my feet.

The stranger reaches into his suit pocket and pulls out a silver envelope. "I have an invitation for you and I'm required to wait until you read it before leaving."

My brow furrows. "What kind of invitation? From whom?"

"I'm afraid you'll have to open it up to get that information, Miss Rockwell." He thrusts the silver envelope towards me.

I'm not sure what to do other than take it, so I lean over the gate that separates us—it barely comes up to his waist—and take the envelope.

The paper is thick, the kind you use for weddings or fiftieth anniversary parties. And it's sealed with a sticker made to tear easily if anyone tries to open it. The card inside is not folded, more like a postcard. It's silver, like the envelope, and just as exquisite. The paper has fibers in it, like that handmade stuff you get from craft stores. And the lettering is embossed.

It says:

You have been selected to interview for a managerial position with Delaney Resorts in Borrego Springs, California. The time and arrangements will be contingent upon your acceptance. Please notify the delivery man of your decision.

"What?" I ask, looking up at the impassive delivery man. He does not look like any delivery man I've ever seen. He looks rich, and a lot like a man who is used to getting what he wants. I try to see his features behind the dark sunglasses, but can't come up with anything very identifiable. "What's this about?"

"A job interview, Miss Rockwell."

"Obviously," I say, but not meanly. "Delaney Resorts? I never applied for this job. I think I'd remember applying to a resort in California."

"I'm not able to comment on that, Miss Rockwell. I'm simply here to get an answer, and if you say yes, I'm to have you sign a non-disclosure agreement about the job and give you the transportation details."

I blink. *Non-disclosure* agreement? "What is Delaney Resorts? I mean"—I laugh a little—"I can't possibly be expected to pick up and go to California without a little more information. Especially when I'm being asked to sign a NDA."

"As I said, all the details will be provided once you accept and sign."

"I have to accept before I get any more details? And agree not to talk about it?"

"Yes, Miss Rockwell."

"I don't know," I say, suspicion taking over. "It sounds fishy. Too good to be true."

"You can tell your family about the interview, just not disclose anything else."

"What if I get the details and change my mind?"

"There is a number to call should that happen," the stony man says. "So the private jet can be cancelled and you can be briefed on the legalities of the NDA."

"Private *jet*?" I have to shake my head for a moment.

"I'm afraid I can't comment further."

"Well," I say, turning away from him so he can't see how uncomfortable this is making me. What kind of invitation is this? I've never heard of such a thing. A phone call is a nice personal way to invite someone to interview. An email is typical. But sending a messenger with news of a private jet tucked inside expensive printed cards? That's weird. "Can I have a moment to look up Delaney Resorts before I comment?"

"Of course, Miss Rockwell."

I nod. "OK, one sec. Let me go inside and get my phone." My phone is in my pocket but I need a moment to compose myself. If this is a real job interview, then I need to take it seriously. I've applied to dozens of places since graduating last spring and had no bites at all. I need a job. Soon. But looking at the man in black and the limo he arrived in parked in front of the townhouse is making it hard to concentrate.

I enter the house and close the door, peeking out through the front window at the stranger. I wait for him to shift his stance or pull his phone out to relay the progress of his mission, but he simply stands there, hands in his pockets, staring at the door.

"OK, Ivy, get it together." I pull my phone out and do a quick search for Delaney Resorts. "Oh, hell." The

JA HUSS

information I'm looking for comes up immediately. And I suddenly understand who it is I'm dealing with.

"Nolan Delaney," I whisper. The infamous Mr. Romantic. No wonder he has all this hocus-pocus privacy stuff.

I stare at his picture longer than I should, but I can't help it. Nolan Delaney is the hottest guy I've ever seen. Of course, I've seen him before. His face was all over the TV when I was a teenager, but not in recent years. He was young back then. My age now. Looking like a college kid looks. But today, ten years later, he looks every bit the businessman he is.

It's real. This invitation might be unorthodox, but it's real. I'm sure if Mr. Delaney feels he needs this kind of privacy protection he has a good reason for it. He was, after all, accused and almost tried for serious crimes back in college. He must still be feeling the sting of those long, depressing years.

I open the door and say, "OK, I accept."

Delivery man in black says, "Perfect," as he once again reaches into his suit coat and produces another silver envelope, which he places on the brick post of my tiny gate. "The arrangements are in there. If you need to cancel there is a number to call. But first," he says, producing a more conventional white envelope, "I'll need you to sign this." He hands the white envelope to me and then finds a pen.

I open the envelope and look it over. It's one page, three paragraphs, and doesn't say anything weird. It all looks like legal speak for a simple NDA.

I sign, then reach out and take the silver envelope from the brick post, and before I can even say thank you, the man in black turns on his heel and walks back to the car. My mouth is hanging open from surprise as I watch the long car pull away from the curb and disappear down the street.

****

"Wait," my best friend, Nora, says later that evening. "A private jet? You got a top-secret invitation to interview for some random billionaire and he's flying you to California in a private jet?"

I have to pinch myself, because yes, that's all true.

"How?" Nora exclaims.

"Remember when I told you my dad wanted me to go to the Brown Alumni dinner with him last month?"

Nora nods, still dumbstruck.

"Well, that afternoon there was a job fair in the library, so I went just to get away from him for a few hours. And I left my résumé all over that room. Maybe he got it that way?"

"So you met him? This Nolan Delaney guy? You do know who he is, right?"

"No," I say. "But yes. I didn't meet him and I do know who he is." Everyone knows who Nolan Delaney is. One of the infamous Mister Browns from Brown University.

"Mr. Romantic," Nora says. "They call him Mr. Romantic. That cannot be good. Your father is going to flip out."

"I know. But there's no way I'm getting this job. I mean, this has to be some kind of mistake. We just graduated four months ago. No one is hiring me to run their new resort. But it's a free trip on a private jet to an exotic place. I should at least go, right?"

"Oh," Nora says, "you're going. There is no way you're not going. I've never even been on a private jet and we have loads of money. You need to take pictures. Of everything. Especially that delicious Mr. Romantic. How long will you be gone?"

"It says a weekend working interview. Is that normal?"

Nora squints her eyes as she considers this. "Hmmm. I'm not sure. What do I know about working interviews? I've only managed to get three meetings with no call-backs since graduation. And that's with all my father's influence. It does sound a little unconventional. But I guess it's a big job. He must want to make sure he hires the right person."

"Yeah. I just can't believe it. What if I do get it?" I have pictured it in my mind for the last six hours since the man appeared at my townhouse door with the hand-delivered invitation. It would be a huge break for me.

"Don't get your hopes up, Ivy," Nora cautions. "I know you're smart and talented and he'd be lucky to get you, but I bet there's going to be some exceptional people there."

"I know." I sigh. "I'm not really expecting to get the job. It's probably some kind of mistake." How could it not be? I have no experience and this is a managerial position.

"When do you leave?"

"Tomorrow. They are sending a car for me at six AM. I'll be back next week. Unless they have some kind of elimination process and send me home early."

"A *Survivor* job interview," Nora says, more to herself than me. "Weird. How many people do you think will be there?"

I shrug as I refill each of our wine glasses. "It didn't say. It didn't say anything. Technically I'm not supposed to be telling you so much. I signed a non-disclosure agreement when I said yes. I was told to only tell my family where I was going, not who it was with."

"Oh, my God. That is super mysterious."

"Right?" I ask back. "It's kind of... hot."

We both fall back into the couch cushions and laugh. "What do you know about hot, Ivy?" Nora snorts. "Still a virgin at twenty-two. I don't know what to do with you. Your father's influence runs way too deep."

"I know," I say, biting my lip. I had a guy all set up for V-day after graduation, but I chickened out at the last minute. "All that episcopal education growing up."

"Honey, we went to the same boarding school and it never stopped me."

That's all true. My father is the episcopal pastor, and dean, of the Bishop School for Girls in Bishop, Massachusetts. I grew up on that campus, in that chapel and with all the rules one might expect from being a pastor's daughter.

"You know what I should do..." I say, the wheels in my mind starting to turn with an idea.

"What?" Nora asks, impatient when I hesitate too long.

"I should lose my virginity this week."

Nora laughs so loud, it echoes off the cathedral ceiling. "With who? The *billionaire?* You want a guy like Mr. Romantic to be your first? Please. You need to work up to a player like him, Ivy. He would fuck you inside out!"

"Don't talk like that!" But I bite my lip just thinking about it. I admit I don't know much about sex, but I was in a sorority in college and I was the only virgin in that house. Those girls were wild, including Nora. "He'd be perfect, though, right? An older, more experienced man. He'd know just what to do."

"He'd hear the word virgin and run the other way, Ivy. Men like that aren't into the whole first-time thing. He wants a yes girl. *Get on your knees, Ivy*, he'd say. And he'd expect you to do it. You've never even given a man a blow job. No, that's a very bad idea. I don't like it. It won't be a good first time. Start small, Ivy. Like Richard. Why didn't you ever do it with Richard?"

Richard. Boring Richard. He was my significant other all through college. In fact, we just broke up three months ago. "I didn't love him. I was never going to marry him."

"So you're saving yourself for marriage all these years and now you're ready to give up your V-card to a playboy billionaire? No," Nora says, like she's putting her foot down. "Don't do it."

I can feel her judgment. She thinks my idea is ridiculous. And I wonder if she thinks that way because it's just stupid? Or if she thinks I don't have a chance in hell of getting the infamous Mr. Romantic to 'fuck me inside out'.

"It was just a silly fantasy," I say, trying my best to diffuse the situation. "You know I would never go through with something like that."

"I know." Nora laughs. "You're just not that kind of girl."

Her words echo through my head. *Not that kind of girl.* All my life I've been living with that label and most of the recent years I've been asking myself... why *can't* I be that kind of girl? My strict religious upbringing? Probably. But there's this fear inside me. A fear of taking risks. I've never been a risk-taker. I've always played it safe.

My childhood was spent sheltered on a rambling four-hundred-acre campus in New England. It consisted of school, my parents, and chapel. I didn't even get to live in the dorms with the other students until Nora talked my father into it in tenth grade. Those last three years of high school were some of the best of my life. And going away to Brown for college was exhilarating.

Having Richard as my boyfriend seemed so scandalous at the time. I didn't even tell my father until we'd been dating for over a year.

But now, Richard is just so... boring. And I'm tired of New England. I don't know anything about Borrego Springs, California, but getting that job would be the best thing to ever happen to me. Moving away would be the best thing to ever happen to me. And I love Nora to death, but she has been my only close friend for practically my whole life.

I feel like I'm missing out on things. Especially sex.

I've heard all her stories. And the stories of the other girls in the house at Brown. They made me watch porn with them on my twenty-first birthday and holy hell, I never masturbated so much in my life after I went to bed.

I have secretly been watching porn quite a bit since then. So I know what girls do. Maybe I'm no expert, but I've seen how they give blow jobs. I even took notes. Look him in the eyes—the men seem to like that a lot. Try to take him deep. I especially like how the men react to that. I love when they tip their heads back and moan. How they fist the girl's hair and urge her on. God, I'm getting all hot and bothered just thinking about it.

Nora is chatting about the stuff on TV now, drinking her wine. But I'm picturing Mr. Romantic as he dips his face down between my legs. What would that feel like?

I almost groan with longing.

I'm not going to admit it to Nora, and maybe it won't be Nolan Delaney, but I need to have sex with someone. I can't take it anymore. This is my week. And hey, if it does turn out to be Mr. Romantic, all the better.

Who am I kidding? I think to myself as I take a sip of wine to hide my smile. I want it to be him. I bet Nolan Delaney fucks like a porn star. I bet he could make me writhe and moan just like the men do to the girls in those videos.

Nora helps me pack as we finish our wine, but as soon as I have my suitcases lined up at the front door, I tell her goodnight.

I have a date with my vibrator and I want to picture Mr. Romantic's face as I make myself come.

CHAPTER TWO

IVY

The next morning I'm a bundle of nerves. Nora gets up to see me off, looking blurry-eyed and a little hungover in her pink nightie. I wish I had something like that to wear for Nolan when I have sex with him this week.

Mental note. Buy lingerie as soon as I get to California. I don't know how, but I need it. My first time is going to be perfect. Candles, flowers, and sexy underwear.

Additional mental note. Don't call him Nolan in person.

A door slams outside and I peek out the window at an older man walking up towards our townhouse. He came in a shiny black car and he's wearing a crisp dark suit.

"Well, I guess that's my ride."

"Hey, babe," Nora says, giving me a hug and handing me a travel mug of my favorite coffee. "Have a good time, OK? And text me pictures."

I nod as the doorbell rings. "I will, I promise."

"And don't do anything too crazy," Nora says.

"Do I ever?" I say, opening the door.

Nora laughs. "No, never. I'm not worried one bit."

"Miss Rockwell?" the driver asks.

"That's me." I smile.

"Let me get your luggage."

He does, and I follow him down the walkway, looking back to wave at Nora, my stomach all aflutter. I'm going to enjoy this week. I might not come back home with a job, but I will come home more experienced.

The driver sets my case down on the sidewalk and opens the back door of the car for me. I slip into the soft leather seat and get settled with my purse as he loads my yellow carry-on into the trunk. I don't need much for a weekend. I packed a bathing suit because it's summer and I'm going to California. I'm wearing my nice cream-colored linen suit. I picked it out last spring and this is the first chance I've had to even put it on. And a few other things. That's about it.

When he gets in, he glances back at me in the rear view mirror and says, "You're flying out of a private airfield."

"OK," I say, a little too quickly. I'm nervous.

"I just didn't want you to wonder where we were going." And then the driver shoots me a warm smile. "Top-secret stuff like this can make a young girl like you anxious."

Hmm. What does that mean? Do I look so sheltered and scared that this complete stranger picked up on my innocence?

I need to do something about this. I realize I have no hope of getting *this* job, but I will *need* a job. If a driver who's known me all of two minutes can pick me out as one of the weak ones, how will I ever impress big, important people enough to give me a chance on the business world?

Ivy Rockwell, you need to grow up. And not just in the sex department.

I make a vow to myself. This week is an opportunity to step out of my comfort zone and I'm going to accept every invitation that comes my way. I need to see more of the world. I need to do new things. I need to put myself out there and take risks.

Welcome to Opposite Ivy Weekend. Where every time I get the urge to say no to unfamiliar things, I will say yes. And every time I get the urge to say yes to familiar things, I will say no.

I think I saw this on an old episode of *Seinfeld* once, so it has to work. And the next time I have an interview I'm going to walk in there with an air of worldliness.

I bite my lip as we drive.

Can I really remake myself in one weekend?

I think I can. No one there knows me. They know nothing about me aside from what was on my résumé. And on paper, I look pretty good. Honor student at an exclusive private school growing up. Ivy League education at Brown. I graduated *magna cum laude*, which is very hard to do at Brown. They have a strict policy about giving out awards of distinction.

I have loads of hours under my belt for various Fortune 500 companies during my summer internships and I was a mentor sister to ten underprivileged girls in the entrepreneurial program in the New England area.

In fact, maybe I do deserve this job? I don't have a lot of outside experience, but I am smart, hard-working, and...

Wait, Ivy.

You can't sleep with the boss and *get the job.*

No, that would be the definition of awkward.

I let out a long breath as I take in the drive. So which one do I want more? The job? Or the sex? The odds of making either one come true are low. Very low, I admit. But if I don't try...

I smile as I think about last night. I pictured Nolan Delaney's face the entire time I was masturbating. Yeah, him. I think I want him more than the job. But if there's no way I'm going to lose my virginity to the infamous Mr. Romantic, then I'll take the job.

I'll know right away if he's even interested, right? Our eyes will meet across the room. He will look me up and down like he's hungry, mentally undressing me in front of everyone. He'll find ways to get me alone, make excuses for his fingertips to brush against my bare arm.

That's how it works. I've read it in books.

So if I don't get any of those signals today, then I'll just go for the job. Problem solved.

The driver drops me off right on the tarmac of a small private airstrip where a jet is waiting. "Wow," I say, getting out with the help of the driver. "It's kinda big."

"It's a long trip, miss. Needs to be big to have enough fuel for a non-stop."

That makes sense. But. Wow. I don't think I've ever been on a plane this size. It looks massive. "Does he fly everyone around like this?" I ask the driver as he gets my carry-on out from the trunk.

"Only the ones he wants to impress, miss. I have you returning Sunday. But they'll call me and let me know the exact time. Have a good time and good luck." And then he tips his fancy driver hat at me and someone is there to take my case.

I smile at the driver and redirect my attention to the new guy. He says, "I'm Jerry, Miss Rockwell. I'm in charge of getting you safely to Borrego Springs per Mr. Delaney's orders. It's a long flight, I'm sorry to say." We start walking towards the jet and I suddenly have a case of the butterflies. "But there's plenty of entertainment on board. TV, gaming, if you like that. A full kitchen if you're hungry and an office if you feel the need to work. If you get tired, we have two bedrooms to choose from."

"Holy shit," I say before I can stop myself.

"I know." Jerry laughs. "Believe me, I've been working for these guys for eight years and I'm still not used to it."

"These guys?" I ask. "You mean, like, all the Misters?"

"Yeah. Don't let them scare you. They're good men, not exactly what the reporters made them out to be."

"So they're still good friends. That's nice."

"Well," Jerry says, waving me forward to ascend the stairs up to the jet door first, "not exactly. They hardly ever talk these days. They all went their separate ways a while back. But they purchased this jet together as a show of solidarity eight years ago when the charges were dropped."

When I get to the top of the stairs I step inside and have to take a breath. It's like a house in here. A narrow one, for sure. But it's just as wide as the townhouse I share with Nora. And better equipped.

We enter what looks to be a living room, complete with flatscreen and a long sectional couch. There's a bar, with a bartender, who smiles and says, "Hello," as I gawk at him.

"Hello," I say back, a little timid, even for me. *Stop it, Ivy. Be assertive.* I walk forward to the bartender and stick out my hand over the shiny burl wood bar. "Nice to meet you. I'm Ivy Rockwell. What should I call you?"

"Jonathan," he says with a smile. "Now, what can I get you to relax?"

A drink. He's asking me what I want to drink. I don't really drink, but I'm Opposite Ivy now. So I say, "What do you think a girl like me drinks?"

He tilts his head at me, grinning. "You don't look like a drinker, Miss Rockwell. Would you like a sparkling water?"

I let out a small laugh, like I've seen powerful women do in movies and TV. "Well, I'm flattered you think so, Jonathan. But I like…" Shit. The only drink names I know are the stupid ones the sorority girls used to serve me in the house. So I choose my father's drink. "Cognac." I say it with as much confidence as I can muster.

"Really?" Jonathan says with raised eyebrows. "I'd have never guessed that one. My grandfather drinks cognac. In fact, I think Nolan's father drinks cognac too."

"Well," I say, forcing myself not to wipe my sweaty hands on my business skirt, "I like to keep people on their toes. And it's a man's world, right? Might as well try to fit in."

"Hmm," Jonathan says, turning towards his bar and looking up at the top shelf. "I have this." He reaches up and pulls down a very pretty bottle and grabs a glass at the same time. "I typically serve this in a balloon snifter, but that's far too manly for such a pretty young woman. So the tulip snifter it is." He pours a small amount as I fidget and look over my shoulder. Jerry is standing behind me, my case already stowed, smiling.

Jesus. They already have me pegged as an impostor. But I know a little bit about this drink. My father was really into it and I've watched him taste cognac my whole life. So I take the glass, and swirl, doing my best to not look nervous, and then take a small sip.

Holy hell. It's strong. I can't stop the grimace and Jonathan chuckles. I swallow it down and breathe out forcefully, my eyes tearing up.

"Too strong?" Jonathan asks.

Very strong. But I smile and say, "Is this XO or Hors D'Age?"

"Ah," Jonathan says. "So you do know something about it. But don't waste your time trying to impress us, Miss Rockwell. We're not part of the interview."

"Shit," I say. "Am I that obvious?"

"Very," Jerry says, coming up next to me at the bar. "But it was a bold move, Miss Rockwell. And no doubt it will have the effect you're looking for. A woman who knows cognac is impressive."

I laugh and then say, "I don't really drink. But I'm being Opposite Ivy this week for this interview. I want to impress Mr. Delaney and I don't want to come off as some newly-graduated millennial who has no real-world experience. So I need all the help I can get."

"Well," Jerry says, "Jonathan can tell you all there is to know about cognac if you'd like. And if you want to know how to impress Mr. Delaney, I'm happy to help as well."

"Please," I say. "To both offers." I ease up onto one of the barstools as Jerry takes the one next to me. "I'm listening."

I spend the next six hours drinking, laughing, and getting many, many tips on what Mr. Delaney is looking for in an employee.

Smart. Ruthless. Take-no-prisoners kind of people. That's what they tell me.

"He wants go-getters, Miss Rockwell," Jerry says just before we land. "People who know what they want and go take it. The way he has. He likes a challenge and he's looking for people who are as bold as he is."

I am good and buzzed from all the drinking, but it was worth it.

If Mr. Romantic wants balls to the wall, I'm all in.

CHAPTER THREE

NOLAN

The Smitten Kitten.

I can't. I just can't in good conscience do this. I press Mr. Corporate's contact on my screen and call him up.

"Mr. Weston Conrad's office, Janet speaking. How can I help you?"

"Janet, it's Nolan. I need him." And why the hell is Janet answering his private line?

"He's out of the office today. Shall I take a message, Mr. Delaney?"

"When will he be back? I really need to talk to him."

"He didn't say. But I presume tomorrow since he has a full schedule."

"All right. I'll try him at home. Thanks."

I end the call and press Corporate's home number but it just rings through to voicemail. "I agreed to your little plan, but the Smitten Kitten? You're joking, right? He will eat that shit up, West. And not in a good way." I stare out the window, watching a limo pull into the long drive that leads up to Hundred Palms Resort. Who is this? "Call me back, asshole. We need to make new arrangements."

I end the call and stand up to get a better look at the car. It winds its way down the long drive, half hidden by the wall of palm trees that line it, and then pulls smoothly into the valet area, disappearing from view.

I look down at my roster for today. We've got two guys here interviewing. Oh, yeah. I see the folder that Claudette mentioned peeking out from under a stack of papers. I forgot all about this one.

I sit back down and open the folder. Ivy Rockwell.

She's a Brown alumna, which is probably why West sent her over. He has this stupid loyalty to our almost-alma mater that it most certainly does not deserve.

I never graduated from Brown. None of us did. They treated us like criminals. Accused us all of rape, kicked us out, bad-mouthed us to the press. And if that wasn't enough, I have it on good authority that the president of Brown at the time called all his buddies and ruined all our plans of applying to other schools.

By the time the charges were dropped, it was too late. All five of us had moved on to making money and going back to college was the last thing on our minds. I am the first person in my family in over one hundred years to *not* go to college.

Well, fuck them. I didn't need a fancy education to pull off a win. I won. *Am* winning. And I'm certainly not interested in this Ivy girl, that's for sure. West sent her, so I'll see her, but that's all I'll do. She's on the next flight back to... I check her file real fast... Rhode Island. Jesus. She still lives near Brown. Obviously not the kind of person I'm looking for right now. Probably some timid do-gooder who is afraid to fly the nest.

West might be the best headhunter in the country right now, but I'm afraid he missed his mark on this girl.

I guess the Smitten Kitten fiasco West has gotten me into will have to wait until tonight. Now I've got three people here interviewing and I need to make a decision about going forward. I grab the new girl's folder and head out of my office to the stairs. Voices carry in the large cathedral foyer where the guests check in. I can make out Claudette and the new girl chatting.

She has a nice voice. Too bad I don't hire managers based on sweet pitch. I descend the stairwell that takes me from business offices to resort and emerge just to the left of the front desk.

We have two people running the desk today. Only about a dozen guests right now, since our soft opening on Monday, but this is our dry run. We're ironing out wrinkles and preparing the marketing campaign for the grand opening next month.

Miss Rockwell is… well, easy on the eyes.

Don't fall for it, Romantic. Don't do it.

I don't need the internal monologue to warn me of the dangers of an office romance. I had my fill with the last manager.

She quit. And she's probably going to sue me for sexual harassment.

Fucking women. Can't trust them.

Nope, I need a man to do this job. Preferably one of the two middle-aged guys currently laboring away in separate offices upstairs, working on an innovative way to improve guest experience and make this place work.

But… Miss Rockwell is pretty. And by pretty, I mean, hell, yeah. I wouldn't mind some of that action.

Just not at work, Romantic.

Got it.

Miss Rockwell is wearing a cream-colored linen suit that says professional. But it's cut just above the knee, so it also says sexy. Her silky blouse is light pink, which tells me she's girly. I like girly. And she's got her blonde hair up in a tight bun, so I can't tell how long it is.

Yeah, Miss Rockwell says buttoned-up businesswoman by day and unbutton-me party girl by night. I know her kind.

I walk over, extending my hand. "Miss Ivy Rockwell, I'm Nolan Delaney. Welcome to Hundred Palms Resort. I trust you had a nice flight?"

"Oh, yes!" She laughs. Has she been drinking? I think

I smell alcohol. Well, I've had a drink or two on a flight. But it's barely noon.

Hold up. She's on East Coast time. I guess that makes it afternoon for her. Must've been a lunch cocktail.

"Nice to meet you, Mr. Delaney." I hate hearing that word mister. Every time someone calls me Mr. Delaney all I hear is Mr. Romantic. She smiles confidently and shakes my hand with a soft grip.

Normally I hate the soft grip, but only with men. The only thing worse than a soft grip on a man is a firm grip on a woman. Every time I get a firm handshake from a woman I picture those overly muscular female body builders.

Miss Rockwell's soft grip is so feminine, I almost bring her hand to my lips and kiss it.

Instead I laugh at my ridiculousness.

Her smile falters and she lets go of my hand. "Am I late?"

So... not that confident after all.

"Not really," I say, checking my watch. "I knew you were coming today."

"Are the others already here?" she asks, looking around.

"Already working, in fact. Denise," I call to one of the front desk girls. "Put Miss Rockwell in room twenty-one. And then—"

"Mr. Delaney?" Denise interrupts. "We booked that room. The Gurrods wanted separate rooms."

"Jesus Christ. Can't those two get along for one goddamned weekend?" I roll my eyes. Mr. and Mrs. Gurrod are old family friends. I only asked them here for the soft opening because my father said Mr. Gurrod wanted to see the place before he invested money into it.

I don't need the investors, but it would be nice, for

once, to have help. God knows, my father hasn't helped one bit. *Nolan*, he said. *You have a trust fund. If you don't want to finish college, then everything you do from here on out is going to be with your own money.*

And so it has been. But Mr. Gurrod's investment would go a long way into making Hundred Palms everything I envisioned when I bought the land five years ago.

"How about—"

"All the finished rooms are full, Mr. Delaney," Denise says, grimacing. "We weren't expecting her."

"Surely there is a room for Miss Rockwell, Denise? You were expecting her. I told you—" Well, I didn't tell them. I hardly talk to them. "*Claudette* told you this yesterday."

"We have a room, Nol. Just relax." Claudette's hands latch onto my arm and she smiles up at me. "Go do something and I'll take care of Miss Rockwell."

I look down at my sister and manage a smile. She has been helpful, at least. She's a big part of why I'm even giving this whole resort thing a go. I have seven nightclubs in Southern California, but the club scene is starting to bore me. And it's filled with partiers. I'm sick of partiers. I'm ready for high-end hotels and high-class people. People who spend a lot of money, and not on drinks. They spend money on thousand-dollar spa days and outrageous green fees.

But land in San Diego is expensive. Land out here, practically worthless. I spent a lot of money building this resort and I'll be damned if I'm going to let the project flop.

"Fine," I say, prying Claudette's hands off my arm. "We have a meeting tonight at six, Miss Rockwell. I'll introduce you to the other candidates, then we can discuss how you might contribute."

It's only after the words are out of my mouth that I realize I meant to have her on a plane back to Rhode Island tonight. Well, maybe the meeting can be short? Maybe one of the two men upstairs will have a brilliant idea and I can get this interview business over with?

I don't amend, just turn and walk back upstairs to my office, eager to figure out where the hell Weston Conrad is so I can tell him his Mr. Match plan is shit.

CHAPTER FOUR

IVY

Claudette introduces herself as Claudette Delaney, and it takes me a few dizzy minutes to figure out she is his sister, not his wife. Drinking on the plane ride wasn't a good idea. My head is fuzzy and I'm very tired. I could definitely use a nap. It's only Claudette's overly sweet perfume that keeps me from falling asleep on my feet right now.

But every room Claudette takes me to ends up being filled with unfinished projects. One has no working bathroom. Another has no bed. Several more, on the opposite side of the main swimming pool, are filled with construction workers.

"OK," Claudette says, a bit exasperated. "We do have a few rooms over on the family side of things."

"Family side?" I ask.

"Yes, the private residences we're using at the moment. When the resort opens these will be the luxury bungalows, but I didn't want you too close to Nolan. He's not fun to be around, Ivy, take my word on that." Claudette sighs. "Apparently we have no choice. I'll try to get one of the other rooms finished and move you over there. But just so we're clear, you did sign the NDA, right?"

"Yes," I say, feeling unsettled. "I did."

"So you understand that whatever you see or hear during your time with us is never to be repeated to anyone."

"Sure."

Claudette stops walking to look at me. "I need a more

confident acknowledgment than that, Ivy Rockwell. We're not playing around. Nothing. You see or hear. Will be repeated to anyone or the family will sue you. My father is not the least bit interested in more controversy. And while he and Nolan have had their differences, he will not allow the Delaney name to be dragged through the mud again."

"I understand," I say with as much confidence as I can manage. "I do. Not a word, I promise."

"OK." Claudette physically relaxes, so much so that I can see the tension release from her upper body. "And while I would love to have a woman here helping me with the resort, Nolan has a very bad track record with female managerial staff, so your chances of landing the job are not good."

"What?" My hands are suddenly very sweaty. "What do you mean?"

"He likes to fuck his staff, Ivy. The last one would sue us if she hadn't signed the arbitration agreement upon hire. In other words, Nolan thinks with his dick. Stay away from him. Under no circumstances will you be alone with him. I have half a say in who gets this job since I've been the one managing the project since inception. And if I find out you and Nolan are involved in any funny business, you're on the next jet out, Ivy."

I swallow hard and nod. Just what kind of man is Nolan Delaney? Maybe all those accusations were true after all?

We walk silently back across the main courtyard where the large pool is and then make our way through a fence that leads to a private walkway with small cabana-type places that face another, more private pool. There are about half a dozen of them and Ivy stops me in front of the last one and points. "You can stay in here until the other room is ready."

"Wow," I say when she opens the door and waves me in. "This is nice."

"Very nice. I stay in the one next door and Nolan is in that first one we passed. It's as far away from him as I can manage for now. But don't worry, I'll be close by."

"Why would I worry?"

"I told you," Claudette says. "Nolan might make a move. You are to tell him no if that happens and then notify me immediately, so I can take control of the situation."

"Is he going to try to..." I can't even say the word.

"No." Claudette laughs. But she's not convincing. Is Nolan Delaney a rapist? Did they let him get away with something back in college and he's been victimizing women ever since? Jesus Christ. "No," Claudette repeats. "He's just very... God, how to put this about your brother. Just very... charming, OK? Charming. Charismatic. And... oh, God, I can't believe I'm talking about my brother this way... but handsome. Right?"

"Right," I sigh, before I can stop myself.

"Well, don't fall for it," she snaps. "He's not Mr. Romantic, no matter what anyone says. It was a joke, Ivy. Back when they gave out those names, Nolan's Mister name was a joke. He was a total player asshole. He still is. Don't fall for the joke."

"I won't," I say, biting my lip as I think of my ridiculous plan to seduce him. Little did I know that it would be so easy.

"All right then. I know Nolan isn't expecting you to produce a campaign tonight at the meeting, but if you really want a chance at this job, you should. The mission of the recruits, as we like to call our interviewees, was to come up with a way to make the customer experience more enjoyable so we can garner word-of-mouth buzz. So if you'd like to ruminate on that this afternoon and show up in the main lobby at six with an idea, it will go a long way towards needing that room I'm making ready for you tomorrow."

I'm nodding in agreement all the way up to the last part. "What do you mean make it to tomorrow?"

"We're sending someone home tonight. I have a feeling that will be you."

"But the invitation said one weekend working interview. Won't I get a real chance?"

"Of course, if you make it past the first hurdle tonight."

"But that's not fair. I just got here. And I didn't arrive late. I was only invited yesterday."

"Look," Claudette says. "Nolan didn't want to interview you. Weston Conrad insisted you were right for the job. He's our headhunter for this position. I'm sure you recognize his name." When I stare at her blankly for a few moments, she expands. "He's Mr. *Corporate*. And since Nolan hired him to find us the best candidates, he didn't want to turn you away when West sent us your file at the last minute. So you're here. But come on, Ivy. You're what? Twenty-two years old? Fresh out of college? I didn't read your file, but I didn't have to. You're way too young for this position."

What does young have to do with it? I want to ask. But I don't. Old Ivy is back and New Ivy is nowhere to be found. I'm silent as a church mouse as I stand there.

"Don't take it too hard. It's good experience, at any rate. Not many people get a chance like this. So work on a presentation for this evening and then try not to feel too bad when we send you home tonight. There's towels in the linen closet and complimentary shampoos and stuff if you forgot yours."

Claudette gives me the mini-tour of the cabana as she talks. But all I'm thinking about is what a fool she thinks I am. She assumes I'm so stupid I forgot to pack my own travel shampoo?

Young is not the problem. I'm inexperienced, sure. That's the problem. But assuming I'm not qualified based on my age is not right.

"See you at six then?" Claudette asks, standing in the doorway, ready to make her exit.

"Six," I say. "I'll be there and I'll be ready."

She smiles an indulgent smile and turns her back, walking out of the cabana without even bothering to close the door behind her.

Holy shit. This is weird.

I watch her walk off. Her body is slim and her clothes expensive. It's hot as hell out here. I didn't realize that Borrego Springs was the middle of the desert, but I do now. So I close the door and go hunting for the air conditioning. There are no towns around this place. It's totally secluded. In fact, it looks as if the Delaney family bought up some useless desert land and decided to make a go of starting something from nothing.

Who would want to come all the way out here for a vacation? It seems silly to me. I get out my phone to make sure I have reception—I do—and then do a search for Borrego Springs.

The map pulls up a small town in the Southern California desert. San Diego is two hours away and Palm Springs is an hour and a half. The closest attraction, if you can call the weird Salton Sea an attraction, has been abandoned and is now mostly used to film post-apocalyptic indie films and sad documentaries of ecological disasters.

Luckily, Hundred Palms Resort is on the western side

of the town of Borrego Springs, and it's not likely that anyone heading out here would venture so far as to see the disaster a little farther east in the desert.

What the hell was Nolan Delaney thinking?

I do a little more research on Borrego and after about an hour decide it draws a lot of people who come to see the desert bloom in the early spring each year. I'm not one for cactus flowers, but I can see that it can be pretty at times.

August isn't one of them, unfortunately. I can't imagine how he's going to attract visitors out here.

I guess that's why he's looking for a manager with marketing experience, Ivy.

For whatever reason, he wants this place to succeed and the three interviewees have been brought in to make sure that happens.

I don't care for Claudette Delaney. She's got the makings of a spectacular bitch. And it's quite possible that Nolan Delaney is everything the reporters said he was back when he was accused of raping that girl in college. But everything has value and the job of a good marketer is to find that value and exploit it.

Challenge accepted, Mr. Delaney.

I didn't come all the way across the country to be thrown out like trash, and even though he's expecting me to fail tonight, I'm not going to let some over-privileged family make me look like a fool.

I think I'll keep my virginity for someone special and go for the job.

CHAPTER FIVE

NOLAN

Even though I spend the rest of the miserably hot day locked in my air-conditioned office, the desert is making me crazy.

Crazy. That's what my father called me when I said Borrego Springs. *You'll attract hipsters with tents. Eco-freaks or throwback drug addicts who want to hunt down their own wild peyote. We already have Palm Springs, and even that is too much action for the wasteland out there.*

But I don't think the desert is a wasteland. I kind of love it out here. I can deal with the heat of the day when I know the cool nights are coming. But July and August are the worst. And every time the temperature climbs up to a hundred and ten these days, I forget all about how nice it is in the winter. All I can see are people huddled in their air-conditioned rooms, counting the minutes until check-out.

Was I wrong to take on this risk?

I've had many moments of doubts. In fact, without Claudette, I'd have never gone through with the project. She's the only one in my family who understands. The only one willing to put in time and effort to help me make this happen.

Why can't you build resorts where people like to go, like everyone else?

Because building resorts is fucking expensive. I have plenty of money, but most of it is tied up in the San Diego clubs. And that is my future, like it or not. Even if Hundred Palms does get off the ground, the clubs will be paying for it until it can turn a profit.

And knowing what I do about resorts, that might take a while.

The golf course is going to cost a fortune to maintain. The water to keep the greens healthy is a whole other political matter. I had to invest millions in alternative energy to even get the initial permits to build.

Why are you such a disappointment, Nolan?

I grab my phone and press West's home contact again. It rings through to voicemail, so I just hang up. I don't know what the hell he's doing. We have this little thing going between the Misters. Like we used to do back in school. Fucking with each other for old time's sake.

Now that Mr. Perfect has settled down, Corporate's been hounding me to do the same. All of us, actually. And so he concocted this little plan to set up Oliver—Mr. Match—with a girl who frequents the online dating site he runs with his sister. That's how Oliver made his money since college. Online dating.

"Don't you think it's strange that Oliver has no girlfriend when he runs an online dating site?" West asked when I saw him last. "It's the wrong kind of business for him."

But it's no worse than feeding people drinks in a club, I guess. I say let Oliver take over the virtual world if he wants. Who are we to say it's not the right path for him?

But West didn't agree. He says it's time to grow up and make a difference. Like Perfect. But there's a reason everyone called Mac Mr. Perfect. He is, after all, pretty fucking perfect.

Maybe Oliver and I aren't interested in making the world a better place? And who the fuck knows what Mr. Mysterious is up to? Perfect's engagement party a few months ago was the first time I saw him in ages. He lives in LA. Knows lots of important people. I've heard people whispering his name at the clubs. And even though I was pretty sure at the time it was only because of who he was in the past, I think it's more about what he's doing now.

There are no five-star hotels in Borrego. There are two four-stars that do a passable job and an RV park masquerading as a hotel that doesn't even count.

It's a good plan, Nolan.

That's not my father's voice in my head. It's mine. My father hasn't said a nice thing about me since my mother walked out on him and took me with her back when I was twelve. She didn't take Claudette, just me.

And even though Claudette should hold a grudge about that, she didn't. Doesn't. She's far too much like my father to foster feelings of abandonment.

Still, I need ideas. Fresh ideas. Ideas that no one's thought about. Ideas that will build interest in this resort besides what it has to offer in amenities. There are a million spectacular hotel pools. There are many professional golf courses. Why should people come *here*?

That's what I need from the two men I have working on the marketing campaign. They are the best in the business right now. And both of them have excellent jobs. They don't need *this* job. They are here, on my dime, using their own vacation days in order to interview. They are taking a risk on me and that is the only good thing I have going right now.

At least two people, outside of Claudette, believe in me.

Well, Corporate believes. But he believes in everyone. His job is to see the potential in people and match them up with employers looking for what they do best.

Which brings me to Ivy Rockwell. I scan my desk until I see the folder, then open it up and take out her résumé.

She looks good on paper, but what the hell, West? Twenty-two years old? I get that she's smart. But twenty-two? There's not enough real-world experience there to offset her *youngness,* no matter what kind of go-getter she's proven herself to be in school.

I can't send her home tonight. I have to at least give the impression she has a chance or she might pull the woman card on me. Call me sexist. Imply that she didn't get the job based on her sex.

The fact is, she's too pretty. Claudette would never give the thumbs-up to hire a woman as beautiful as Ivy Rockwell, so tonight I'll give her an assignment and have her present it tomorrow morning. She'll be on the jet back to Rhode Island before noon and then I can get the guys started on the next project. I only have a few days to come to a decision that might make or break my success here at the resort, so I can't waste time on placating Ivy Rockwell.

I really should consider hiring both these guys I have here interviewing. They are talented.

But it's a big risk to tie up that kind of potential.

I grab a few things and stuff them in my briefcase, then head over to the cabana I'm staying in. I need a dip in the pool. I need the sun to burn this negativity off me. I need to relax.

I pass the few guests who were personally invited as I make my way through the main lobby. They are huddled in the bar, mostly, where the AC is kicking out full force. I smile, and wave, and say pleasant things as I continue walking, then drop the smile when I walk through the back doors to the main pool.

The heat is suffocating and there's no one at all lounging under the umbrellas. The misters, which go off in strategic locations every thirty seconds to keep sunbathers cool, are a waste of water.

Don't think about it, Nolan. You have six couples here, that's all. If the place was full there'd be plenty of action at the pool.

But I don't believe it. I just don't believe it.

I go through the gate that separates the residence section from the hotel and I'm already taking my suit coat off before I even get inside. I throw it over the couch, the briefcase follows, and I go to work on my dress shirt.

Two minutes later I'm wearing swimming trunks and diving into the private pool in front of the cabanas.

When I come up for air I look straight at Ivy Rockwell in a bright yellow bikini.

I flash her a Romantic grin out of habit, then catch myself and let it fall into a frown. "I'm glad you're having a nice afternoon at the resort, Miss Rockwell."

She lowers her white sunglasses and peers down her nose at me. "I'm testing out the facilities, Mr. Delaney. The misters are off-target and the pool water is too hot."

"Is that so?" I ask, swimming over towards her lounge chair. "Feels good to me."

"That's because you just got out of that stifling suit. But if you were me, sitting in this chair, aching for a refreshing dunk to cool down, you'd know better. Because I was thoroughly disappointed when I dove in ten minutes ago."

I stand up in the pool—the depth is only three feet. And as the water rushes down my chest, I don't miss the fact that her eyes follow those little droplets all the way down to my dick. She recovers quickly, and her eyes find mine again.

"Furthermore—"

"Are you trying to impress me with your analysis, Miss Rockwell?"

"Furthermore," she repeats, "the AC in my cabana"—she nods her head behind her—"isn't up to par with what one might expect when it's a hundred and thirteen degrees outside. It only goes down to sixty-seven."

"Sixty-seven isn't cool enough for you, Miss Rockwell?"

"Hardly, Mr. Delaney. I'd like it to be sixty-six. But I can't adjust it. Well, I can. But it doesn't get any cooler because you have some sort of temperature threshold built in to prevent the AC from making it any cooler."

"Did you know that they charge you to use the AC in Paris hotels, Miss Rockwell?"

"I did, actually. I've experienced it first-hand. But we're not in France, Mr. Delaney. We're in the United States. And people expect the freedom to choose their own temperature in a five-star hotel room. *Especially*," she continues, "when it's a hundred and thirteen degrees outside."

I walk over to the edge of the pool and lean down, resting my chin on my hands. Her feet are right in front of me. Her little toenails are painted yellow, like she was trying to match her suit.

My gaze travels up her body, lingering on her legs for a moment, before continuing to her breasts, which are spilling out of her top. She shifts her legs, bending one knee into a sexy scissor arrangement, and stares me down.

"Energy is expensive, Miss Rockwell."

"I realize that, Mr. Delaney. But people expect to be comfortable, whatever that word means to them, when they pay top dollar for a room. So my first suggestions would be to retarget the misters, nix the heaters on the pool at night—it's simply not necessary since the water can't possibly cool off enough to matter—and lower the threshold on your AC to sixty-two."

"Is that your professional opinion?" I ask.

"It is."

I place my hands flat on the concrete and pull myself up and out of the pool, bringing a rush of water with me that splashes onto her perfectly tanned legs. She has to tilt her head up to me now, and I like the way that makes me feel.

"Thank you for your suggestions," I say, grinning that grin that drives women crazy. "I'm going to take care of this immediately."

"It was my pleasure to help, Mr. Delaney," she calls. "That's why I'm here."

I shoot her a look over my shoulder and shake my head.

Don't do it, Nolan. Don't start fantasizing about your face between her legs. She's going home tomorrow no matter what.

CHAPTER SIX

IVY

Holy shit. I did it. I stood up for myself and made an impression on Nolan Delaney. My heart is beating so fast, I need a moment to calm down.

"Miss Rockwell?"

Claudette's voice startles me, and when I look over my shoulder, she's standing a few feet in front of her cabana, door open wide.

"Yes?" I say, getting to my feet and wrapping my towel around my waist.

"I thought I told you not to interact with my brother?"

"You did, but he approached me. It's not in my best interest to be rude to the man responsible for choosing the next manager of Hundred Palms Resort when I want the job."

"Want the job?" Claudette asks, walking forward a few more paces. "I've already explained the situation, Miss Rockwell. You're not getting the job. You're here as a favor and nothing more. You'll be sent home after the meeting tonight."

"Probably," I say, forcing myself to stay brave. Why is Claudette so intimidating? Nolan was far easier to deal with than she is. "But until that happens I'm going to do my best to show that I'm worthy of the position. That I have things to contribute. And that I might just have an opinion that could help this resort."

Claudette scowls at me, annoyance all over her face. "It's two o'clock. The meeting is at six. We'll finish up at eight. You'll be on the jet by nine. Don't get too comfortable."

I nod and smile. But I don't answer. I just walk towards my cabana and go inside.

When I close the door I'm breathing hard, sweat pouring down my body. And not all of that has to do with the extreme heat.

I did it.

A small smile creeps up my face as I replay my first real interaction with Nolan Delaney. He was arrogant, sure. But he wasn't demeaning. He listened to my assessment and took note on my observations. Which are correct. I was one hundred percent right and he knew it. And maybe the temperature of the rooms and pool water aren't groundbreaking revelations, but it's all in the details, right? That's what makes a resort worthy of five stars.

I can do this, I decide. I can. I might be right out of school, but I'm smart. I like details. I live for details.

I quickly change out of my bathing suit and throw on some tan slacks and a silky white blouse that should help keep me cool in this abominable weather. I need more details between now and six o'clock. I need to walk this entire place. See all of it. Come up with a plan. It was dumb luck that I was frustratingly hot when I got to the room and decided to take a swim. Dumb luck that I figured out that the pool water was too hot. And dumb luck that Nolan Delaney came along at just the right moment to hear my complaints about them.

But I did it.

I take a deep breath as I dust my face with powder and reapply my eye makeup.

Nolan Delaney is hot.

I can't stop thinking about that pool move. The way his muscles bulged in his arms as he drew himself up and out of the water. The sight of his body when he stood up.

The little river of water that fell down over the curve of his chest and the six pack abs. The way he stared at *my* body, those hypnotic green eyes lingering on my breasts for the briefest of moments.

He thinks I'm pretty. I can tell.

But the way Claudette tells it, he probably thinks everyone is pretty. I mean, I *am* pretty. I'm not strikingly beautiful or anything. But I'm cute. My blonde-brown hair might be just another ordinary color, but my eyes are blue. A blue so light, they almost look gray. People say it's one of my best features.

Richard liked my eyes, but does Richard even count? I don't want to brag, but I was a lot cuter than his last girlfriend. He pointed her out to me enough when we were walking across campus and saw her—all huddled up with her serious friends. She didn't wear make-up or fashionable clothes like I did. She was one of those people who go to college to join things. Movements and marches. And she was off-putting any time Richard said hi to her and we were together. Turning up her nose at me like I was some kind of pariah.

Richard was the one who said I was too pretty for her. She loathed people who took an interest in their appearance.

Well, I hope she's happy working for whatever stuffy non-profit she ended up in after finishing her degree. Maybe she and Richard got back together? I haven't talked to him since I broke up with him before graduation.

At any rate, the point of this whole thought exercise is that I'm worthy of this job, of Nolan Delaney's attention, and of things I never thought possible until that very moment when I stood up for myself out at the pool.

I have what it takes to succeed in this world, regardless of the sheltered life my father wanted for me.

And if Claudette is hell bent on getting rid of me ASAP, then what's the harm with a few flirtatious moments with Mr. Romantic? What's the harm in testing the waters?

No, he's not going to be the one to take my virginity. I sigh, because it would've been fun. And there's no way in hell I'm actually getting this job, especially with Claudette gunning for me to be sent home. But I could make an impression and get a reference.

Yes, I decide as I exit the cabana. I'm going to scour this resort looking for details that might make all the difference and come up with a plan. With any luck, I'll walk out of here firmly embedded in Mr. Delaney's mind.

I make my way over to the main building and enter the cool back of the lobby. The smell of food being served in the restaurant grabs my attention and I wander over to the hostess station.

There's no one there. I wait a few moments before craning my neck at the people in the dining room and get a wave from a server.

"Seat yourself," she calls. "We're not fully staffed yet."

I nod and wander through the empty tables, taking a seat at a booth that overlooks the pool. There's a couple out there. The older gentleman is swimming while his wife looks uncomfortably hot under a large shade umbrella, leaning into the misguided misters.

Nolan appears, no longer wearing swim trunks. He's in casual clothes now, like me. Dark slacks with a white shirt. No tie. Sleeves rolled up to reveal is perfectly tanned forearms. He says something to the woman, smiling, as he leans in and redirects the mister so that the water will soothe her skin properly.

She smiles and says something. Probably a heartfelt thank you. This heat is not good. People still go to Las

Vegas and Palm Springs in the summer, but they stay inside. I looked over the amenities book in the cabana before taking my swim. This resort seems to have a lot of outdoor activities and very little to do inside except the spa. No one will want to come here in the summer if that's all there is to it. I wouldn't.

"Hi," the server says, coming up to my booth. "I'm Elizabeth and I'll be preparing your food today. I'm still finalizing the menu, but we're stocked with just about everything, so choose your favorite dish and I'll whip it up."

"Really?" I ask. "Anything?"

"Pretty much," Elizabeth says. "I've been cooking for about fifteen years now and not much can surprise me."

"Hmm," I say, taking my gaze back to Mr. Delaney out by the pool. I'd like him on my menu. *Focus, Ivy.* "Where did you work before coming here, Elizabeth?"

"Oh, I was teaching at a culinary school in New York."

"Big change, huh?"

"Very big." Elizabeth laughs. "But it's exciting too."

"Well, I'd like something light for now. Maybe you could just give me a nice green salad? Do you have croutons? That's my favorite part of a salad."

"I can make them fresh in just a few minutes. Anything else?"

"No," I say, once again distracted by Nolan Delaney. "That's all."

She walks away and leaves me to my thoughts. Which is all aflutter when I notice Nolan making his way inside. I watch him as he stops at the restaurant. *Come in here and talk to me*, I silently beg.

He catches my eye and shoots me the same disarming smile from our encounter at the private pool earlier.

I practically melt. His sister was right. The charm oozes out of him, even from a distance. How does a man with so much negative baggage have the right to be so damn handsome?

Shit, here he comes. What will I say? I look around nervously, aware that I've already pissed off Claudette once this afternoon.

Be cool, Ivy. Be cool.

"Miss Rockwell," Nolan says when he's close enough to my table to talk in a normal tone.

"Mr. Delaney," I say back with a smile. "Your sister doesn't want me to talk to you. She says you're quite a player."

What the hell, Ivy? That is not the definition of cool!

"Is that right," Nolan says, slipping into the booth across from me. "Mind if I sit?"

"Of course not."

"Claudette's warnings aren't enough to scare you off?"

"I'm not afraid of a challenge," I say back. *Smooth, Ivy. Smooth recovery.*

One eyebrow lifts up and his grin becomes lopsided. His expression says, *Oh, really?* and *That's interesting*, at the same time.

Yes. He's got all the moves.

"Mrs. Watters sends her thanks."

"Who?" I ask.

Nolan waves his hand towards the window. "Mrs. Watters. I adjusted her mister and told her you discovered they were misaligned. She is eternally grateful for your attention to detail."

"I like to please, Mr. Delaney." Too late I realize how that sounds. And so does he, because that other eyebrow is raised now, and his expression is one of keen interest.

"I have to admit, Miss Rockwell, you intrigue me."

"How so?" I ask, my heart suddenly beating fast. His gaze goes to my chest, which is heaving as I try to breathe through my mistake. Can he tell that he's having this effect on me? Can he see how flustered I get when he speaks? When he looks at me?

"Weston Conrad is an experienced headhunter. He supplies the perfect candidates for the perfect positions in every Fortune 500 company in the US, and many lucrative businesses overseas as well. And yet he sent *you*."

It's my turn to raise my eyebrows. "You say that like it's a surprise."

"It is, Miss Rockwell. West doesn't normally make mistakes. I'd ask him what he was thinking but he's conveniently out of the office today. I have a feeling it was a joke."

"A joke?" I can't stop the sudden anger in time to keep the disgust out of my voice. "I'm not a *joke*, Mr. Delaney. And your sister has already informed me that this was a pity invitation, so I am expecting to go home very soon. But since you're forced to see me today, I will give you my expert opinion about your resort."

"Is that so?" Nolan says, leaning back in his chair. "Then by all means, commence with said expert opinion." He waves his hand at me like some sort of king talking to a subject.

"I'm still making my assessment, Mr. Delaney. You'll get a full report at the meeting tonight."

"Will I?" he asks, grinning like a boy.

Why is he so fucking handsome? I'd like to slap his face right now. I even picture it in my head, but decide Nolan Delaney would not tolerate that kind of outburst from a woman.

Stay away from him. Claudette's voice is in my head.

I can't quite decide if she's exaggerating about his personality or not. But I am certain of one thing. Nolan Delaney is not a man who likes to be fucked with.

"You will," I say. "I was right about the misters and the temperature of the pool. I bet you've already called engineering and asked that they adjust the threshold on the AC."

"I have," Nolan says. "I know good advice when I hear it. And yours came with proof. It was clever to take a dip in the pool. Especially wearing those few scraps of clothing you're calling a bathing suit."

"It was the only thing I packed, Mr. Delaney. I won't wear it again if it distracts you."

"It was very distracting, Miss Rockwell," he says, sliding out of the booth. "But it would be a shame if you weren't able to enjoy the pool tonight when it's cooler out. So don't let me stop you from swimming."

"I have it on good authority that I'll be on a jet back to Rhode Island tonight, Mr. Delaney. So it will hardly matter."

"I have it on good authority that you won't, Miss Rockwell. But if you'd like to scale down the reaction you'll get when I see you out in my private pool half naked, you can pick up a one-piece suit in the women's shop on the west end of the hotel and charge it to your room."

He makes this little bow with his head and says, "Good day, Ivy. I look forward to the meeting." And just as he turns he whispers, so low, I might not have been supposed to hear it, "And our midnight swim tonight."

I stare at his ass until he disappears out of view. He called me Ivy. He's flirting with me. But why?

"Miss Rockwell," a familiar stuffy voice says from behind me.

Shit. "Ms. Delaney," I say, standing up and turning

around.

"Are you deliberately trying to piss me off?" She hisses the words in a whisper through clenched teeth. That sweet perfume smell is there again and I realize I hate it. I might even hate her.

"Uh... no."

"Then why can't you follow my simple instructions? I already told you not to interact with my brother. How much clearer can I make it?"

"He came up to me. Sat down uninvited. What do you propose I do? Blow my chances at this job by telling him to get lost?"

"We've already discussed this—"

"We have, Ms. Delaney. And I'm done discussing it. Your threats are highly inappropriate. I'm here as an applicant, on Mr. Delaney's request. How that got screwed up and these silly details about your friend the headhunter are not my concern. I'm here and I'm applying for this job. End of discussion."

"For now," Claudette snaps.

"For now," I agree.

"He's dangerous."

"I've been warned."

"Then I wash my hands."

"Consider them clean." My last words stand final in the ensuing silence and then Claudette shoots me one more angry look and turns away. I don't watch her as she disappears. Just take my seat and try to pretend that all four diners in this room didn't hear that.

They aren't looking at me, so maybe they didn't. I'm not sitting close to any of them, but still. Who the hell does Claudette think she is? I might be inexperienced in the bedroom but I'm not one to let people walk all over me. I can be a competitive bitch with the best of them and that

Claudette has another think coming if she thinks I'll cower.

There's no way in hell I'm getting this job now. Not with Claudette on the hiring team. But I can show these people what I have to offer. I don't even want their recommendation anymore. Screw all of these people.

My new objective is to show them what they'll be missing when I leave.

CHAPTER SEVEN

NOLAN

"Goddammit, Corporate! Where the fuck are you?" I tab the screen on the phone and end the call. I need to know more about Ivy Rockwell and her file doesn't give me nearly enough information. Maybe I can call Mr. Mysterious? He's got connections. I'm not sure what kind or with who, but I am sure that if you need info in LA, he's the guy you call to get it.

Nah. I hardly talk to him anymore. And we were never tight. Not tight enough for him to owe me a favor. Plus, Ivy is from the East Coast. He probably won't have a lot of connections out that way.

Still, I'm dying to know more about Ivy Rockwell. And if I can't get it through prying, then I need to get it the old-fashioned way.

Seduction.

She's so self-assured. And while I'm not really turning on the charm or making a play—yet—she's not very intimidated by me.

I like it.

I know Claudette will throw a fit, but I like it. And I need an excuse to get rid of Claudette this evening so I can have that midnight swim. Maybe Ivy will wear that tiny yellow bikini again? Maybe she'll take my advice and try to find something more conservative in the women's shop? Maybe she won't wear anything at all?

I call Shadows, my main club in San Diego, and get Travis, my long-time head of operations. "Hey, how's everything down there?"

"Good, man. Good. No problems. We've got that new DJ tonight. Expecting a big crowd. Called in extra security, got a few more waitresses to take an extra shift. It's gonna go well, I think. Your presence is not necessary."

"Not what I wanted to hear, Travis."

He laughs. "Tell me why."

"I need to get rid of Claudette tonight. She's cockblocking me, man."

"Who's the girl?"

I hesitate.

"Dude," Travis says, dragging out the word. "Do not tell me it's a new hire."

"She's not a new hire. She's an applicant." I sound a little smug with myself for differentiating.

"Same thing, Nolan. Jesus Christ. Do you want to get sued for sexual harassment? Because that last one is still pretty pissed off. You can't afford another fuckup."

"I fucked that one before I hired her. And then fired that one before I fucked her again, so she has no case."

"It's not good for business, man. You've got a bad rep in this town. Stay away from the employees."

"I told you, this one is only an applicant. Claudette wants to send her home tonight anyway. Which is fine with me. But I'd like to fuck her after she's fired and before she leaves. So I need you to create an emergency and call Claudette to come down and take care of it."

"What kind of emergency?" Travis is wary of my plans. As he should be.

"Something about me, obviously. That's all she cares about, right? That's the only thing aside from my father that will get her attention. So tell her a girl is there saying I knocked her up or something. Make me look bad, Travis. Make me look bad and I'll co-sign the next time you need a loan for one of those fancy boats you like to collect."

"It's not hard to make you look bad. And you're conveniently forgetting that you were accused of knocking someone up a few months ago."

"All lies, my friend. You know I don't fuck without a wrapper."

"You're sick."

"Will you do it?"

"What time?" He sighs.

"Six thirty. Thanks, man. I owe you."

I sigh as I end the call. Ivy Rockwell. Maybe I can do a search for her online? I open up my laptop and type in her name, adding Brown University to the search.

Nothing for Ivy Rockwell at Brown, but there is a whole bunch of stuff for Ivy Rockwell at the Bishop School for Girls in Bishop, Massachusetts.

Holy fuck. She's in a uniform. *Don't look, Nolan. Don't look.*

But I look.

Her hair is long and blonde in this picture, flowing down over her shoulders, partially hiding the school insignia on her left breast of the navy blue jacket. Her face is probably the sweetest thing I've ever seen. And she doesn't look much different than she does now. She has a very innocent vibe going.

A man and a woman are standing next to her. I read the caption. *Rev. William Rockwell and his wife, Sophia, celebrate the graduation of their daughter, Ivy Rockwell, from the Bishop School for Girls.*

Oh, fuck no. She's a pastor's daughter?

I think I get hard just from reading that.

Well, I might need to up my game for this girl. She's probably been schooled in the fine art of saying no. And I can see it, actually, now that I know her little secret. The manners. The high opinion of her virtue. It comes out in ways that are unnoticeable, yet still there, in everything she's done since she arrived.

Classy.

I had class once. I went to private schools too. Was brought up in with lessons in manners and all sorts of stupid rules. Rules I preferred to break, but still. I can play that game with the best of them.

Well, little Miss Ivy Rockwell might deserve my A-game in order to break through her walls. But one thing is for certain. I will fuck this girl before I send her packing.

CHAPTER EIGHT

IVY

I wander down a wide hallway after I eat my delicious salad in the dining room—the homemade croutons were to die for—towards the west end of the resort. Not really looking for the women's shop, but if it happens to come up in front of me, I might as well take a look inside.

I can't stop thinking about Nolan Delaney. He was flirting. It excites me in ways I'm embarrassed to think about. I mean, I actually wish I was at home right now so I could masturbate, that's how horny his attention makes me.

And he's counting on me still being here tonight. He wants to have a midnight swim with me.

What else does he want to do?

I spy a fancy window filled with pretty lingerie and stop to look at it. The mannequins are faceless and thin, yet still graceful and slender enough to spark a bit of jealousy in me. How is it fair that a fake woman can pull off sexy far better than I can?

"It's pretty, isn't it?" A salesgirl is watching me covet the expensive bits of lace, and silk, and chiffon.

"Very," I say. "But all I really need is a one-piece swimsuit. Mr. Delaney said I could charge it to my room? I'm in family cabana number six." I can't help but hide the disappointment in my voice. And even though it's somewhat dishonest to take him up on his offer for a free swimsuit when I know I'll be leaving soon, I'm going to do it anyway.

"Well," the girl says in a low voice. "We have the *best* selection in that area. Would you like to see your options?"

"Certainly," I say, following her inside the shop.

She stops in front of more mannequins and waves her hand at the display.

"These are... swimsuits?" I ask.

The girl laughs. "Yes, and technically, a one piece." She winks at me for obvious reasons.

The tops and bottoms of the suits are all *technically* connected, just as she said. But connected is a matter of degree. Slim straps, and in some cases, silver or gold chains, are what keep the two small pieces of fabric from being called a bikini. The one I'm looking at is definitely a bikini, with just a single chain linked from the middle of the bra piece to the middle of the panty piece.

Would Nolan Delaney die if I wore this for our midnight swim tonight or what? I chuckle, and then stop. Maybe he sent me here on purpose?

"Do you have anything more conservative?" I ask.

"Not in this shop. This is what I call the naughty store. We have another shop on the east side with more traditional pieces."

So he *did* mean for me to stop by this place. Hmm.

"Would you like to try one on? I bet you'd look great in this." She points to another suit with slightly more coverage than the first. It's all black and the bottoms have straps of fabric that burst out from between the legs in a starburst fashion and connect to the bra.

Nice way to draw the eye down to... well, the goods.

"Yes," I say. "Yes, I really would."

Twenty minutes later she's wrapping the suit up as I stare at the lingerie again.

"Want to continue shopping, Miss Rockwell?"

"No," I say, coming to my senses. A provocative bathing suit is enough for one day. Besides, I've already decided I won't be sleeping with Nolan. That lingerie I long for will have to wait until a more suitable man comes along. I sign the slip that will charge the suit to my room, and then notice there is no price on it. "How much was this? I completely forgot to ask."

"We haven't priced them yet. We're still setting up shop. None of the ladies Mr. Delaney invited to the soft opening are interested in this store. It's for younger women, like yourself."

"OK. But how much?"

"Sorry," the salesgirl says with a shrug. "Mr. Delaney stopped by earlier and said you might be by. He said to make sure you left with something pretty and not to tell you the price."

"He did, did he?"

"He did," the girl answers back, as she hands me the fancy bag.

That snake is very sure of himself. *Very* sure of himself.

And you walked right into it, Ivy.

What was I thinking? Why would I ever want to lose my virginity to a man like him?

"Well, thank you so much for your help," I say, taking my bag and walking out of the shop.

"See you around, Miss Rockwell."

Not for much longer. I'm fairly certain my time here is just about up. Claudette Delaney will get wind of this transaction, and the instructions from her brother that precluded it, and have me on that jet in no time. I'll probably be lucky to make it to the six o'clock meeting.

When I get back to my cabana it's almost five thirty. There was no sign of Nolan when I walked past his cabana, but I assume he's already in the office getting ready for his applicants' presentations.

I put my cream-colored linen suit back on from

earlier today and freshen up my face and hair before walking out of the cabana and heading over to the main building. *Here goes nothing, Ivy.*

Oh, stop. It's not like I have a chance in hell of getting this job. Even if Nolan is impressed by my analysis, Claudette won't be. Face facts, I'm out of here tonight, tomorrow morning at the latest.

But I'm going out in style.

The front desk ladies greet me by name when I approach, and then point to a set of stairs that wind up to the office. I arrive on the second floor at five minutes to six, and smile self-consciously at the two men sitting in the outer office waiting room.

"Hello," I say.

"Hello," they say in unison.

I'm screwed. They are both in their mid thirties, slightly older than Nolan. They are both wearing expensive suits, and they both look like men who have most certainly done this before.

Well, there goes my grand exit. I bet they have all the same ideas I've come up with for adding value to the Hundred Palms Resort customer experience, and then some.

"Oh, good," Claudette says from off to the left. "Ivy has finally arrived so we can get started."

I was early. Five minutes. She is really out to make me look bad.

"Come on in to the conference room, everyone. We're doing this together. Nolan?" she calls. "She's here."

God, I wasn't late.

Nolan Delaney appears from an office down the hallway and smiles at us. He's wearing a suit again. Perfectly tailored, black suit with a yellow silk tie. "OK, everyone. I can't wait to hear what you've come up with."

We file in and take our seats around a long oval table. I sink into my chair when I notice the two other candidates pulling out presentation material. One guy is setting up a projector.

I have nothing and even worse, this is painfully obvious to everyone in the room.

"Ivy," Claudette says from across the table. "Do you need to grab anything?"

"Um, no." I smile and tap my head. "I've got it all up here."

I look self-consciously at the two men, but they don't seem to be gloating quite as much about my lack of props as Claudette is.

Suck it up, Ivy. You're smart, capable, and you have good ideas for this place.

I glance over at Nolan and find him smirking at me. He cocks his head and raises an eyebrow, but doesn't comment.

"Mr. Miller," Claudette says. "You can present first."

"Thank you, Ms. Delaney. Mr. Delaney. As you know—"

"Wait, wait, wait," Nolan says, interrupting him. "We haven't all met. Let me introduce everyone for Ivy's sake."

Well, that was nice.

"Ivy, this is Bram Miller, current brand manager for Beachwood Resorts in the Caribbean. How many resorts do you oversee, Bram?"

"Ah, seventeen, Mr. Delaney."

"Bram got his MBA at Harvard and specializes in golf course promotion. Our professional course will be competitive and we think it will be a major draw for Hundred Palms."

"I have you covered, Nolan," Mr. Miller says with a confident smile.

Bram? Nolan? Well, they got cozy fast.

"And this," Nolan says, pointing to the second candidate, "is Daniel Davies. He got his MBA at Stanford and is the project marketing director for the Shell Island Luxury resorts in North Carolina."

"That's right," Mr. Davies says. "I'm particularly interested in the high-end amenities. Aside from the golf course"—he chuckles as he trades a smile with Bram—"I think of the spa as a gold mine, Ivy. It's usually the most expensive service, and the most lucrative, offered by luxury resorts. Who can't resist some pampering on vacation?"

"Right," Nolan says, pleased with his two options. "Well, Miss Ivy Rockwell just recently graduated with honors from the IE Brown Executive program."

Wait. What? Did I just hear him correctly?

"Ivy might be inexperienced and young"—they all have a nice chuckle at my expense—"but she comes highly recommended from Weston Conrad."

"Ahhhh," the two other men say. As if that explains everything about my sudden presence here.

"He knows his stuff," Bram says. "He chose me too, after all."

Hahahaha from the gang of men.

Jesus Christ.

But I'm still wondering why Nolan Delaney thinks I have an MBA. I'm twenty-two. He knows this.

"Ivy worked on her MBA at Brown simultaneously as she completed her undergrad degree," Claudette explains, like she's reading my mind.

"Wow," Davies says. "I've never heard of such a thing. Impressive, Miss Rockwell."

"Thank you?" I say weakly. But what the hell is going on?

"Ivy has no formal experience, of course," Claudette adds. A sudden wave of fear threatens to overtake me. "But if Weston Conrad says she's up for the job, well, we can't just dismiss her outright, you both understand, right?"

What a bitch.

"Of course," Bram says.

"Totally understand," Daniel adds.

I smile through my humiliation and nod as the formal presentation about the golf course starts, headed up by Bram. But I can't even begin to pay attention to what he's saying, even though he's got a full-on PowerPoint presentation on screen filled with data tables and projected profits for the next ten years.

Why the hell do the Delaneys think I have an MBA? And why would this Weston Conrad guy tell them this?

I look nervously at Nolan, who is sitting on the same side of the table as me, but two chairs forward. He's asking Bram something about a slide. I glance down at three folders open on the table in front of him. One for each of us, I presume. Two are thick, like there are many documents inside them. But it's the thin one I'm interested in. That has to be me. I crane my neck a little to get a glimpse of what's in there and see a fancy letterhead on a résumé.

My résumé. But that's not my letterhead. My letterhead is an elegant embossed gold script and this one is in bold black.

What is happening? Do they have me mixed up with someone else?

Someone else named Ivy Rockwell, Ivy? Don't be ridiculous.

But what other explanation is there?

Should I stop this? Should I tell them they're mistaken?

I ponder that for a while as the meeting continues. Bram has all kinds of thoughts about the golf course that I'm not even remotely interested in. And then before I know it, Daniel is standing—not with a PowerPoint, thank God, but he's got handouts. Full-color graphs and charts, documenting every detail of the most profitable spas around the world and what services they offer.

My hands start sweating as I volley my options back and forth. Tell them the truth? Or give it my best shot and walk out with my dignity intact?

I can't stomach the thought of standing up and admitting that my meager accomplishment is a lie. Will they accuse me of lying? Of tricking them into this expensive meeting? How much did it cost to fly me across the country in that private jet?

Everything inside me is screaming to do the right thing and tell them the truth. My father's words in my head, all growing up. *Never lie, Ivy. Lying is the worst sin because it fosters undeserved trust and loyalty.*

But… I didn't do anything. I didn't fake my résumé. And I don't even know how they got a hold of it. Why should I have to humiliate myself because—

"Miss Rockwell?" Nolan asks.

I look up and realize the room is silent. Daniel is seated again and all eyes are on me.

"Yes?" I ask, meeker than I'd care to admit. *Suck it up, Ivy. Suck. It. Up.*

"Are you ready?"

I nod and stand, smoothing out the wrinkles in my linen skirt as I walk to the front of the room. I'm out of here tonight anyway, right? I was a pity interview. I'm only part of this meeting at a friend's suggestion. I don't have a chance in hell of getting this job.

Right. Nothing to lose.

I straighten my back and force a smile. "I know I'm inexperienced," I say, referencing Nolan's introduction. "And all the ideas I've heard here are great."

Chuckles from my male counterparts. They're so damn sure of themselves. So confident that they are better than me. Smarter, more deserving. But I do have good ideas and they're about to hear them.

"Well," I say, sighing a bit. "They were all great ideas about ten years ago."

"What?" Daniel says. I don't look at anyone, just focus my gaze out the window.

"The world of marketing has changed, gentlemen." I pause, then look at Claudette. "And lady. And yes, I'm not quite up to par with what's worked in the past. That's true. But my youth gives me many advantages. Let me tell you what I'd like to do with this sorry excuse for a resort in the middle of a desolate wasteland, whose closest attraction is a dead saltwater lake."

My eyes dart to Nolan and he's smiling. Everyone else is staring at me like I just choked a puppy.

Keep going, Ivy.

"Oh," Claudette says, her hand over her heart like I have personally insulted her. "I can't wait to hear *this*."

I turn back to Nolan. "Mr. Delaney. I'm going to assume you chose this location based on the price of land, the proximity to San Diego, and the fact that this wasteland actually blooms once a year and manages to pull off the impossible—it becomes pretty. But you've got a big problem and it's got nothing to do with your golf course, which I understand was created by some famous someone or other."

Snickers from Bram. I ignore him.

"And it's got nothing to do with your spa services."

"Enlighten me, Miss Rockwell," Nolan says.

"OK," I say, taking a deep breath. "Your problem is no one wants to come here except when the cactus is in bloom in the late winter and early spring. That's a great time of year. The temperatures are mild, the desert is pretty, and it's close to the city. It's a day trip for most. But you have ten more months of the year to book. And you're new. Everyone in San Diego equates Borrego Springs with a day trip. It's not a place to vacation. You can stay in San Diego and get a better vacation. Or go a little further north and get a real desert experience in Palm Springs."

"Tell us something we don't know, Miss Rockwell," Claudette snaps. "We are well aware of the resort's limitations."

"Fine," I say. I take a deep breath and spit my idea out with the exhale. "Give the rooms away for free."

"What?" Claudette laughs. In fact, everyone laughs.

Except Nolan.

He's scratching the stubble on his chin like he's actually listening to me.

One brownie point to Mr. Romantic.

"Give the rooms away for free," I repeat. "Bram here has already told us that the golf course is exceptional. Upcharge it. And Daniel has already said the spa is spectacular. Raise the prices. Give the rooms away for free and make your profit off the amenities."

"That's your plan?" Claudette sneers.

"Oh, no," I say. "I've got a lot more plans, Ms. Delaney. But since you've informed me that I don't have a chance in hell of getting this job, I'm going to keep them to myself." I walk across the room towards the door and look at Nolan as I pass. "I'm ready to leave when your jet is ready to take me."

"Miss Rockwell," Nolan calls after me.

I take a deep breath and turn. "Yes?"

"It's bad manners to leave the interview early." He turns to Daniel and Bram and says, "Please wait outside while my sister and I discuss things, will you? Miss Rockwell," he repeats, turning back to me as Claudette marches the men towards the door. "Please have a seat with the other candidates."

He stares into my eyes. Dead on. And if I thought he was intimidating before, it was nothing compared to this smoldering gaze he's giving me now.

I breathe again. Swallow hard. And take a seat.

You're weak, Ivy. You don't have to listen to him. He's not the boss. He's no one to you.

"That was quite possibly the dumbest thing I've ever heard," Claudette says as she smacks the door closed, sealing them up inside the office.

I glance over at Bram and Daniel, both of whom look shell-shocked over what just happened. "Sorry," I say. "I didn't mean to insult you guys. It's just not fair the way they brought me here just to throw me away on the first day."

They give me small nods, but neither look at me.

I can hear arguing inside Nolan's office.

Well, Ivy. You've certainly made an impression now.

CHAPTER NINE

NOLAN

"Just what the hell was West thinking bringing that girl here?" Claudette asks.

I have no answer. I'm still thinking about the way Ivy Rockwell just stunned the room.

"Nolan?"

"What?"

"Let's decide tonight. Send her home. She's no longer welcome here."

Claudette's phone buzzes on the other side of the table. That would be Travis calling. But Claudette is too wound up to even bother with her phone.

"Did you hear me, Nolan? Let's decide now."

"Well," I say, sighing a bit. "I want both of them."

"What? We don't have budget for that right now, Nolan. One is enough. Pick or I will."

"I want both, Claudette. And while you might have a say in my decision, you do not dictate. Understand?"

She stares daggers at me. She has always been little jealous of my power. Even before I became Mr. Romantic and had four filthy-rich instant best friends. The five of us Misters weren't even close before that girl dragged our names through the mud. We lived in the same frat house, sure. And we partied together like most brothers do. But once we were all implicated in the same crime, everything changed.

Perfect has been proper billionaire from birth. His trust fund is, fuck. More money than I can even imagine.

Corporate comes from a similar situation, though not as global.

Mysterious comes from Hollywood money. Bastard Hollywood money—hush money he always called it—but money is money all the same.

Match comes from some motorcycle empire. His dad is some famous bike builder. Had a reality show back in the day, the way Match tells it. Plus a little somethin' somethin' on the side that Match was never too keen to talk about.

And all that money came out to play when the shit hit the fan. We were like brothers—real brothers, not just frat brothers—for two years.

Claudette hated it. I remember that now. I try not to think about that time in my life too much. It's depressing. It made my father hate me. He always thought I was guilty. He thought we were all guilty.

And Claudette picked up on it. She thought we were guilty too. I waited for her to turn on me. For my father to turn on me. My mother was there, right by my side. She never believed a word. And even though Claudette never acted out when my mother took me away in the divorce and left her behind, it had to sting. I expected her to betray me. Give some kind of tell-all interview about how I was a total player back in boarding school. How Perfect and I used to sneak off campus and go drinking and fucking every weekend.

But Claudette kept her mouth shut back then and she keeps her mouth shut now. She is high-strung. She's bossy and authoritative and I'm not in the mood. "Ivy can go-"

I stop talking when her phone buzzes again. She ignores it. Again.

"Ivy can go home tonight," I continue. "I'll call for the jet." I pick up my phone and pretend to call the travel scheduler, then have a fake one-way conversation about fuel and flight plans before ending the call. Claudette stares out the window the entire time.

"All set," I say. Claudette turns to look at me when her phone buzzes yet again. "Are you going to get that? Or are you going to let it buzz all fucking night?"

"Why do you need both men, Nolan? It's a waste."

"Because they have unique talents. Besides, Corporate told me they would build good synergy. That's why he sent them. You know he's not the kind of guy to send multiple candidates."

"Exactly," Claudette says. "So why did he send Ivy Rockwell?"

"I don't know." I shrug. "He thought she was cute?" I smile but Claudette just sneers at me. Her phone buzzes and this time I make a grab for it to force her to see the message.

She beats me to it, as I knew she would.

I watch her face process the message I know Travis sent. All of the many expressions that flash in an instant. It changes from angry, to puzzled, to shocked.

You know what I've always wondered? Why she believes all these accusations girls throw at me. Why is it so easy for her to believe everyone but me? Sure, I have had my share of workplace relationships. But I never did anything the women didn't agree to. I never pressured them. I *never* got anyone pregnant. But Claudette has always been willing to see the dark side of me no matter who was making the accusations. Even back in college when all that shit happened, Claudette's first words were, "We'll get the best lawyers. You won't go down for this."

I never did anything wrong. That's the part she never understood. She simply waved her hand at me and said, "Neither here nor there," each time I proclaimed my innocence.

But it's both here *and* there for me.

"I have to go back to San Diego."

"Who was that?" I ask.

"It's nothing, Nol. OK?" She smiles that fake smile I've become used to when people accuse me of things I never did. "I'll handle it and be back as soon as I can."

"OK," I say. "I'm keeping both guys."

Claudette waves her hand at me and walks over to the conference room door, opening it up wide. "Congratulations, Bram and Daniel, you've both got the job. We'll meet again on Monday. Until then, please enjoy the complimentary facilities. Miss Rockwell, sorry. You've been dismissed. The jet will take you home tonight. Please pack your things and be in the lobby in—" Claudette pauses and looks over her shoulder to me. "When is she leaving?"

"They're going to call. I'll handle this. You go. Take care of whatever it is that's so important you refuse to tell me about it."

"OK." She sighs. "Call me if you need anything." And then she steps through the door and closes it behind her.

I won't be calling. The only thing I need is some alone time with Ivy Rockwell.

Claudette called her suggestion to offer the rooms for free dumb. But I don't think it's dumb at all. There's more to it, I can tell by the coy smile Ivy had on her face as she was talking. She has an idea. Maybe more than one. And she thinks it's good.

I knew this resort was a risk when I bought the land but I figured I'd come up with something. The golf course and the spa. Those were my ideas. And while they're not bad ones, Ivy Rockwell is right. They're not enough to pull people in the way I need.

So now what?

I'd like to fuck her, that's for damn sure. I can see the headline now—*Mr. Romantic pounds preacher's daughter.* Maybe she's wild in bed? Maybe she likes it in the ass? Maybe she was a little buttoned-up schoolgirl until college and then went crazy as she vented her sexual frustrations?

I wonder how well she can suck cock?

It amuses me so much, I laugh out loud.

But...

If I want her ideas about the resort, then she's probably off the table for a kinky one-night stand.

Decisions, decisions.

Maybe I'll just play it by ear?

The conference room phone buzzes, so I reach over and grab the receiver from the middle of the table. "Yeah," I say.

"Mr. Delaney, Miss Rockwell is packed and ready at the front desk. She says you're making travel arrangements?"

"Tell her to go back to the bungalow and unpack, Denise. And tell her to grab some dinner from the restaurant and charge it to the room. I'm going to require another meeting with her tomorrow."

"Ummm. Yes, sir. I'll do that."

I look at the candidate files in front of me, then ease Ivy Rockwell's closer. She's amazing on paper. How fucking smart do you have to be to get your BA and MBA at the same time? I've heard of people doing it, but not at a school like Brown. And all the guys I knew of completed most of their BA's in high school, before they ever got to college. Dual track, I think they called it. I bet that preacher father of hers was all about overachieving.

I can see it, actually. I can picture her in that little schoolgirl outfit, studying late on Saturday nights in the library as she completed two sets of courses in high school.

She's amazing in person, as well. I picture those perfect pink lips wrapped around my cock, her big blue eyes staring up at me as I grab her hair and force her to take me all the way down her throat.

God*dammit.* Why did she have to come up with a unique idea?

What if… what if I fuck her senseless tonight and then hire her tomorrow?

It just might work.

Oh, Nolan Delaney, you are one sneaky bastard. That should've been my name back at Brown. Mr. Sneaky Bastard.

CHAPTER TEN

IVY

"Mr. Delaney wants you to go back to your cabana, unpack, and then get dinner and charge it to the room."

"What?"

"I'm sorry, Miss Rockwell. That's what he said. I don't know any more than that. He wants another meeting with you tomorrow."

"Another meeting?" I whisper to myself.

"Yes, ma'am."

"OK." I sigh. "Thank you." I grab the handle of my carry-on bag and go back out the lobby, past the pool, and into the little secluded residence section. It's not quite dark yet, but the sun is low in the sky and the unbearable heat is finally starting to fade.

When I pass the private pool I think of the swimsuit I bought. I left it in the pretty bag, sitting on a chair in the cabana. I couldn't make myself take that suit. I don't want to take anything from these people. But Nolan Delaney said to stay. What can I do about it? He's the one with the jet. If he doesn't call it to take me home, then I'm stuck doing his bidding.

But another meeting is a good sign. I bite my lip as I think what it might mean.

What it might mean, Ivy Rockwell, is that he knows you're on to something, regardless of what Claudette says. I tiptoe past her bungalow, but I don't think she's in there because the curtains are open and I can see inside.

When I get inside I unpack my clothes and change into a yellow sundress and a pair of flip flops. I pull my hair up in a ponytail and wash my face, relieved to be rid of the day's makeup.

I should call Nora and tell her everything. Tell her what a supercunt Claudette is. Tell her how weird the infamous Mr. Romantic is.

But she will keep me on the phone for hours and my stomach is rumbling. That salad this afternoon wasn't enough to satisfy me through the night.

Besides, Nora will see right through me and start asking about how hot Nolan is. And that's not something I can deny.

He is damn hot.

And the way he stared at me when I finished my presentation, the way he saw me—like he was undressing me with his eyes. Imagining my body naked before him. Imagining me doing things to him. Or himself doing things to me.

Oh, shit. I suddenly remember the fake résumé. If he wants to talk to me again that will surely come up. I can't lie about it. I'm not a very good liar.

But I can't tell him, either. I have no explanation for it. And they won't believe me, anyway. They will say I dropped it off at that job fair and that's how that other guy, Mr. Corporate, got a hold of it.

Of course someone with that kind of academic history would be of interest to a headhunter, right? It makes me out to be some kind of business-school prodigy.

I'm going to sit on that little detail for now. Even though Mr. Delaney asked for another meeting tomorrow, I'm probably still on the next jet out of here.

Might as well get some dinner. Bossy Mr. Romantic practically ordered me to.

I open the door and come face to face with the deviant himself.

"Oh," I say, stepping back. "You startled me."

Nolan notes my change of clothes with an appreciative glance. The sundress isn't overly short, but it's a sundress. It stops mid-thigh and the top has a low-cut v that shows more cleavage than I'm comfortable with, now that his green eyes are taking me in.

"Going to dinner, Miss Rockwell?"

"Yes," I say with hesitation. Why is he here? And now that he is, I begin to notice what he's wearing as well.

Gone is the suit. Replaced by faded jeans that hug his muscular legs and… well, let's just say there's a healthy bulge right where you'd expect said bulge to be. I stare at it, unable to stop. Is he hard? Or is that just… I look up and find him smiling at me. Oh, my God. He caught me staring at his dick. And then, before I can even be properly embarrassed, I notice what else he's wearing. A white cotton dress shirt, with only the bottom few buttons buttoned up, and nothing else.

His nipples are beautiful.

I did it again. And when I find his handsome face I get lost in the five o'clock shadow of his strong, square jaw.

His smile becomes a laugh. "Good." And then he takes my hand, places it on his elbow like he wants me to hold on to him, and says, "I'll walk you."

I'm speechless. I have no idea what to do other than grab hold of his arm and walk with him as he steps forward.

"I'm sorry we didn't hire you, Ivy. But there's a very good reason for it."

I roll my eyes, but I'm looking straight ahead, so he can't see them. "Let me guess. The reason is because your sister is a bitch?"

Nolan sighs.

"Sorry," I say. "I'm sorry. I understand. I'm not really

73

qualified for the position and I knew that when I accepted the invitation. I only came for the ride in the private jet and a chance to meet the infamous Mr. Romantic."

"Hmmm," he says. And even though I can't see him, I know that little *hmmm* came with a smile. "What do you think so far? Do I live up to the hype?"

"Not really."

"No?" He chuckles as we walk past the pool. "Why not?"

The whole thing becomes surreal for me in that moment. The emptiness of the resort. The heat and the sun. I am two thousand miles from home and I'm clutching Mr. Romantic's elbow like we are lovers taking an evening stroll.

"You're a little bit quiet so far."

"Is that right?"

"Your sister is the bigger personality. I'm surprised *she* wasn't accused of something inappropriate in college. I think she has it in her."

Nolan laughs. "That's kind of true. She's a handful to most, but she's been good to me. She's very protective."

"She called you dangerous."

"What?" He stops walking and looks down at me. "When?"

"Today. She told me to stay away from you. Didn't you know that?"

"What exactly did she tell you?" His mood has changed. Not a lot, but there's an edge to his words.

"She said something like..." I struggle to remember her exact words, but can't. I shouldn't have said anything. He'll probably confront her and use me as an example.

"Like?" Nolan pushes.

"You're not romantic. Something like that. They called you Mr. Romantic when all that stuff happened because it was a joke."

"And the dangerous part?" His words are low and when I look up at him, the easygoing expression has changed into something else.

"I don't know why she said it. She was telling me to stay away from you all day. And I was angry that she was so dismissive of me. She said I was here by mistake. So I told her I was going to do my best to get the job anyway. And while I agree those men you hired are far more qualified, it was not fair of her to dismiss me so quickly. I'm not as innocent and inexperienced as I look, Mr. Delaney. I have ideas and I'm smart. Hiring everyone in the applicant pool but me was about the most humiliating thing I've ever experienced."

Nolan continues our walk, silent for a few seconds. "You're lucky."

"I am?" I ask, a small laugh escaping. "How so?"

"You're lucky that you've never been humiliated the way I have."

Oh, shit. Way to go, Ivy.

"Do you think I'm dangerous?" Nolan asks, staring down at me in that way he does.

It makes me uneasy. "Maybe."

"You're willing to take that chance?"

"Maybe."

"Well, good," Nolan says. "Let's have a nice dinner and I'll tell you why I sent Claudette away and kept you here against her wishes."

He did *what?*

My heart starts to beat faster. Why would he do that? Maybe Claudette was right to warn me? There's hardly anyone here at the resort. Especially now that all the construction people have left for the day. The main pool is empty when we pass, and even the desk clerks are missing when we enter the lobby.

The dining room has two couples eating dinner and Nolan greets them by name as he leads me to the rear part of the restaurant. Back into a dimly lit room with a single table, white linen tablecloth flowing over the sides. Candle glowing in the center. Set for two.

"This is… unexpected." My mind is filled with possibilities. And even though I came here with the intention of getting his full attention, possibly losing my virginity to him—and even though I've talked myself into feeling ready to take on a man like him, both professionally and personally—I am not excited. I am suddenly scared.

There's not enough people. There's not enough noise. There's not enough of anything to make me forget just who I'm having dinner with.

Mr. Romantic. A man accused of raping a woman ten years ago. A man who was not prosecuted for that crime because the woman died before she could testify. A man who might be guilty.

Nolan pulls out a chair and waits for me to sit, sliding it in perfectly the way a gentleman does, before taking his seat across from me. "I like the unexpected, Miss Rockwell. Get used to it."

I am in way over my head.

CHAPTER ELEVEN

NOLAN

I make Ivy Rockwell nervous, but I like that. A lot. I like keeping women off guard, never quite knowing what I'm up to. I like that my reputation makes them have doubts and second thoughts. And what I like most about all that is the fact that they never say no.

There is just something about me that draws them in like helpless little birds.

Ivy glances at everything in the room but me. Her hands flatten her linen napkin in her lap and she reaches for the glass of water, taking a small sip that leaves her lips with a shine I'd like to lick off.

They always say yes. Even when they want to say no, they always say yes.

Ivy Rockwell is no different. She will say yes to everything I have planned for tonight. And when she wakes up in my bed in the morning, she will say yes to everything I have planned for tomorrow too.

I like getting my way. I like having power. I like bending the will of resistant people, arcing it so far back from what they consider normal, they don't recognize themselves the next day.

It might be sick, but I don't think so.

I think every man wants the power I have.

"We don't have menus," Ivy says when our silence becomes uncomfortable.

"We don't need menus, Ivy." I watch her take in a small breath of air, like the way I say her first name excites her and terrifies her at the same time. "I asked the chef to make us something special. I hope you like Italian."

She nods, but her shoulders are stiff. "Why are you having dinner with me?"

Ah, so she's not that scared. She's pushing for answers. Good. "Because you're beautiful and I want to have dinner with a beautiful woman tonight. Are you seeing anyone? Do you have a boyfriend?"

"Mr. Delaney—"

"Nolan," I correct her. "Call me Nolan. You're not here at dinner as a candidate, Ivy. You're here as my date. So let's stick with first names, OK?"

"You didn't really ask me on a date, Nolan."

"No? I thought I did. And you're here, so it must be true."

"To answer your question, yes. I do have a boyfriend."

"I don't believe you," I say back.

"What?" Ivy laughs, but it's an uncomfortable laugh. "Why would you say such a thing?"

"Because if you did have a boyfriend you'd be on the phone with him tonight, telling him all about how inappropriate the Delaney clan is."

"I was, actually. I told him all about it. He's expecting me home tomorrow afternoon, so I hope you have that jet all fueled up and ready."

"It won't be, Ivy. So relax. And you don't have a boyfriend. I can tell. I'm good at that."

"His name's Richard, Mr. Delaney." She scoots her chair back and places her napkin on the table, but I grab her wrist and hold it down.

"Sit," I say.

"Let go."

"No. Now sit and relax and tell me that the boyfriend was a lie so we can enjoy ourselves."

"You really are something. Your sister was right. I

should stay far, far away from you."

"Forget my sister, Ivy. Don't you want to learn the truth about me? Learn some secrets, maybe? Secrets very few people know?"

"No," she says forcefully. But she sits back down. Which is a yes, in my book. "I don't, actually. I think that what they wrote about you ten years ago was probably all true."

"Well, that's a shame," I say. "Because they left out all the interesting stuff."

"I can see you're a man used to getting what he wants, but I'm a woman who is well-practiced in the art of saying no."

"I bet you are," I say with a small laugh. "Preacher's daughter. All-girls' boarding school. Still living close to home."

"What are you doing?" she snaps.

"Intriguing you, Ivy. I'm making you curious."

"You're making me uncomfortable."

"Same thing," I joke.

She shakes her head and blows out a loud breath of air. "Why didn't you send me home tonight?"

"So we could have dinner. And talk. And fuck. And talk some more."

She is speechless. Her mouth is opening and closing, opening and closing, but no words make it past those beautiful plump lips.

"So relax, enjoy it. And if you really want to say no when I start taking your clothes off, I'll back away. I'm not a rapist, Ivy. And if you think I am, then you're not as smart as that résumé makes you out to be."

She scowls at my words but stays silent.

"I don't need to force women to have sex with me. I get them to the point of begging and then it… just happens."

"It won't happen with me."

I honestly think she believes that. But she has no idea what's coming, so I wave it off with a hand gesture. "So, Richard is your boyfriend? How long have you been dating?"

Ivy tips her head up, like she's got the upper hand here. "Yes, Richard. We've been dating since my freshman year of college. And he's a lawyer."

"What kind of lawyer?" I ask, wondering how far she'll take this boyfriend thing.

"He works for the district attorney's office in Boston."

"Boston, huh. He's a close-to-home guy as well?"

"You live in the desert, two hours from your father's home in San Diego. So you're one to talk."

"I didn't grow up with my father, Ivy. My mother divorced him when I was twelve and we lived in Palm Beach when I was at home. But most of the time I was in boarding school in upstate New York."

"Oh," she says, taking a moment to think this through.

"I came back to the desert because I like it here. It's a place people hide."

"Are you hiding?"

"Isn't everyone?"

"No." She laughs. It's not a real laugh. Not like the ones I saw earlier. But it's a start.

"You're hiding behind a fake boyfriend. Why? To keep my sexual advances at bay? It won't work."

She shakes her head as she lets out another nervous laugh.

"What?" I ask.

"I just can't believe what an asshole you are. I mean,

I expected some of this—"

"Which parts? I love hearing what people think of me before they actually meet me."

"Jesus Christ—"

"Ah, so that religious upbringing is wearing off." I *tsk* my tongue mockingly at her and then say, "That's good to know."

"I figured you were a jerk but I really had no idea you were this bad."

"Because I'm self-assured?"

"Because you are the definition of arrogant, Mr. Delaney."

"Nolan," I say. "I thought we were in agreement on that?"

"We're not in agreement on anything, Nolan."

I smile and she falters for words.

"We will be by the time this night is over."

She's just about to respond to that when the servers come with a basket of bread and wine.

"I hope you like wine."

"I do," she says.

"Good," I say. "Then I did something right. This is a fantastic Ornellaia Vendemmia d'Artista Special Edition Bolgheri Superiore that comes straight from Tuscany. Have you ever had it?"

"No," she says crisply. "It sounds a little out of my price range for dinner drinks."

"Well, enjoy then. I like the finer things in life, Ivy. I won't skimp on this date, don't worry."

The servers leave us alone again and Ivy gathers her nerve. "It's not a date," Ivy says, once they're out of earshot. "And I won't be fucking you tonight, Nolan. No matter how pricey the wine or how good the food."

"Oh, don't worry, Ivy. I don't get girls in bed by

wining and dining them. It's the talking that lowers all those keen defenses and inner voices telling them to run away as fast as they can."

She laughs. And this time, I think it's real. "Well, the rumors seem to be true all the way around. You certainly are charming. And charisma? You've got it in spades. But I don't fall for charm."

"Is that why Richard is boring? I mean, come on. District attorney's office? Tell me, does he have grand dreams of public service once his five years are up? State's attorney, maybe? Federal judge? I'm practically falling asleep as I talk."

"It's a noble profession. Putting criminals away."

"Criminals like me?" I ask with a wink.

"You were never tried."

"Correct. I never was."

She presses her lips together, wanting to reply, but afraid to.

"Say it, Ivy. Go ahead. I know you want to."

She swallows hard and goes for it. "Did you do it?"

I smile as she fidgets in her chair. "Wait until we've been dating a week and then I'll ask *you* if you think I did it."

"A week?" Her eyebrows knit together.

"Do you think I'm a one-night kind of guy?"

"Absolutely. But I think you probably make your targets think it's more, just to get through that one night."

"Well, I guess you'll have to wait and find out."

She gives me an indulgent smile this time. It's funny. She doesn't even realize what I'm doing. Putting her through this emotional rollercoaster. Watching her expressions change. Watching her fight her instincts and give in.

"After this dinner I'm going back to my room to

sleep—alone—and tomorrow morning I expect that jet to be ready and waiting to take me home."

"What if I want to hire you tomorrow?'

"What?" She says it loud, too. It echoes off the high ceilings of the small private dining room. "You are too much."

"No really. I liked your idea, Ivy. And I know there's more to it. But I really do want to fuck you. So I can't hire you today or that would be inappropriate."

Her mouth hangs open.

I reach over and close it up with a fingertip to her chin. "Close your mouth, Ivy Rockwell," I croon. "You're making my dick hard just thinking about how you'll suck it tonight."

She blinks. Twice.

"Does Richard talk dirty to you, Ivy?"

More silence.

"I'll take that as a no. I will. I'll talk dirty to you. Is Richard the jealous type?"

It takes several more seconds for Ivy to catch up on the conversation and then she squints her eyes at me and says, "Yes. He is. And he comes from a mob family in Providence. Ever hear of the Providence mob? It's infamous."

"You're lying. Richard is some stuffy career man who wouldn't know a mobster from his flaccid little dick. And no one you're sleeping with is more infamous than me."

"I'm not sleeping with you, Nolan. That's final."

"Not yet," I say, leaning back in my chair and wishing we were somewhere more private so I could masturbate as she fights my seduction. "Anyway, I know Richard is fake. I even know why Mr. Corporate sent you here."

"What?" she says quickly. "Why?"

"He's trying to set us up."

"What?" This time she's loud.

"Yeah," I say, taking a sip of my wine and reaching for the bread. I pull off a piece, butter it, and then place it on the little plate to her left. "Eat that. It's fucking delicious. This chef I hired can bake like a motherfucker."

"Why did he send me?" Ivy asks again, ignoring her bread.

I butter a piece of my own and then take a bite and another sip of wine to wash it down. "We're playing games."

"What kind of games?" She's angry now.

"You know Mr. Match?"

"No," she says, huffing out air that makes a little bit of hair blow up from her forehead. "Not really. I don't know his real name. But I've heard of him."

"His name is Oliver Shrike and he runs this dating site. Online dating? You ever done that?"

"Absolutely not," she says, shaking her head and blushing. Which means she totally has. I'm going to get Oliver to look that shit up for me. If she was dating online, she was probably doing it at his website.

"Well, Oliver and his sister own this big dating site. But I was at Perfect's engagement party a few weeks ago and Corporate comes up to me and says, 'Don't you think it's weird that Match has no date today? Shouldn't he have a date if he runs the country's largest online dating site?'

"I shrugged and said, 'Maybe?' So then he goes into this whole plan about how he's going to headhunt a girl for him. And he sends me this ridiculous online dating dossier this morning. A girl for Match. Right as you were pulling up in that limo, to be exact. So I think he sent you here to fix us up because I was dateless at that party too. Which means there's no Richard. Maybe there *was* a Richard, once. But he's not in the picture now. Mr.

Corporate is very thorough."

I have rendered Ivy Rockwell speechless too many times to count today. It gives me a lot of satisfaction. "You're not eating your bread, Ivy. It's good. And that fucking chef, man. She even has people making the butter from scratch. Take a bite."

"Are you for real?" Ivy asks, all her defenses down. "No man is really this full of himself."

"One hundred percent genuine. You're getting me tonight, Ivy. I hope you can handle it. Because I'd hate to disappoint Mr. Corporate at the next party."

CHAPTER TWELVE

IVY

I... have no idea what to make of him. None. This whole day, this whole experience, has been one mind trip after another. "Why would he do that?"

"I just told you," Nolan says. His voice is low and filled with ego, and self-assurance, and charm—all wrapped up into one low rumble. His voice is filled with power.

"He's trying to set you up? On... a date?" It seems silly.

But the look on Nolan's face tells me I'm reading it wrong.

"What?" I ask.

"Nothing," he says back. "So about those ideas you have."

Hmmm. So that's why he kept me here another night. He wants to pump me for information. "I don't work for free, Mr. Delaney. So you're wasting your time with this dinner."

"I don't expect it for free, Ivy." Those green eyes practically burn into mine. He doesn't blink, or avert his gaze when I stare back.

I break away first. "So you really do want to hire me? For like, a job?"

"No." He shakes his head. "More like a contractor. And not until tomorrow."

"Because you're going to fuck me first."

"Now you're catching on."

"Well." I laugh, looking out into the empty restaurant beyond the arched doorway. "You're mistaken. I'm not interested in you like that."

"Then why did you come? Hmmm? Good girls like you, Ivy Rockwell, don't get into a private jet and travel two thousand miles for an interview with someone you've never even met."

"Don't assume things about me, Nolan. I'm not as innocent as I look."

"Well." He smiles, unleashing a dimple in his chin I hadn't noticed before. "That's good to know. I was afraid I'd be wasting my time with a virgin."

I huff out an uncomfortable laugh before I can stop it.

"I mean, twenty-two is late, but it happens, right? And you are a preacher's daughter."

My heart is beating fast and I have a sudden fear that panic will overtake me and I'll say something stupid. So I shut it down. "I'm not discussing my personal details with you. So change the topic of conversation or I'll get up and walk out. I don't give a fuck who you are."

"Sure you do. That's why you came, right? The infamous Mr. Romantic. I've heard that said enough times on the news reports to accept it. They don't call Perfect infamous. Hell, they don't even call Mysterious infamous, and he's far more dangerous than I'll ever be. So I know when you figured out who the interview was with, those words danced across your tongue. And I like the swearing, Ivy. I see you haven't fallen for the bullshit your father probably sold you all growing up."

"Don't talk about my family like you know them. You have no idea what kind of man my father is."

Nolan shrugs. "Don't need to know. It's the type. The strait-laced type. The kind of people who judge before they know the whole story. I bet he sat in front of the TV and asked his God to punish me for the atrocious sin I took part in. Did he do that, Ivy?"

I huff out some air, disgusted. What does anyone see in this asshole? And he is not even a class-act asshole, like some of the boys Nora or the other sorority girls dated in college. He's the scum variety.

"He didn't, *Nolan*." I sneer his name. "He's a kind man who was very good to me."

"Except for the religious brainwashing?"

"Did you ever consider if I liked the religious brainwashing?"

"Do you?"

"I don't mind it." I shrug. "In fact, I like a lot of it. It's made me the person I am today and I'm quite proud of that. So this stupid idea you have of making me uncomfortable, or trying to get in my good graces because you think I want nothing more than to rebel against the things I was taught—well, it's not working, Mr. Romantic. You're not exactly playing your A-game today."

"Noted," he says, like he's done with the topic.

"So I would appreciate it if you'd be professional, if, in fact, you really *do* want to have a professional relationship with me. Got it?"

"Your plan," he says, not missing a beat. "Did it involve the free room idea you pitched in the meeting? Or was that just a decoy?"

"It does. Somewhat. But I already told you, I'm not discussing the plan unless we have an agreement on how you'll be paying for my expertise."

He leans back in his chair, hands in his lap. "I have no intention of taking advantage of you."

"No, you just want to fuck me." It was meant to be like a slap. And he was meant to recoil. But he doesn't react, and I find myself throbbing between my legs just from saying it out loud.

He smirks. Like he knows. I close my eyes and take a deep breath, willing that excited feeling to go away.

It doesn't take very much to turn me on. And even though there is something about him that says, *Run. Get away. Don't participate in this conversation. Go back to your room, lock the door, and don't close your eyes until you're safely back in your own bed.* I can't... I can't stop thinking about the reason I came here.

I bite my lip and wonder how crazy I'd be if I actually let him do what he wants?

"Ivy?"

"What?"

"What's on your mind?"

"Going home."

"Should I call the pilot and let you go home?"

"I thought you wanted to hear my ideas?"

"After I fuck you, I said."

I don't know what to say after that, and thankfully the servers come with the food. A plate of shell pasta filled with ricotta cheese, topped with melted mozzarella—surrounded by a perfect circle of red sauce that smells so delicious, my mouth starts watering—is placed in front of me.

The chef appears, all smiles, hands behind her back as she looks at us. "I hope you like it. It's one of my specialties. Nolan asked me to make my favorite dish for you, Miss Rockwell. And I don't want to mess up your first date, so I'm nervous."

I look at Nolan, one eyebrow raised.

He looks back, both eyebrows raised. "Taste it, Ivy. Elizabeth is waiting."

I cut off a small piece because the sauce is still steaming, and place it in my mouth.

Jesus. Yes. I'm very hungry, but this dish is amazing.

"Wow," I say, after I swallow. "It's perfect."

Elizabeth bows to me, then Nolan, her smile even bigger than before, and then backs off, and turns away, walking to the kitchen, doing a little fist pump in the air as she disappears through a door.

"Well, you made her night."

"It's really good," I say, our heated conversation over. "I was talking to her earlier. She told me some interesting things."

"Things you took note of?" Nolan prods as he takes a taste of his own pasta.

"Yes," I say, unwilling to give him any details.

"Things you won't discuss with me until tomorrow?"

"*If* I stay."

"You're staying," he says. "I already know you want to, so let's get past that. Forget about tomorrow for now, we'll do it your way. I will hire you, we will sign a contract for your consultation services, and then we'll discuss it. But tonight—I'm sorry, Ivy. Tonight, we're gonna do it my way."

I take a sip my wine, considering my options. Would it be so bad to have this very experienced man as my first?

I mean, beyond my father hating him. My father can't ever know anything about Nolan Delaney. No way. And beyond the fact that Nolan might catch on to my secret and put a stop to it, thereby humiliating me as I beg him to keep going, even though I insisted we were not going to have sex tonight.

If I could control those two variables, then would it be so bad?

"I would die to be a mind reader right now." Nolan is smiling at me, his expression nothing but cocky. Nothing but ego and self-assurance.

Nothing but the power he knows he has.

To render women powerless against his charming advances.

He knows I want him. Hell, I'm sure every woman he meets wants him.

I have never felt desirable. I have never felt wanted, not like this. I have never known the touch of a man and what that touch might mean. And I have never made a man want me so badly, I knew, no matter what I did or said, he'd never want to walk away. No transgression would be big enough for him to say no.

I can imagine Mr. Romantic being one transgression after another. And I can imagine all the hearts he's broken in the process. I can imagine all the ways in which he walks out. All the ways in which he is begged to stay.

"I would die to have your confidence right now," I say back.

And then he frowns.

CHAPTER THIRTEEN

NOLAN

I frown. Thinking about that statement for a moment.

But then she laughs. "I mean, holy hell. You are so full of yourself, Mr. Delaney, it's like ego is your superpower. Your picture is the definition of narcissist in college psychology text books. You're the cover model for self-help books that tell people to believe in themselves."

Is she insulting me? I can't tell. "I wrote a self-help book once."

"I'm not surprised. Was it called *How to Make a Woman Defenseless?*"

I narrow my eyes. "Are you implying something?"

Ivy shrugs. "Just curious."

"It's called *Rising Above*. Maybe you don't know this, but Maclean Callister has done some pretty significant things since our days at Brown. He inspired me"—I eye her, gauge her reaction—"to rise above the bullshit. And so I wrote that book."

"Did you publish it?"

"No. The title is ironic. And my lawyers thought it would ruin my chances of building up the resort and garnering investors."

"So it's not about rising above?"

"No."

She waits for me to continue, but I don't. Fuck it. If she wants to be nasty, I can play.

"It's about taking the low road?"

"Maybe."

"And that's why you're the most infamous of them

all?"

"What do you think?"

"I don't know *what* to think."

"You sure knew what to think a moment ago."

"I guess that was before I saw something real."

I lean even farther back in my chair, studying her. She really looks the college-prep boarding school part. I know. I've seen enough of those girls. Hell, I was part of that world myself. But I'm not now.

Ivy Rockwell looks like she never left that world. She looks as protected, and secluded, and every bit as innocent as I imagined, regardless of her proclamation a few minutes ago.

"I told you, this is the real me. All of it. So don't fool yourself, Ivy. You were right about me."

"So why admit it before you get what you want?"

I shrug. "Maybe I've already lost interest in you."

"Why? Not that I'm interested in you. But why? It's like one second you're into it, and then..." She realizes. She knows. She's got me. "You're still sensitive about it, aren't you? Behind that facade of bravado, you're still pissed off."

"Wouldn't you be? If you were accused of something you didn't do?"

"I think I probably would've handled it differently. Gotten better advice."

"How so?"

"Well, you guys all lawyered up. Refused to talk. That's what they said anyway."

"Is that what they said? I really wouldn't know. I didn't watch TV for five years after the charges were filed. You don't know what it's like. You have no idea what it's like."

"But if you're innocent—"

"Then I have nothing to hide? Do you really believe that? Doesn't everyone have something to hide? Well"— I laugh, shake off the anger—"it would've been very stupid to talk. That was the best advice I ever got. *Just shut the fuck up*, Match said. We were all there, fucking bewildered. No idea what was happening. No idea we'd be arrested within a week. No idea that every asshole in the country would have an opinion about our personalities, our pasts, our habits. Our guilt."

"The Misters."

"Right," I say. "Do you know why they call me Mr. Romantic?"

"Claudette said it was ironic. Like your book title."

"That's not why. I—" But I shut the fuck up. I hear Match in my head. *Just shut the fuck up until my friend gets here. He'll know what to do.* And so we did shut the fuck up. We didn't even tell each other what happened that night. No one knew what I was doing. I don't know what they were doing. None of us had alibis, because that stupid bitch was our alibi. Every single one of us.

"She set us up, Ivy. Set us up. Someone was pulling her strings, but we never figured out who. There's enough enemies to go around, I guess. But I didn't do anything wrong that night. Not one goddamned thing."

She looks down at her plate and lets out a long breath. "Sorry for mentioning it."

Sorry. She's one of those girls. Sorry. The confrontation makes her uncomfortable. Well, I'm not an apologizer. And I love confrontation. "Don't be sorry for me. It's a waste of time."

"I'm not hungry," she says, pushing away from the table. "I'm going to bed. If you want to hire me tomorrow, well, fine. I'll talk about it. But I'm done talking tonight."

I stand up and put my napkin on my plate, our food

hardly touched. "Hey," I say, taking her hand and placing it on my arm, the way I did when I walked her over here. "I'll walk you back. And I'll still fuck you tonight, Ivy. Still give you the option to suck my cock. Because once I pay you for your time, it will never happen again."

She slaps me in the face and walks out.

CHAPTER FOURTEEN
IVY

My heart is beating so fast, I feel like I might pass out. I push my way throughout the maze of tables, trying to get out of there before it happens, trying to get fresh air before I suffocate from the conversation I just had with a very fucked-up man.

But Nolan grabs my arm, jerking me to a stop. "What was that for? Why the fuck did you hit me?"

I jerk my arm away and place my hand over my eyes, swaying slightly. *I'm going to faint.* I hear the words in my head, and that shakes some sense into me.

I am not going to faint.

"I'm sorry. The heat. I'm not used to it. I feel dizzy, I want to go lie down." I jerk away from him and walk out of the restaurant, straight through the back doors, and out into the pool area. I want to jump in so bad, but my feet keep walking. Right around it, towards the private bungalows. When I look over my shoulder as I enter the narrow walkway surrounded on all sides with palm trees, Nolan is following.

I look forward again, urging my feet to go faster. But the water in the private pool looks too good to just pass by. The sun is just setting, the light is dim, but not dark. And I know if I hang out just a few more minutes, it will completely slip away and leave me alone.

How do people live out here in this heat?

It's not the heat, Ivy. It's him you need to get away from.

I reach my bungalow, open the door, and practically throw myself across the threshold. Inhaling the cool AC and dropping into a chair.

"Ivy?" Nolan knocks on the door. "What the fuck is happening?"

"I don't want to talk to you anymore."

He goes away. I know it. I don't need to get up and look. I just sit there in the chair and breathe deeply.

Why did I slap him?

Because he said he wanted to fuck me?

Wasn't that why I came here?

And he's offering me a job tomorrow.

Wasn't that what I really wanted? Both the job and the sex?

It was. But not anymore. I don't know what I want. I don't know anything. I don't understand this man, I don't trust him, and I don't think I should say anything else to him. At all.

By the time I calm down the room is dark. I make out shadows of furniture. A love seat, the bedroom door, the little kitchenette.

The bag on the other chair that holds the bathing suit I bought today.

You didn't buy it, Ivy.

I get up and grab the bag, taking the suit out of the tissue paper it's wrapped in, and hold it up.

I hear a splash from outside and walk over to the window.

Nolan is swimming. It figures. I was just thinking I'd like to go for a swim and he's already out there.

Wait. Why am I turning back into that timid girl I left behind in Rhode Island? Didn't I come her to say yes to everything I'd normally decline? Didn't I come her to say no to everything I'd normally accept?

Then why the hell am I letting him control me?

I slip my sundress off and rip the tags from the suit with my teeth and step into it. I wriggle the top part up to cover my breasts and adjust the starburst pattern of straps that point a path directly between my legs.

Screw him. I'm going to let his filthy mouth control me? Unsettle me and make me run away like a child?

No.

But… That timid voice is insistent. *But I don't even know what I'm doing.* He's going to know and if he finds out I'm a virgin, he'll stop. I just know it. Even though Claudette called him dangerous, I *know* he will stop.

If I go out there and commit to losing my virginity to Nolan Delaney, then I can't let him be the reason it doesn't happen. I will be humiliated if he figures out I'm a virgin and refuses to participate in my little plan.

Google.

Yeah. That's what the internet is for, right? I can Google it. I can look up what it's like to lose your virginity and then get ready. Prepare myself.

Oh, God, what if he really does want a blow job? I don't think I could fake that. I've seen it done, sure. But I've never, like… practiced.

I grab my phone, desperate for some advice, and type in, *What does it feel like to lose your virginity?*

I scan the results, pick the second entry, which is people telling their losing it story in a forum.

Hurts.

Feels like your vag is stretching.

Amazing.

Hurts.

Hurts.

Hurts.

There is only one story that says amazing, so I go with that one. If I'm going to do it, I want it to be amazing. I didn't save myself up all these years to let my first time be a disappointment.

My boyfriend has the biggest cock. I've seen a lot of them watching porn, so I was scared. But he was careful with me. And let me be on top. It made all the difference. I eased down at my own pace, and instead of letting him fill me, I pretended like I was covering him. I rocked my hips a little when he was inside me and that just stimulated my clit like crazy. Before I knew it, the pain was over and I was enjoying myself. I even came. I know people will say I'm lying, but he was playing with my clit the whole time. And it just felt so good.

OK. I'm feeling a little better about this. Better not ruin it with any more stories. I go back to Google and type in, *How to give a blow job.*

I get a how-to video from a porn star this time. I need visuals and I need a professional. She qualifies. I watch the girl wrap her lips around the guy's dick, her tongue flicking in and out. And then she explains the hand movements. Her palms twist as she sucks, bobbing up and down his shaft as she licks and tries to take him deep. The guy moans, so she is definitely doing it right.

I make a mental list. Suck the tip, lick it, pump my hand, twist them a little, take him deep, and then…

Ewww. She lets him come in her mouth. And when she's done, she says that's mandatory.

I don't know about that. I don't think I can. I've seen videos where they come on the girl's face. In fact, most of the time they do that.

But in a porno, the girls always lick it, which is disgusting.

I'm not going to do either of those. I'm going to let him unload in a condom.

That makes me laugh, which makes me brave.

You can do this, Ivy. He's going to make it amazing, I just know it.

I tear the hair tie out of my ponytail and shake my long blonde hair out a little. And then I step outside.

Nolan is looking directly at me, arms stretched out along the blue-tiled rim of the pool, treading water in the deep end. "Well," he says, "I didn't expect to see you again."

"Why not? Think you scare me?"

"Yes."

I lift my head up, defiant. "Well, you don't."

"Maybe you should reconsider."

I step into the pool and walk down the steps until the water is deep enough for me to sink into.

"I like the suit. It's a good choice."

I sigh, because I was brought up to be polite. And this was basically a gift. "Thank you. I do too. I can pay you for it—"

"I don't need your money."

"Whatever."

"You want to explain what set you off back there?"

OK, here goes nothing. Be Opposite Ivy. "I don't like being talked to that way."

"No?" he says back with a smile. "Why not?"

"It's rude, for one."

"It's hot."

"To you maybe. I'm not—"

But I stop short. Opposite Ivy wouldn't say that, would she? Opposite Ivy *would* like it.

"Just admit it, it's hot. I get it, you're not used to it. But that doesn't mean you have to close yourself off to it."

I don't know what to say. I'm not *really* Opposite Ivy. I wish Nora was here. She'd know what to say to a guy like Nolan Delaney. She'd have quick, witty comebacks all ready to go. She'd stand toe to toe with him and come out winning.

Nolan pushes off the wall of the pool and comes swimming towards me. Slowly. One leisurely stroke at a time. "You're not what, Ivy? Hot? Desirable? Ready for something... new and different?"

I am ready for something new and different. Even though he scares me. I am ready. I swim forward, doing a side stroke into the middle of the pool, and meet him halfway.

"What happened back there?"

"Nothing happened. I was mad. That's all."

"Because I said I wanted to fuck you? Put my cock in your mouth? Are you really that timid?"

"I'm not used to it."

He moves closer, his arms wrapping around my waist, and my hands automatically go to his shoulders to keep afloat.

"That's a step forward."

"Look—"

"No, you look. Don't be so uptight. Just relax, for fuck's sake. Enjoy it. It's a hot summer night, we're in the middle of the desert, at a huge resort that has a total of thirteen guests including you. We're in a secluded pool, total privacy."

Oh, my God. I think he wants to fuck me in the pool. This is going way too fast for me.

"Your heart is beating so fast. Do I scare you that much? Do you really think I'm a rapist?"

"That's not what—" But I stop again. Because he's going to ask me what I'm really worried about if I continue.

"Then what?"

"I mean, yes, of course. You have a very bad reputation, Nolan. It's something I can't forget about."

He looks me in the eyes for a few seconds. "You only see what they want you to see. A bad guy. A player. And yeah, I've had my share of fun and most of it has been with women. But I'm not that guy in the news. I'm just Mr. Romantic."

I make a noise that might be a laugh if I wasn't so nervous. "I'm not sure that's any better than Nolan Delaney."

"It is," he says. His hands slide over my hips in a very provocative gesture. One even slips over the curve of my ass cheek, his fingers lifting the bathing suit up a few inches. "Trust me, it is."

I stare at his eyes, the green shimmering with the light reflecting off the water. "You said it was ironic. Like your book."

"It was meant to be. But if you ever get to know the real me, you'll see what I mean. I'm not all irony, Ivy. I have a very serious, straight side too."

"Show me," I say, surprised by my bravado.

He leans in and kisses me. His hand leaves my hip and grabs the back of my neck, preventing me from pulling away.

I don't pull away, so it's a wasted gesture. And as soon as he understands that, he fists it and pushes me closer. I wrap my legs around his waist and feel his hard cock rubbing the sensitive skin near my ass.

I could go all the way tonight. Let him tease me into the adult world of sex, and dirty talk, and midnight fucks in a swimming pool. I could let him just... be him. And tomorrow this will be over. I'll just be Ivy again, minus one intact cherry. And we'll talk business.

I could do this and go home feeling new and ready for whatever comes. A new man, a new job, a new life.

"Have you ever done it in a pool, Ivy?" he says into

my mouth.

I shake my head no.

"Well." He reaches one arm out, pulling us through the water towards the shallow end. And when his feet touch the floor, he walks forward. My arms are still holding onto his perfect shoulders, my legs still circling his muscled waist. "It's not as fun as it sounds." He carries me up the steps of the pool and walks over to his bungalow. "So we're going to take this inside."

CHAPTER FIFTEEN

NOLAN

She clings to me. And even though that little display back in the restaurant should be nothing but warning bells going off in my head, I ignore them. Something is wrong, but I'm not sure it's about me. So I'm going to ignore it.

Her heart is beating so fast against my chest, I almost ask her what the fuck. But I figure it's just a little residual fear over what Claudette told her. I'm dangerous.

I'm mad about that, and I will be confronting Claudette about it later.

But not now. She's hundreds of miles away. Right now the only thing I want to do is fuck this girl. I get it, she's inexperienced. Probably only ever fucked one guy. I like that, to be honest. I like her inexperience.

"Don't be nervous," I say in her ear when we step into my bedroom. I set her down and say, "It's fine. I'm good, I swear."

"I don't doubt it. But I'm—" She stops short.

"You're what?"

"I'm not that good."

"It's OK. I'll be patient. I'll tell you what I like and if you tell me what you like, it will be a lot of fun. Don't you want to have fun, Ivy? Say screw tomorrow and have some fun?"

"Yeah." She sighs. "I want to think I do, anyway."

"OK," I say, dragging the strap of her bathing suit down her shoulder. "Did you buy this to drive me crazy? Because it's sexy as fuck."

"No." But then she stops and reconsiders. I know because she blushes. Even though there is only one small

105

light on in my room, I can see the redness of her cheeks. "Maybe a little."

"So you were thinking about me? About how I wanted to fuck you."

She nods.

"Say it."

"Say what?" she whispers.

"Say you want me to fuck you."

She bites her lip and I can't control myself. I lean in and kiss her. My tongue is more demanding now. "I'll lick your pussy like this if you want. Do you want me to lick your pussy?"

She swallows hard and nods. "Yes."

"How do you like it? Fast and thrusting? Or slow and swirly?"

"Um…" She stops, like she's really considering this question. It's cute. She takes it all so, *so* seriously.

"Say it, Ivy. Tell me. The more you tell me, the better it will be. I'll do whatever you want. Lick you, suck you, squeeze your tits until you whimper. I'll fuck your ass if you want. I bet your asshole is a virgin, isn't it? I bet you have no idea how good that feels, do you?"

"No," she says.

"I can show you. Maybe not tonight. Maybe tomorrow night. Would you like that?"

"Yes," she breathes into my mouth. "Maybe tonight. Maybe we can do that?"

"Ah, you horny little slut. You want me in your ass? Fuck, yeah, Ivy Rockwell, I'm going to make you wish you met me years ago, before anyone else got to you first. Ruined you with boring intercourse. I won't ruin you, Ivy. I'm going to make you wish I was your first. Make you beg me to do it again, and again."

"Make me wish that, Nolan."

"I will. I will." I lower her other strap, and then yank her wet bathing suit down her body and peel it off, asking her to step out of it, one leg at a time, as she holds tight to my shoulders.

I throw it aside and she says, a little breathlessly, "I want to be on top."

"OK, baby. I'm not gonna argue with that. But take my shorts off first. You can't suck my cock with my shorts on." She takes a deep breath and I start wondering just how much BJ experience she has. "Have you ever sucked a cock before?"

She shakes her head, just a little bit. Like she's embarrassed.

Jesus. That makes me so fucking hard. "Don't worry," I say, petting her hair, the silky blonde strands slipping through my fingers until I reach her breast. I pinch her nipple and she moans. "I'll tell you just how I like it. OK?" She presses her lips together, like she might not be OK with this. "For a girl who wants me to fuck her ass tonight, you sure seem nervous about all this other stuff."

"Sorry," she says.

"Don't be. I love it. I love knowing I'll be your first. I'll teach you everything, Ivy. Now get on your fucking knees and take my shorts off so I can stick my cock down your throat."

She starts breathing heavy, almost panting. But she drops to her knees. I place her hand on my hard cock and make her squeeze it.

"Do it," I say, grabbing her hair and yanking a little. She moans again as her fingertips ease under the waistband of my swim trunks, tugging them down my legs until they drop on the floor.

I fist my cock, pumping it a few times, and say, "Are

you ready to blow me?"

"Yessss," she hisses through her teeth.

"Then put your hand right here, Ivy." I take her hand and place it over my shaft.

"You're so hard."

"You make me hard. Now pump it. *Yeah*," I say, "just like that." She's got a little technique going and I'm pleasantly surprised, a twisting motion as she slides her hand up and down my dick. "I want to be inside your mouth, Ivy. I want to feel your throat. Open up."

She opens her mouth, leaning forward, but then she hesitates.

"It's OK," I say. "I won't go deep. *Yet.*" Her eyes dart up to meet mine and I grip her hair even tighter. "Jesus, Ivy. Are you sure this is your first time?"

She smiles, gaining confidence.

"Open wider, Ivy. It's not going to fit like that."

She opens wider, waiting for me to move forward, but instead of doing it that way, I surprise her when I thrust her towards me and my dick slips inside her hot, wet mouth. Her lips seal around it automatically, her teeth scraping along my skin. I wince, but I don't chastise her. I'll take what I can get right now. If I scare her, she might not want to finish me off.

I ease deeper and she gags. I love the fucking gag reflex. I love when I'm fucking a girl and I stick my fingers down her throat to make her gag. Her pussy clamps down, every time.

I want to feel that with Ivy Rockwell.

I need my fingers in her pussy. I need to make her gag on my cock as I'm fingering her, just so I can feel the muscles clamp down.

"Get up," I say, pulling on her hair as she stands. "Shhh," I say, when she looks worried. "I love it. But I want to finger you as you suck. So come here."

I sit down on the bed and lie back. "Turn around, Ivy. Sit on my chest and suck my cock while I stare at your pussy."

She takes a deep breath and lets it out. But she climbs on, and positions herself just as I asked. Her ass is perfect. Two round globes, her pussy peeking out at me, practically dripping. Practically begging me to fuck her.

"Suck, baby. Keep going."

She lowers her mouth to my dick again, her hot breath covering me, until her wet tongue is licking and swirling around my head.

"Deeper," I say, scooting her down so she will be able to take me in. I grab her hair and push. She responds by opening wider, gagging a little.

I shake my head. Damn. Everything she's doing is perfect.

My fingers can't get inside her fast enough. I slip one in and she startles, gasping for air. But I just say, "Shhh," and keep her head in position.

I go slower this time, easing in and out of her pussy. It's slick enough, so I stick another finger in. This time she wriggles until my fingers fall out.

"You don't like it?" I ask.

"I do," she says, the air cold against my wet dick. "I just like it… slow. Can you do it slow?"

"Sure," I say. "I'll do anything you say, Ivy. So don't be shy. The key to fantastic sex is talking. I like it fast. I want your head bobbing up and down my dick like you want to eat it. So if you do it my way, I'll do it your way."

She inhales and then resumes, her motion much faster now, just the way I like it.

I go slow. So painfully fucking slow. It drives me crazy to do it her way. It makes me so fucking hard, I just want to explode.

Easy, Nolan.

"Fuck, yes, Ivy. That's perfect." I can feel her smile around my cock and I take my attention back to her pussy. I let go of her hair and use my fingers to spread her open, then sit up a little so I can lick her clit.

"Oh, my God," she says, my dick falling out of her mouth.

"What?"

"That feels so good."

Shit, that boring boyfriend guy must not know how to lick pussy, because this is basic stuff.

Well, I have no complaints about that. She will never forget the way I eat pussy. I'm going to ruin her for life with this night.

I ease a finger in and wish I could lick her everywhere, finger her, and fuck her all at the same time.

She moans and wiggles, but she doesn't stop again. Her mouth is so full of saliva, I can feel it dripping down onto my balls. So I pump her a little harder. Soft and slow is nice, but the hard fuck is what makes girls come.

"Do you like it?" I ask.

"Mmmm," she moans.

"Come," I say. "Come like this and then I'll make you come again. I'll make you come all night if you want, but I want to taste it right now."

Her moans get deeper and I know she's close, so I grab her hair again and start thrusting my cock inside her mouth. She gags, pulls back. But I hold her there. Waiting for it. Waiting for her throat to constrict, to grip me tight. And when that happens, she clenches her pussy, gasping for breath, desperate to get my cock out of her mouth as she comes all over my fingers.

I lean forward and lick her juices as I blow my load

into her throat.

CHAPTER SIXTEEN

IVY

I have never. Ever. Had an orgasm like that. And if this is what sex is like, and he's not even inside me yet, it is amazing.

But then I feel his cock tighten, and then there's a rush of come, filling my mouth, sliding down my throat. I pull back, gagging, choking. His come drips out of my mouth. The taste of salt and something else I can't identify—*come*, I say in my head.

"Turn around, Ivy. You want to be on top? Get the fuck on top. I can come again and again."

"Condom," I say, wiping my mouth.

"Fuck," he says. "I'm clean. Aren't you on birth control?"

"No," I say. "Condom."

"OK," he says, pushing me off to the side as he gropes around for a towel. He wipes my face with a smile. "You like that? You came pretty hard. I felt your pussy gripping my fingers."

That's... a thing? "*You* liked *that*?" I look at his legs, all wet with the come I spit out.

"Liked?" he says. "Fucking loved it. You're a blow job natural, Ivy." And then he leans down and kisses me on the lips. "That's what I taste like," he says, pulling away. And then he slips his fingers inside my mouth and says, "This is what you taste like."

I taste sweet. He tastes salty.

He kisses me on the mouth again. "I gotta go find a condom. Just relax for a second."

I rest my head back on the covers and stare up at the

ceiling. I came. My fingers dip between my legs, amazed at how wet it is down there. I came with a guy. And I sucked his dick. And I liked it.

When he had his fingers inside me, it hurt. I thought for sure he'd know. I thought for sure there'd be blood or something to give away my secret. But he didn't. He just kept going.

I'm smiling when Nolan returns, rolling the condom over his still fully-erect cock.

He bounces on the bed next to me, lying back and patting his stomach. "Climb on, Ivy. Face me this time so I can squeeze your tits and slap your ass at the same time."

Jesus.

But it surprises me how happy he seems. All the walls he had earlier are down.

Is that all it takes to get a man to open up to you? Sex?

"Come on, baby. I'm ready to go again." He pulls me towards him, and when I swing my leg over his middle, he slaps my ass hard and says, "Hurry. I need to be inside you."

This is when I get nervous. A finger or two is not that giant cock I just had in my mouth. "I like it slow, remember?"

"I'm OK with slow." And then he winks. "At first."

Oh, God. All my bravery is gone. I'm really going to let him put his dick in me.

And it's going to hurt, hurt, hurt. Just like those girls said on that forum.

I hover over him, hesitant. And just as I'm about to tell him maybe this isn't a good idea, he says, "Wait."

"Wait?"

"Yeah, hold on." His fingers slide between my legs, pushing into my pussy. "Let me get you good and wet."

Oh, yeah. I've read about lube. We're not using lube, but I'm slick down there.

"Fuck, Ivy."

"What? What's wrong?"

"Nothing." He laughs. "Nothing at all. You're just so goddamned wet. I want to lick your pussy so bad."

"We can do that instead," I say, hopeful.

"Fuck that. We can do that all night. Right now, all I want is for you to push yourself down on my cock and let me fuck you—"

"Slow," I remind him.

"Right. We can do it slow."

I take a deep breath and ease myself down. He guides the tip of his dick into my opening, pushing against my folds.

It fucking hurts! Those girls were right. It fucking hurts!

"Relax," Nolan says. "Why are you so tense?" He massages my shoulders for a second and I try to relax. I think I read once that tensing up makes pain worse. But that was for like, a broken ankle or something. Not losing your virginity.

"That's better," he says. "And I get it, you like it slow. But not too slow, right?"

He likes it fast and hard. He's said this a few times already. So I smile and say. "Not too slow."

"Good," he says, like he really means it.

I don't want to disappoint him or make him suspicious. So I ease down a little more. It's feels like my vagina is being ripped open. But I bite back the moan of pain and bury my head in his shoulder.

Nolan responds by wrapping his arms around me and moving his hips in a gentle sideways motion.

It feels good. The pain recedes, and the way he's

moving makes me arch my back. Somehow, he's hitting my clit.

"Do you like that?" Nolan asks when a soft moan fills the room.

"Yes." I don't even recognize my voice. My mind is filled with the pleasure.

I ease my hips down a little more, sinking over his cock. Covering him, like the girl described in her post. I feel in control. Like I'm the one calling the shots.

"Move your hips with mine, Ivy. Yeah," he says, when I respond. "Like that. You're driving me fucking crazy with this slow stuff."

But I like it. It's perfect. I'm used to his thickness now. The stretching feeling is going away. I'm actually enjoying myself.

"I'd like to flip you over, Ivy. Push your face into the mattress. I'd pound you hard. I'd pull your fucking hair so hard, pull your head so far back, you'd have to look me in the eyes as my other hand wrapped around your throat. I'd kiss your mouth as I made you come all over my dick."

I can feel my next orgasm building. I'm bewildered by all of this. The way he's talking to me. What he's doing to me. It's everything I thought it'd be. He is everything in bed. Everything a girl wants.

"Come, Ivy. Come right now."

I do. I come. I come and he holds me close, makes me feel so close to him. I bite his shoulder as the wave of pleasure makes me shudder. And I wait for him to do the same. But he doesn't. He doesn't stop, his hips never stop that motion. And before I know it, he's thrusting up against me. I realize then that he wasn't fully inside me... *but he is now.*

I scream from the pain, and all Nolan hears is the pleasure of my orgasm. Because he breathes hard in my ear, saying, "Yes, yes, yes," over and over again. And then he stops. "My turn, Ivy. My way now."

He rolls us over, his crushing weight pushing me into the bed, but all I'm thinking about is the relief of not having him pounding his dick into me.

A second later I'm face down on the mattress, his chest pushing hard against my back. His mouth on the back of my neck. "Now you'll see how I do it. None of that soft shit, Ivy. I like it hard. And when I'm done, you'll like it hard too."

He grabs a fistful of my hair, yanking my head back. just the way he told me he would.

He pulls hard, making me look up at the ceiling. I concentrate on it as he thrusts his dick back into my pussy.

I scream again, the pain shooting through my body.

"Fuck, yes," Nolan says, his face hovering over mine now. Hiding the view of the ceiling. "Scream, Ivy. I like the way you scream."

He fucks me.

Hard. And when he's ready, he pulls out, rips the condom off, flips me over, and says, "Open your fucking mouth."

I do it automatically. Like I'm under some kind of spell. And then he comes all over my face, my tongue, my hair.

And when he's done, he collapses on top of me, rolls to the side when I grunt and try to escape, and wraps his arms around me. "We're going to do this again. Later, when I'm not so sleepy and content."

I cry into my pillow, sticky and wet from his come. I wipe as much of it as I can on the pillowcase and then just lie still as the hours tick off. I don't fall asleep until there's a crack of light coming through the closed blinds.

I feel like I just barely closed my eyes when Nolan

gets up and walks into the bathroom. I roll over and watch him disappear inside, then scoot over on to the other side of the bed so he won't get any funny ideas about fucking me again when he comes back. I pretend to sleep. I squeeze my eyes closed and start breathing heavy. Faking it.

He returns a few minutes later, but he doesn't join me in bed. I feel a wave of relief. I can't fuck him again. Ever. He's too much. Way too much. That hurt so bad last night. It wiped away all the stuff I loved. I will never have sex again, I know it. My vagina is permanently damaged.

"What the fuck, Ivy?" Nolan asks, annoyed. "Why didn't you tell me you were on your period? I would've put a towel down."

"I'm not—" I stop. Because I realize what's on the bed. Blood. Evidence of my lie.

But before I can say anything else, someone is pounding on his door.

"Nolan!" Claudette's voice booms from outside. "Open this fucking door, right now!"

CHAPTER SEVENTEEN

NOLAN

"I thought you said your sister was out of town?"

I just stare at Ivy, ignoring my sister's tantrum. "What do you mean you're not on your period? Then why were you bleeding last night?" It's not a lot of blood, but it's definitely blood.

"Nolan," Ivy says. "I can explain."

"Explain what?"

Claudette is still pounding on the front door to the room. In fact, she might be kicking it.

"I just..."

"Wait," I say, putting the pieces together. "No. It's not possible. You're... you were a virgin? Jesus Christ, Ivy! What the fuck is wrong with you?"

She jumps up from the bed as I pull on some shorts. "What are you doing?"

"What does it look like I'm doing?" I look around for her clothes, realize she came here in a bathing suit, and then fish through my drawers until I come up with a shorts and t-shirt for her too. "Put these on," I say, throwing them at her.

"Why are you mad?"

I grab my hair to think this through as I pace the room. Claudette is still throwing her fit. "I took your virginity?"

Ivy pulls the shorts up and then hastily drags the t-shirt over her head. "Why are you mad about it?"

"Why didn't you say something? Holy shit. I fucked you hard, Ivy. You can't tell me that it felt good!"

"Some of it did."

"Some of it?" I just shake my head at her. "Why didn't you tell me?" When she says nothing I get angry. "Ivy Rockwell, I need that fucking answer. *Now.*"

"Because you might not have wanted to."

"Is this the reason you came here? To trick me into taking your virginity?"

"You're the one who invited me here!" she yells. "You came on to me!"

I need to calm down. I need a deep breath and about ten minutes to think about this, and I can't fucking do that with my goddamned sister screaming outside.

"I didn't trick you, Nolan," Ivy says.

"But you didn't tell me, either. Why not? And don't say because I might have put a stop to it. That's fucking lame. It's my right not to fuck you, isn't it? So what you did, Ivy, was fucking dishonest. Do you have any idea how bad this looks from my point of view?"

"Nolan, look—"

But before Ivy can finish, Claudette comes barging in, having apparently given up hope that I will answer the door and used her master key. "Get away from him, Ivy."

"Jesus Christ. I'm not dangerous, Claudette. She doesn't need your protection. Believe me, she's got her secrets too."

"That's why I'm here, Nolan. She certainly does have her secrets. Did you know she lied on her résumé?"

"I did not lie!" Ivy yells.

"Are you trying to tell me that you actually did graduate Brown with an MBA, Ivy? Because I've already checked, honey. You're as fake as that blonde hair you have."

"I don't dye my hair!"

"Enough!" I say. "Enough. Now what the fuck is going on here?"

"That résumé she sent us is a lie!" Claudette yells.

"I didn't send you people a résumé! You came knocking on my door!" Ivy's face is red and she's breathing hard, clutching the t-shirt at her chest like she needs something to hold onto.

I took her virginity. I made her give me a blow job. I flipped her over and fucked her hard. I thought she was screaming out of pleasure, but it was fake. It was all a lie.

I hold absolutely still. And in that moment, *everything* goes still. Ivy goes still. Claudette goes still. And there are about three seconds of complete silence before I look at Ivy.

"You lied to me."

"Nolan," she says, taking a step towards me.

"Stop," I say. "And answer my question. Did you graduate Brown with an MBA?"

She shakes her head, her face nothing but a frown.

I glance at Claudette and find a satisfied look on her face, her arms crossed over her chest, her chin tipped up in smugness, like she's so very proud that she caught Ivy in this lie. And she doesn't even know about the other lie yet.

Two lies. Two. I don't put up with lies. Not even one lie. So the fact that Ivy Rockwell tricked me into taking her virginity *and* lied on her résumé... well, I can't.

"I think you need to leave, Ivy. It was nice meeting you."

Ivy sighs, then nods her head, walks across the bungalow, and out the door.

I look back at Claudette.

"I knew there was something weird about her, Nolan. I told her to stay away from you."

"Yeah," I say, angry with her too. "You told her I was dangerous. Just what the fuck, Claudette? Why the hell would you say something like that?"

"I'm not the bad guy here, Nolan. I told her to stay away from you for your protection. And it's clear I was right. She was lying to get close to you, don't you see it?"

I can see it, that's the part I hate so much. Ivy wanted me for *something*, but she didn't want me.

She wanted to tell her friends that she tricked the infamous Mr. Romantic into taking her virginity. She wanted me to believe she was something she's not. She played with me, from the moment she stepped off the jet, right up until the moment she left my room.

I fucked her.

I can't even think about what it felt like for her last night. I can't even think about how she will probably twist this story. I can't even think about seeing my face on the news again.

I don't fuck virgins for a reason. I don't want to be careful and I don't want to be someone's trophy. I don't want to be a story that gets told over and over.

"You slept with her," Claudette says. "Didn't you?"

I nod, but I don't look at her. I just go back to my bed and start ripping off the sheets before Claudette—

"Is that blood?"

Fuck.

"Nolan, please tell me you didn't get rough with her. We don't need any more shame brought on our family name because of you."

"Of course not," I snarl. And I didn't. It was definitely rough by virgin standards, but I'm not someone who likes sexual blood play. "And fuck you for even thinking that."

"Then why are you changing the sheets? Why is there blood—Oh, good God. She wasn't a virgin. Was she?"

"Yup," I say. "She was. But she isn't now."

"I cannot believe that sneaky little bitch."

I sigh. Because I can't either. I never saw it coming. I saw exactly what she wanted me to see. An innocent college grad looking for her first big opportunity.

Well, she got more out of this than I did, that's for sure. So even if she's not the business-school prodigy I thought she was, she's damn cunning. She got me.

"I'm calling the pilot right now," Claudette says. "She's out of here, Xavier," Claudette says into her phone. "I need the jet fueled and ready to take Miss Rockwell back to Rhode Island immediately."

"That's probably the best idea," I say, balling up the sheets and tossing them into the corner for the maids to take care of. I sit back down on the mattress and hang my head in my hands, scrubbing them up and down my face for a few seconds.

I'm disappointed.

I'm really fucking disappointed. How could I have been so blind? How could I not have noticed the way she was writhing when I flipped her over and started fucking her from behind? How could I not have seen this coming?

How could Mr. Corporate make such a huge mistake?

I reach for my phone on the bedside table and thumb through my contacts until I find his face. Claudette is still talking, her words coming out in a rush that I need to ignore. I can't.

I press Corporate's contact. But it goes to voicemail, even when I try his office. Not even his assistant is answering his calls today. It's Saturday. And she said he had a full schedule of meetings today.

It's not unusual for him to work weekends. He does whatever it takes to headhunt the perfect corporate executive. Meets them wherever they are. Travels all over the world.

And maybe it's not so weird that he doesn't pick up? How would I know? I've barely talked to him over the years. I'm only talking to him now because Perfect and I are still sorta close and he recommended I ask Corporate for help in finding a manager.

I end that call and tuck my phone in my shorts pocket.

"I'm outta here," I say, dialing the front desk on the hotel phone. "Get my car ready, Denise." I hang up and look at Claudette. "I'm going back to San Diego for the rest of the weekend. You can hold things down?"

Claudette stops rambling on about Ivy Rockwell, and she nods. "Of course, Nol. Of course. I'll take care of everything. Don't worry. I'm sorry you got hurt by this. You know I just want to protect you, right?"

"I know," I say as I pull a shirt on and slip my feet into some old Chucks I've had since college.

We walk out of the bungalow together, make our way into the main building, and then say goodbye in the lobby.

My little silver Porsche Carrera is already waiting and I can't get in fast enough. I tip the valet and slide behind the wheel, eager to forget about this day before it even properly starts. It's only nine AM.

I shift into gear and speed down the resort driveway, the tall palm trees I paid almost half a million dollars to ship and plant blurring by as I pass.

Why? Why did Ivy do this? How did I misread her so badly? Was it Claudette? Did she somehow taint my instincts? Was I just being stupid? Horny? I've been out here for two weeks. No girls, no clubs to run, no fun.

But Ivy has to have an explanation.

Doesn't she?

CHAPTER EIGHTEEN

IVY

I am already packed since I barely brought anything. So all I have to do is slip my shoes on and grab my carry-on bag.

I guess you blew it, Ivy.

I guess I did.

I make my way to the lobby and inform the desk staff that I will be waiting in the bar until the plane is ready. There's no bartender. It's not even nine in the morning. But I don't care. I'm not looking for a drink, I'm trying to hide.

And I'm eternally grateful that I didn't sit in the main lobby, because a few minutes after I sit down Claudette and Nolan appear. There's a quick, awkward goodbye, and then Nolan leaves.

I can't believe how badly this all turned out. And maybe last night's mistake is my fault, but I'm not responsible for that résumé.

Claudette talks to the desk staff, and then the girl points towards me. Claudette turns around, and I swear, even though she is all the way across the lobby, I can see her eyes squint down in anger.

Here we go.

I guess I won't get out of here without some bruises after all, even if it's only to my ego.

Claudette's shoes make a tapping sound as she comes closer, but she stops just at the edge of the bar entrance. "The jet is ready, Miss Rockwell. The car to take you to the airstrip will be here momentarily. Please, wait outside." She turns on her heel and walks away.

Banished. I've been banished from their resort forever.

I don't bother trying to explain. What does it matter? My fancy weekend is over.

So I get up and drag my carry-on case behind me as I make my way through the lingering haze of Claudette's sick perfume to the front of the lobby. There is no car outside, but I have my orders. So when the automatic doors open, I step into the unbearable summer heat.

A hot desert wind blows my hair and I catch Nolan's scent coming off the shirt I'm wearing. It's an old Padres t-shirt. San Diego. Very… *him.*

I will never tell anyone about this. Ever. I will take this humiliating experience to my grave. No one will ever know that Mr. Romantic took my virginity. I will lie to Nora when I get home and tell her nope, no job and yep, still a virgin.

Just like you lied to Nolan.

Did I lie to Nolan? It didn't feel like a lie. But his words, they are ringing in my head. *Do you have any idea how bad this looks from my point of view?* It was meaningful. It was heartfelt. It was the most emotion I've ever seen from Mr. Romantic.

He was referring to the way that girl lied about him back in college. He must have a lot of trust issues. And who can blame him? If I had gone through that, I'd have trust issues too.

And I earned his distrust. Because he's one hundred percent right. I did come here to lose my virginity to him. At first. But that's not really what I was thinking when it finally happened. I just wanted… *him.* That's all. I just wanted his attention. I liked the way he was flirting with me. I liked holding on to him in the pool. Wrapping myself up next to his hard, warm body.

He felt like... like a possibility. Like maybe he and I might turn into something more. Like he and I were special.

That is so stupid.

I haven't even known him for twenty-four hours.

But... I can imagine, in a fantastical kind of way, that we made a connection. When he talked about himself I only wanted to hear more. When we were having sex, before he got rough, it was perfect. It felt good. *He* felt good.

A long black car pulls up, and while I was almost certain that Claudette would make me take a taxi, she didn't. It's for me. Not the same driver from before.

He puts my carry-on in the trunk and then we're on our way.

I look out the back window as the tall palm trees flash by, and twenty minutes later, we're at the airstrip.

It's not busy here. Who is flying in and out of Borrego Springs in August? Just me.

I thank the driver and take my case.

"Miss Rockwell!" I look up at my name and spy Jerry, the flight attendant, waving at me from the top of the stairs. I wave back. "Did you have a nice stay?" he asks, once I'm in earshot.

"Yes," I lie. "Very nice. But no job offers, unfortunately."

"Well, it's not over for you yet, Ivy Rockwell. I know you're going places, so don't worry too much."

"You're right," I say. "And you know, I'm really tired, so can I take you up on the offer of a bedroom during the flight?"

"Sure," Jerry says, leading me towards the back of the jet. He pulls a panel aside to reveal a small room filled mostly with a large bed. It's tight, but I don't care. I keep my purse, but nothing else, and the minute he closes the door back up, I fall face-first onto the soft comforter.

And cry.

I sit up and rub my eyes. We're still in the air, so I'm still stuck in this nightmare. I get up and grab my purse and open the door. There's a bathroom across the hall. I know this from the last trip on the plane.

I try to close the door as quietly as I can so Jerry won't know I'm awake, but there's a knock as soon as I engage the lock.

I disengage and open the door to Jerry's smiling face. Can't put anything over on him.

"Miss Rockwell, as soon as you're done in there I'm going to need you to take your seat and buckle in. We'll be landing soon."

"We will? Jesus, I must've slept for a long time."

"We've only been in the air for about twenty minutes."

"What? Then why are we landing?"

"We're only going to San Diego." He shoots me a puzzled look.

"What? No, I'm supposed to go home! To Rhode Island!"

"Mr. Delaney came by just before you did and told us to bring you to San Diego. He said you have a second interview."

"He did?"

Jerry cocks his head and gives me a funny look. "You didn't?"

"I… I don't know. We had an unexpected end to our morning. Claudette—"

"Don't say the demon's name," Jerry says, rolling his

eyes. "I completely understand. She's horrible, right?"

"Right?" I ask back, smiling now that I have a friend. "I hate her. She's a liar too."

"Don't get me started, Miss Rockwell. But hurry now. Use the facilities and come up front so you can buckle in. We'll be landing in a few minutes."

I do as I'm told and quickly make my way to the front where I buckle in to a plush leather seat just as the pilot announces our final descent.

The landing is smooth and easy, and my stomach starts fluttering when I suddenly realize what's happening.

Nolan didn't walk out on me this morning.

He brought me here to San Diego against Claudette's wishes to see him.

It's all I can do to hold still as we taxi, and then I have to wait until the stairs are pushed up to the jet and the door is opened. I say a quick, "Thanks," to Jerry and rush out.

There he is. About a hundred yards away, leaning casually on a silver Porsche with his arms folded across his chest. I don't know what this about at all. But the only way to find out is to walk over to him.

I take a deep breath and one step at a time, I get closer. Even in his casual, grungy clothes, he is beautiful. I realize how tan his skin is in the bright morning sun. How muscular his arms are. When I get up close enough to talk without shouting, I realize he's trying very hard not to smile.

"What are we doing?"

He shrugs and unleashes the grin, flipping his sunglasses up onto his head. "I told you, Miss Rockwell, if you let me fuck you last night I'd hire you and get your expertise this morning."

"But Claudette—"

"Fuck Claudette. She has my best interests in mind,

but she's not my mother. I don't answer to Claudette, or anyone else, for that matter. So if I want to have sex with you and hire you the next day, I will."

I sigh in frustration.

"And if I want to have sex with you and then get to know you better, then I'll do that too."

"What?"

His smile fades. "But it was a dick move, Ivy. Not telling me you were a virgin."

"I get it," I say. "You don't trust women, do you? Not after what happened to you in college."

"Not much, no. But I don't think you lied about the résumé, did you?"

"I didn't," I say. "I swear."

"I think Mr. Corporate did it."

"Why is he doing this though?"

Nolan shrugs. "He had to have seen you somewhere. And I guess he just thought I'd be interested in this." He waves a hand down my body. "And I am, Ivy."

"OK, wait. My turn. I actually did think... maybe... you'd take a liking to me and relieve me of my v-card while I was here. I mean, I did know I was not really qualified to get that job. But I came anyway. Because of you. I came because of you, Nolan."

"I did make you come." He winks. "Didn't I?"

The laugh escapes my mouth and I have to shake my head. "Yes. Yes. You did."

"But I was rough too, wasn't I?"

I swallow a little and nod. I feel a lot better than I did this morning. I guess I was overreacting about the 'never having sex again' thing. I'm not damaged. I'm still sore, but it's fading. I'm actually sorry it's fading. I liked being reminded of Nolan's cock inside me. "It was still fun. It was just a little bit scary too." I blush like mad.

"I can do it better, Ivy. I mean—" It's his turn to laugh. "I mean, better for a girl who needs it soft. I loved every fucking minute of last night. And I don't know who's running the blow job classes, but you get an A, woman. It was amazing."

"Some porn star on PornTube was giving lessons."

"Ah," Nolan says, placing his hands on my hips and pulling me up to him. "You like porn? What would your father say about that?"

"He would die of embarrassment. And if he ever met you, he'd probably lock me up in the basement."

"Well, I'm actually a nice guy, Ivy. So I'll deal with him later."

I can't imagine what is going through his head right now. We're talking about him meeting my father? "Who are you and what did you do with Nolan?"

"What?" He laughs. "I grew up in boarding school too, Ivy. I know the drill. And I'd just like you to know if I want to, I can pass inspection. But forget that for now. I'm fucking hungry and Claudette came storming in and messed up all my breakfast plans. Let's just go eat."

He opens the door on his Porsche and I slip inside and try to calm my racing heart as he opens the front trunk and places my carry-on inside.

When he gets in and starts the engine, the whole car rumbles. It all becomes real.

I slept with Mr. Romantic.

I am in his car, going out for breakfast in San Diego.

Yesterday morning, I was in Rhode Island. I had no job prospects, no boyfriend, and no life to speak of.

And now I'm here.

It all seems too good to be true.

CHAPTER NINETEEN

NOLAN

"Where are we going?" Ivy asks when we've been traveling on the freeway for about thirty minutes.

"Del Mar. Do you like the races, Ivy? The horses are running. So we're gonna go on down there to the club and have some brunch before post time."

"I can't go like this," she says, pulling on my t-shirt.

"We can stop by my house and you can change first if you like."

"Yes," she says quickly. "Please. I actually love horses. I've been riding since I was six. And I've been to the races before. It's a fancy affair."

"It doesn't have to be. All kinds of people go to the races."

"Not to the *Club*."

I shrug. "They know me. I have a box there. I go all the time in the summer. In fact, you can see the track from my house. So if I don't feel like going down there, I just walk out onto the master bedroom terrace and enjoy it from afar."

"Wow, that must be some house."

"You're gonna see it for yourself. We're only minutes away."

I pull into the private Boca Del Mar neighborhood and Ivy's eyes go big as she checks out the houses. "Holy crap," she says. "You're really rich. I mean, I see the Porsche and you do own that resort. And I know about the clubs. But this is something, Nolan. I'm breathless."

"You haven't even seen the view yet, Ivy. You know what's funny about this house?" I ask, pulling up to my gate and activating the remote control.

"What?" Ivy asks, as we wait for the gate to open.

"I didn't even want it." I pull the car forward and Ivy is craning her neck to get a glimpse of the house as we weave around the lush landscaping.

"Why not?" she asks, her head tipping up as I park in front of the house. "Wow," she breathes. "It's huge! What's wrong with *this* place?"

I get out and go around to her side, opening her door and giving her my hand to help her up from the low-profile car. "Oh, there's nothing wrong with it. It just wasn't my thing. But Mysterious owned it before me, and he said he needed the cash. But he didn't want to sell it to strangers because he likes the races too much. He said he'd be by to watch them in the summers. But he never comes."

I lead her though the glass front doors, and immediately, there is only one thing to look at.

The ocean.

Well, and the racetrack. You can't help but notice it, since it's directly below my house and I have a clear view of everything. The grandstands are filled with people already, even though the races don't start for hours. The infield is all grassy and ready for the winners who will come, race by race, to be celebrated with trophies and prizes. It's filled up with lots of people on the big race days, but that's not today. And the tracks. One turf, one dirt.

"You know why people go broke at the track, Ivy?"

"Who goes broke?" She doesn't even look at me. Her fingers are pressed up against the glass doors, like she's trying to get closer to the ocean and the track. This magical place where you can hear thundering hooves and crashing waves in the same instant.

"Gamblers, owners, trainers, whoever. The track is filled with the richest of the rich and the poorest of the poor, all going broke together. And you know why?"

She drags her gaze to me and says, "Why?"

"Because they're addicted. Not to gambling. Not the way a poker player is. They're addicted to this sport in a way that has nothing to do with money. They're addicted to that." I point down. "The track. The smell of the dirt and the grass. And the horses. The sleek coats and the silks of the jockeys. It's a different world down there. A different *life*. And people get addicted to it."

"Are you addicted?" Ivy asks.

"If you only go once, you're OK. You know? But if you go back, it's over. The *life*..." I slide the patio doors open and the sea breeze rushes in, blowing long wisps of hair that have escaped her ponytail as she steps outside. "It is pretty cool. I didn't think I'd be into it when I said I'd take the house off Pax's hands. But I really do love it. I love the sound of the races. The trumpet guy? You know, that guy who blows that horn before the race starts? I live for that in the summer now. It sucks in the winter when the seasons ends and everything quiets down. And I've been over there hundreds of times in the past few years. So, yeah. It got me too. But I'm not a gambler. So I'm not going broke paying for the Club or the box. And I'm not an owner. I'm rich, but truthfully, you gotta be some special kind of rich to want to throw away millions of dollars a year on this sport. It never pays out."

Ivy is caught up in my imagery for a few seconds. And then she says, "Why did your friend have to sell it? Was he in debt?"

"Who knows," I say. "Who knows why Mysterious does anything. He never came back to visit, the asshole."

"What does he do? I don't know if I can recall his

face."

"Nah, he hates being photographed. And what *does* he do? I'm not sure, but whatever it is, it's not something typical. Let's just leave it at that."

"Your friends *all* seem to be atypical."

"Can't help it," I say with a shrug. "We got wrapped up in that shit and even though we were never that close before it all started, we got close after. But once the charges were dropped, we fell apart. Just wanted to forget, mostly. I still talk to Perfect. And I hear that Match and Mysterious both talk too. And Corporate shows up every once in a while asking if we're hiring and need him to find anyone. But then Perfect found a girl last year and, well, he's settling down. So we were all at a party for him a few weeks back and that's where Corporate put me on his bachelor hit-list."

"And you think he chose *me*?" Ivy points a finger at her chest. "Why?"

"You're beautiful," I say, tucking that blowing strand of hair behind her ear. "And smart. Even if it's not business-school prodigy smart. You still went to Brown, right?"

Ivy laughs nervously, but nods her head. "I really did go to Brown. That's why I knew about you guys. It's been a while since all that happened, but it's like an urban legend on campus for the freshmen. Some Greek Week ritual."

"Jesus, fuck. Please tell me it's not about gang-rape?"

"No. Nothing like that. I think it's a team-building thing."

"Really?" I can't help but be interested.

"I don't know all the details, but they break all the fraternity rushes into teams of five now. And each team has to complete the Rush Week Challenge together. They either all win, and get accepted, or they all lose, and don't."

"Hmm. Interesting. But enough about the past. Let's talk food. You want to go to the club? Or..."

"Or?" She laughs. Nervously. "I have another option?"

"Well, we can see the races from here. There's really no reason to go out. I can make you breakfast and we can eat on the terrace. And then we can talk business for a little bit. How's that sound?"

It sounds pretty fucking fantastic to me, but Ivy hesitates.

When I got in my car and started driving off, all I kept thinking about was how I fucked her. How I was the first *ever* to fuck her. And she never said a word. It blew my mind. I have never had a virgin before. I've never had anything other than someone's sloppy seconds.

It intrigues me. That I could get to know her better. Date her. Keep her for myself. Me and only me.

What a fucking prize, right?

And even though I have no clue what Corporate was thinking when he set all this shit up, I don't much care.

I think I'd like to be the only man Ivy Rockwell *ever* fucks.

It's a dangerous thought. Dangerous. That's how Claudette described me to Ivy. But once I get an idea in my head I'll usually do whatever it takes to get my way. Even if it means bringing her here. Taking her places. Getting her addicted. Just like the people down there on that track. You don't get addicted to one thing or another. You get addicted to all of it. You get addicted to the *life*. I want her to be addicted to my life.

And it's working, isn't it?

One look at her face as she gazes down at the ocean and considers my offer tells me all I need to know. It's working all right.

I've got her right where I want her.

CHAPTER TWENTY

IVY

I'm wowed. So if that was Nolan Delaney's plan, he's certainly succeeded. But... *But.* None of this makes much sense. Why is he doing this?

Stop complaining, Ivy. He's still interested, that's why.

I'm not putting myself down. I'm quite a good catch. And I did appreciate his blow job compliment. I fooled him, didn't I?

But.

He wants to talk business. Which, in my book, is not compatible with being brought to his home.

And he's more than I thought he was. A lot more. This house. I didn't see this coming. I pictured him living in some ultra-modern high-rise penthouse loft near downtown San Diego where all the action is. Where his clubs are. But this house. I don't even know where to begin.

Nora is rich. And she's been my best friend for enough years for me to understand the word rich. They have a huge house in Greenwich, Connecticut. Ocean view, private dock. Worth millions of dollars. More dollars than I ever thought about having. Everyone at the Bishop School for Girls was rich. Everyone but me.

And Nolan is up there in that kind of rich category.

But how do I trust a guy like him? Accused of rape. *Gang* rape. They all were. He has this air about him that reeks of danger. I'm not sure why, because he hasn't really done anything too unusual. So far.

But.

That one word echoes in my head.

But.

"Ivy?" Nolan presses.

"I'm thinking about it."

"Why is it taking so long to make a decision?"

I turn to face him and almost wish I hadn't. His looks. Damn. They are so distracting. Everything about him makes you want to stare. Take it all in and burn it into your memory.

He's not as intimidating now. Not like he was in his suit yesterday. I like casual Nolan. It puts me at ease a bit.

But maybe I shouldn't be at ease with Mr. Romantic?

"I need to know more about you," I say. "I don't think all this stuff is appropriate, Nolan."

His smile appears. Like he's got another trick up his sleeve. "But last night was?"

"Last night I might've lost control a little, but the light of day—and your sister—have brought clarity to the situation. I don't trust you." There, I said it. "I just don't trust you."

"I should be the one who doesn't trust you. Maybe you did slip that fake résumé in the pile? Maybe Corporate didn't fuck with it? Maybe," he says, that sly grin still gracing his face. "Maybe you came here to seduce me? Get pregnant and trap me?"

"Please." I laugh. "I was the one who insisted on a condom."

"True," he says, taking my long blonde hair in his fingertips and pulling the hair tie out so it blows in the wind. "But how can I be certain?"

"I'm the one who needs to be certain, Nolan. Not you. I'm not dangerous."

"Because you're a woman?" he asks. "I've met my share of dangerous women before, Ivy."

He's got a point. "Well, I'm just not convinced this is

a good idea. I like your house, and your car, and your view. But I'm not sure I actually like *you*."

He stares at me for a few seconds. Just the sound of the crashing waves and a low hum of people coming from the racetrack down below. "Would you like to know a secret about me, Ivy? Something no one else knows?"

"What kind of secret?"

"What do you need to know in order to trust me?"

I take a deep breath and let it out. "What happened that night?"

He shakes his head. "No, not that."

"Why not? If you have nothing to hide?"

"Because we made a pact to never talk about it again. And to be honest, I don't actually know what happened that night."

"How could you not know, Nolan? You were there." What does he take me for? Some simpleton who will eat up his words and accept everything that comes out of his mouth as truth?

"I *wasn't* there."

"What do you mean? Of course you were there. Everyone knows you were there."

"I was…" But he stops.

"You were what?" I'm dying now, and he's not getting anything from me until I understand what happened.

After a long silence he says, "I'll tell you why they call me Mr. Romantic instead. How about that?"

"I already know why. You're a player."

"No," he says. "I told you. That's not why they call me Mr. Romantic. Claudette was lying. Well, not really lying. She has no idea either."

So. A real secret. About his nickname, no less. "OK, then tell me."

"Over breakfast," he says, that winning grin back in place.

I feel like I just walked into a trap. I feel like a rabbit looking up into the eyes of a wolf.

"You want to take a shower?" he asks. "Freshen up while I cook? Come on, I'll show you where."

He takes my hand and leads me inside. The furniture is sparse and there's not much about it that's personal. Maybe that's how he is? Impersonal. And this place says a lot about him. Or maybe all this was left over from his friend and he never bothered to change it?

He takes me through the large living area and back to the front foyer where we climb the stairs and walk down a catwalk that overlooks the view and the living room. It's lined on either side with cables and steel posts. A very modern version of a railing.

We end up in what has to be the master bedroom because it has the same view as the back yard, but better.

"Here, Ivy. You can use my bathroom. I'll bring your case up and leave it in the bedroom. Just come downstairs when you're done and we'll get started."

Get started. We're making a business arrangement. I should stop this. He's going to tell me some far-fetched story about that night back in college. Something ridiculous that will ease my mind so he can take advantage of me.

Maybe.

Maybe that *is* what he'll do.

But I can't seem to stop myself. I feel a little bit like those people down on the track. Like I'm getting caught up in something. Something that might make me feel good in the moment, but be bad for me in the end.

"Go ahead," Nolan says as I hesitate.

I stare out the window for a second, then look back

at him, but he's already walking away, pulling the door to the bedroom closed behind him.

I would like to freshen up. I'm feeling pretty grungy after the sex last night. So I walk into the bathroom and... wow. It's wow.

A tall window on the far side looks out onto the ocean and my feet are in front of it and I'm staring down at the crashing waves before I even have time to think.

What a life. What must it be like to live a life like this?

I've never wanted for anything. I was well taken care of and I had access to the best education. If not in the world, then at least in this country. I grew up with nice things. But that's all they were. Nice. The school was not... this. It was not luxurious. Yes, we had everything boarding schools on the East Coast have. Swimming pools and modern classrooms. Stables filled with several millions of dollars' worth of horses. Pretty uniforms and class trips.

But luxury like *this* is not something I'm used to.

The shower is so extravagant with all the shower heads and knobs, I don't even know where to start. And the white marble floor complements the white marble tiles. The sparkling glass surround tells me Nolan either has a maid or he never bathes, because there's not one water stain to be found. The sunshine from outside washes over the room in a soft, golden glow and the sheer white curtains and tall candlesticks make it feel romantic.

Romantic.

Is he... romantic?

No. My laugh echoes right up to the high ceilings.

I turn back to the shower and step inside so I can turn on the water. It comes falling down from the ceiling in a large square pattern, making me step out to avoid getting soaked.

"Well, if one must clean up after messy sex the night before, this is not a bad way to do it."

I slip Nolan's t-shirt off my body and his scent almost overtakes me. I wish I could keep this shirt on forever.

The shorts slip down my legs and I step away, kicking them aside.

It's steamy now, and I can't wait to get in and stand under that rain shower of hot water. But just as I'm about to step in, the door opens.

CHAPTER TWENTY-ONE
NOLAN

She's talking to herself when I bring the case up to the master bedroom. I walk over to the bathroom door and press my ear against it, but she goes quiet again and all I hear is the water raining down in the shower.

Is she under that water yet? I picture her wet body the way it was last night in the pool. And even though I said I'd cook breakfast while she showered, I'm not in the mood for food.

I'm in the mood for Ivy Rockwell's body.

I just want to see it. Just look at her tits in the daylight. Take in the curve of her hips with my eyes instead of my fingertips as I grabbed onto them and fucked her from behind last night.

So I open the door... and I'm immediately busted. She's not even in the shower yet.

"What are you doing?" she asks.

I expect her to cover herself, but she doesn't. She just stands there. So what can I do but look?

"Fucking hell," I say.

"Get out, Nolan," she says.

But I don't get out. I take a step inside and reach behind my head to grab the collar of my t-shirt. It comes off and I toss it near her shorts.

"Nolan," she says again. "What are you doing?"

"I can't," I say.

"Can't what?"

"I can't just walk away after seeing this." I wave a hand down her body. She is only a few feet away, so I cross the distance and place my hands on her hips. My eyes can't see enough.

She wriggles, but I hold tight as I study her tits. Her nipples are hard, pulling her breasts up. And they are begging me to suck them.

"Nolan," she says again, but this time it's a whisper. "Nolan."

"Keep saying my name, Ivy. It only makes me want to fuck you more."

"Nolan." And then she stops herself.

I look up at her face and she bites her lip. "What?"

"I thought we were having breakfast?"

"I can eat pussy for breakfast."

"Stop it," she says.

"Stop what? I'm not doing anything. *Yet.*"

"We're going to talk business."

"We can still talk business."

"You were going to tell me a secret over breakfast."

"I can tell you a secret in the shower." She's silent. "Come on, Ivy. Give me another chance."

"Another chance at what?" She's exasperated. Uneasy. Unsure of what's happening.

But that's OK. I'm very sure of what's happening. "To make you feel good." I grab her breast and squeeze. She sucks in a breath and makes a little moan. "Let me try again. I won't hurt you this time, I promise."

"I want what you promised me downstairs. I want to know why they call you Mr. Romantic first."

"OK," I say. "But I can do that at the same time." She opens her mouth to protest, but I place a finger over her lips to keep her quiet. "Trust me for a minute. Let me tell you my way. It's so much better than revealing my secret over pancakes."

She's so out of her league with me. I know that. She's inexperienced in almost every way. And I've got all the experiences she craves.

And since she doesn't try to stop me again, I push my shorts down and fist my cock. She stares at my hand as I pump. And it occurs to me, she hasn't gotten a proper look at my body either.

"Do you like it?" I ask, reaching for her hand. Releasing my hand and replacing it with hers. "Do you like how big it is?"

I never take my eyes off her. She swallows hard and all I can think about is how it felt to be in her mouth last night. The way her muscles moved against my dick when she swallowed. I wish she was facing me when I unloaded my come in her mouth. I wish I could see the way it must've dripped out when I took her by surprise.

Ivy nods her head yes to my question and that's all the permission I need. I take her hand and lead her into the shower, pushing her under the water, and then pushing her some more, so she has to bring her hands up and place them on the wall if she doesn't want to crash into the marble.

I press my body against her back, my dick so hard it slips between her ass cheeks, and now it's my turn to moan. "Do you remember asking me to fuck you in the ass last night, Ivy?"

"I take it back."

I laugh. I can't help it. "I'm not gonna, you silly anal virgin. I just wanted to remind you how horny you were. So turned on, you almost begged me for it."

"I couldn't help it, I was scared."

Awww. I actually feel bad. "I can make it up to you."

"I'm sore, Nolan. I don't think I can."

"I'll be careful this time," I whisper in her ear. "I promise."

She hesitates as I wait. "Tell your secret first. I want

to know why they call you Mr. Romantic."

"You know that will change things, right?"

"Why?"

I start kissing her neck, my lips pressing against her soft skin, my teeth unable to stop the small nibbles. "Because it actually is romantic," I say. "The name isn't ironic, Ivy. They call me Mr. Romantic because I was doing something very romantic back in college."

"What?" She turns her head, and I take the opportunity to kiss her on the lips. She opens for me and all I want is to put my cock back inside her. Inside her pussy. Between her lips. But I settle for my tongue. For now.

"I..." I want to laugh. Because it's ridiculous. "I had a thing for drawing girls while I fucked them. And you know what?"

"What?" she whispers into my mouth. "Tell me what."

"They liked it. They thought it was romantic. I was good at it. And it got around school that I liked to do this. And that's why they call me Mr. Romantic."

She pulls back and turns around. I let her because I want to look at her tits again. "You're lying."

"I'm not," I say. "I swear." I squeeze both nipples at the same time and she closes her eyes. "But there's more to it than that. Everything has a catch, Ivy. When you stepped into this house there was a catch."

"You want to fuck me."

"Hell, yes. And I'm going to."

"What if I say no?"

"You won't. Now listen to the catch, OK? Because this is what makes all the difference. The catch was..." I can't believe I'm talking about this again. It's not good. I should shut the fuck up.

"What?" Ivy asks. "Tell me. Tell me what it was."

"The catch is that I like to do things to them during sex. Rough things. And so after I pose them in just the right way, and after I draw most of it, I add those rough things to the drawing and ask them if they've ever done it before. Ask them if they'd like to try it."

"What kind of things?" She's afraid. I can tell. Her eyes are wide and she's breathing faster.

"Choking, for one."

She gulps air as my palm rests on her neck. Her eyes flutter as my thumb presses against her jugular vein.

"So I dangle the bait and see if they bite. Does it turn them on to see the drawing? Or do they walk out?"

"How many walked out?"

I lean into her ear and whisper, "Only one."

I take my hand off her throat and she opens her eyes. "Why do you do it?"

"It turns me on. You wouldn't understand. You've never really been with a guy."

"I was with you. Last night."

I shrug and step back. "I was holding back. Plus I don't do it much these days."

"You still draw?"

"Yes."

"Show me."

"I can't. I burn them afterward. I don't keep the pictures."

"Then draw *me*. And prove it."

"I will, Ivy. If that's what you want. But I like to fuck hard afterward and you need it soft."

"I don't believe you. I think you're lying. I think you're the one responsible for my fake résumé. I think you brought me here."

"Why would I do that?"

"I don't know. But it was you. I know it."

"Then why are *you* here?"

She has no answer for that.

"I know why you're here, Ivy."

"Why?" She straightens her shoulders like she's trying to be brave. Like I'm scaring the shit out of her and she's forcing herself to remain calm.

"You told me. You want me to fuck you. So let me. Let me fuck you again and this time, you won't cry afterward."

Her eyes narrow. "You knew I was crying?"

"No. But I've thought about it. I've run the whole thing back in my mind and I get it. I hurt you. And it wasn't my intention. I just like to fuck a certain way. And if I had known you were a virgin, well…" I laugh.

"You wouldn't have touched me."

"I would *not* have touched you. I can't risk another girl misunderstanding my intentions and accusing me of rape again, now can I?"

"You did rape her, didn't you?"

"I did not."

"She *thought* you did, though. Didn't she?"

"She didn't, Ivy. I swear. It was nothing like that."

"Then tell me what it was like."

"No."

"Then why should I trust you?"

"I never really asked you to trust me, Ivy. I just wanted to fuck you."

"And now you want to fuck me again?"

"Yes. Again, and again, and again. I feel a little possessive of you now. Like I have a claim. Like you're mine."

She licks her lips, but it's a nervous gesture.

"I'll be careful," I say. "I can make it up to you, Ivy."

I place my hand on her cheek and press her back against the tile. The whole shower is steaming up from the hot water and a mist floats between us. A thin mist that might as well be a wall. "I'll show you why they call me Mr. Romantic. You won't be disappointed."

She just stares into my eyes.

"Say something."

"I can't," she whispers.

"Why not?"

"Because I don't trust myself."

I grin. *Oh, you little fucking virgin.* "You don't need to trust yourself, you just need to follow my lead."

"I can't do that either. Something is missing."

"You know what's missing, Ivy? My dick inside you again, that's what's missing. I know you're inexperienced, so I'm gonna talk you through this. Turn around, press your hands on the tile above your head, and open your legs."

"No." She licks her damn lip as she says it. And then she says it again. "No."

"Then what are we doing here?"

"Negotiating, Mr. Delaney. Isn't that what one does in a business agreement?"

"Is this business?"

"It is now."

I tuck my head down to hide the grin. "OK," I say, looking back up at her. "Let's make a deal. What do you want?"

"The truth about that night."

"Can't do it, Ivy. I haven't told anyone. Not my sister, not my friends, not my father, not even my mother. And if I *were* going to tell someone, it would be my mother, not you."

Her shoulders relax and she takes a deep breath. "So

you're a mama's boy?"

I shrug. "Maybe. But I'll tell you what. I'll play the game with you, if that's what gets you off. I'll draw you. I'll pose you and draw you. Naked, out there in bedroom. And then you'll see that what I just said is true."

"What do I have to give you?" she asks.

"Turn around. Press your hands on the tile above your head. And open your legs."

"What will you do then?"

"You'll have to wait and see."

"I want to know *now*, Nolan." Her chest is rising and falling even faster now, letting me know her heart is beating fast. She's scared. Really, truly scared.

"Do it and I'll show you. You know you want to. Or you'd be out of here. And don't give me some stupid excuse that you have no ride or you're on the wrong side of the country. If you think I'd strand you with no ride home, then I don't want you here."

I wait her out as she considers her options, but the seconds tick off and I know she won't make a decision unless I push her. "Decide, Ivy. I've got better ways to spend the day than standing here in the shower waiting for you. How will you ever be in charge of anything if you can't make your own decisions?"

"That's not fair."

"Who said anything about fair? Fuck fair. If life was fair, I'd have my college degree right now. If life was fair, my father would still care about me. If life was fair, I wouldn't have been accused of rape. Life has never been fair. Not for me. Not for you. Not for anyone."

CHAPTER TWENTY-TWO

IVY

I shouldn't believe him. I should just push him away, put my clothes on, and demand that he takes me home.

The problem is… I don't want to do any of that. The problem is… I want to do everything he just commanded. The problem is I feel powerless and powerful in the same instant.

I can walk out or I can make him do things to me that most people only dream about. I can stand firm and go home wanting or I can give in and go home satisfied. I can learn his secret or I can remain ignorant.

I turn around. I stretch my arms up, my breasts rising with the motion, and place my palms flat on the cold marble tile.

And I open my legs.

Nolan bends down and I get nervous. I look over my shoulder and I'm sure I'm going to pass out from the fear coursing through my veins, and the steam I have to inhale, and the heat that surrounds my body.

Nolan places both of his hands flat on my ass cheeks, spreading them apart. His tongue darts in and licks. Not my asshole, not my pussy, but somewhere in between. "That," Nolan says, "is a beautiful fucking sight."

He caresses my opening with his tongue and stands back up. I have to rest my head against the tile too. It's spinning out of control. *I'm* spinning out of control.

"Don't worry," he says, pushing his chest against my back, one leg pressing between mine so he can stimulate me. "I won't fuck you."

"What?"

"You can control that, Ivy. See how generous and fair I'm being? Hmmm?" He nips my earlobe and I suck in a breath. "We can do that your way. But I'm going to make you earn that drawing."

"You want me to suck your dick again?"

"Well, sure. But not now."

His hand fists my breast, squeezing it so tight I let out a squeak from the pain. And then he eases up and his fingertips glide down to my waist, over the curve of my hip, and reach between my legs.

He strokes me in small circles. Tiny, tiny, *tiny* circles when all I want is something big to be right there.

"More," I say. "I want more."

"More what, Ivy?"

"Press harder," I hear myself say. "Push them inside me." Goddammit. Why am I letting him make me do this?

He's not making you do anything, Ivy. You want this.

And I do.

My wish is granted. He strums my clit faster and faster and I start moaning. My moans echo off the walls, and the ceiling, and inside my brain. All I hear is my own pleasure when the strumming stops and he slips a finger inside me.

"You want to know what it feels like to have a cock in your ass, Ivy?"

Oh, Jesus. What am I doing?

He doesn't wait for my answer. I feel pressure and a painful sensation. I cannot keep up and I just know he's tired of waiting for me. He's just going to take what he wants until I stop him.

I bend my head forward, my ass pressing against him. He takes that as encouragement, pressing back, pushing his finger inside my ass a little more as another one keeps pumping my pussy. But I just need this damn wall to hold me up.

"Come, Ivy. Give in, feel this the way it was meant to be felt, and come all over my fingers. And the second you do that, I'll give all the control back to you."

Do I want control?

"You like it," he whispers into my neck. "You want more." He pumps his hand harder. And then harder still. More and more and more and all I can think about is *more*.

I want more fingers, I want more licking, more kissing, more of his hard cock. I want him to make me do these things. Force me, so I don't have to take responsibility. I want to put him in my mouth and suck him until he comes down my throat. I want to taste that salty liquid. I want him to kiss me after and put his fingers in my—

"Oh!" I grunt. My release comes gushing out in waves of heat and pleasure. And even though I'm wet everywhere from the water, and the shower, and the desire, I am even wetter when I'm done.

"You're such a good girl," Nolan croons in my ear.

I slump down, but his strong arms catch me, turning my body and pulling me into his chest. He holds me up now, not the wall. And he walks backwards and takes a seat on the stone bench in the corner.

"Sit on my lap, Ivy."

My eyes are tightly closed as I position myself in his lap. One knee on either side of his thighs. I'm instantly turned on just from the positioning. His arms encircle me as I rest my head on his shoulder, feeling utterly exhausted.

"Now it's my turn," Nolan says, petting my hair as he talks. "I want you to fuck me, Ivy. When you're ready. As fast or as slow as you want. As long as my cock is inside you, I'm happy. And when we're done, I'll show you what you need to see in order to trust me."

The only thing I can concentrate on is breathing.

He lets me do this.

But eventually my heart rate slows and my body relaxes. His fingers begin playing with my ass again. Pushing in and out, just the slightest bit. Sometimes slipping up towards my pussy and sliding inside. Just enough. Just enough to make me want him all over again.

I ease my body up and finally look at him.

There's no charming grin now. No charisma to hide behind. No self-assurance in those eyes.

Just want.

I want the same thing, Nolan Delaney. I want the very same thing.

I reach down between my legs and grab his hard cock, pumping him a few times to get a feel for it. And then I sit up a little higher and position him under my entrance, moving it back and forth the way he did last night.

And then I sit. Slowly, slowly, slowly... sit.

That stretching feeling is back. That feeling of being filled up from the inside out. It still hurts but not as bad. It still scares me, but I know what it leads to.

I place my forearms on his shoulders, my fingertips threading up the back of his head and into his hair, and look him in the eyes. He looks back, his attention only on me. Silent.

My hips begin to move. Just a little rocking motion, back and forth. I'm wet for him again. Or maybe I'm still wet from the way he made me come?

It makes everything easier. His hard cock slips in a little deeper with each thrust. I watch him for something. Some kind of reaction. But he's still and silent until... until that moment when I know he is fully inside me.

And then he closes his eyes and leans his head back.

He enjoys it.

His hips begin to move with mine. His arms wrap me

up in a tight embrace. He fists my hair and I grab his back as we move faster, faster, faster.

His breathing becomes heavy. He is the one out of control. His moans fill the shower when he stands up, presses my back against the wall, and begins to fuck the shit out of me.

"Ivy," he says, over and over. "Come, Ivy. I want to feel your pussy clamp down on my cock."

The wall is cold but his body is warm. So very warm. I cling to him as his hands hold me up by my ass. I wrap my legs around his hips, begging him to pound me hard.

"Come, Ivy," he says. "You're driving me mad. Come."

I bite down on his shoulder to stop the scream.

And obey.

CHAPTER TWENTY-THREE

NOLAN

I sit back down on the bench and Ivy rests her head on my shoulder, both of us breathing hard, our hearts hammering against one another as we calm down.

"I told you I wasn't on birth control, Nolan."

Shit. "Sorry, Ivy. I forgot. I'm sorry. I won't do it again."

"It only takes once," she mumbles.

"I can go get you a morning-after pill."

Her head comes up from my shoulder and I get the most disgusted look from a post-coital girl. *Ever.* "What?" I laugh.

"I don't need an *abortion pill*, Nolan."

Right. Pastor's daughter. I put my hands up and shrug. "Fine. It's your call."

She gets up off my lap with a sigh and stands underneath the water, reaching for the soap.

I get up and take it from her, then place the bar against her breasts and start rubbing her in small circles. "I'm sorry," I say as the lather begins to build. "I just got caught up in the moment."

"It's my fault, so never mind."

"Well, lack of condom buzzkill aside"—I lean down into her ear and whisper—"that was fun. Did you like it better this time?"

"Yes." She hesitates, like she's not sure if she wants to be mad at me or not, then gives in and smiles. "That felt amazing."

I wash Ivy's arms and belly and she squeezes some shampoo onto her the top of her head and lathers up her hair. "My turn now, right?" she asks.

I play dumb. "Turn for what? I got you off."

"Not that, Nolan. You know what I want."

"Why do you want to know what happened that night? It's history. It doesn't even matter anymore."

"It matters to me. I mean I guess you're just using me for a good time this weekend, so what I feel doesn't matter to you. But your part in what happened that night matters to me."

"Who said anything about using you?" I say, getting pissed off. And just what the fuck does she mean by 'your part in what happened that night'? "If I didn't like you, Ivy, you would not be at my private residence in Del Mar. Believe me, I've got plenty of places to take a one-night stand. Besides, this is our second day together, so it's past one-night stand territory."

"Hmmm."

"Hmmm what?" I ask. "What are you thinking so hard about?" But before I can get an answer out of her she ducks under the shower again and I have to wait until her hair is rinsed before I can repeat my question.

"I want you to draw me. Like you said. I want to see a drawing."

"Because you think I'm lying."

"I just want to see," Ivy says, going for the conditioner and massaging it into her long hair that is more brown than blonde now that it's wet. "Can you do it?"

"Yeah. But why should I? What do I have to prove to you?"

"Nothing, I guess. But I'm going home right now if you don't."

"Is this all part of your rules of war, Ivy Rockwell? The fine art of negotiation?"

"Sure," she says, ducking under the water again to rinse the conditioner. I can't stop watching her. Her breasts are lifted up because her hands are above her head. And her nipples are tight peaks that call to my mouth. "If we're going to play this through to the end we might as well negotiate something."

"Instead of your job?"

"What job, Nolan?" She spits out the water dripping down her face, steps out of the stream, and wipes her eyes. "What job? You were never going hire me, were you? You were planning on sending me away before I even stepped out of that car back at the resort yesterday morning. The reason I'm still here is a mystery to me. I have no idea what you're doing. But whatever it is, you're good at it, Nolan. You're good at getting what you want. Me, not so much."

"That's not fair."

"Life isn't fair, remember?"

"Why are you so pissed off?"

"I'm not pissed off. I'm just being realistic. Believe me, if I was mad you'd know it."

"Do you wanna go home, Ivy? Is this how you cut your losses, enjoy the fact that you got me to rid you of that pesky v-card, and go home to tell all your friends who did it?"

"Now that," Ivy says as she covers her breasts with her arms, "was a low blow. And it's my cue to cut my losses, yes."

She tries to step past me but I grab her wrist and squeeze. "Hold on," I say.

"Let. Go."

I let go, but I place an arm in front of her and block her exit. "You want me to draw you? You want to know what happened that night?'

"Yes." She tips her head up. "But don't bother lying

to me. I only want the truth, no matter what it is."

"No matter what?"

"Yes."

"You do realize I never stood trial, right?"

"Yeah, but I need to know—"

"No," I cut her off. "I mean I never *stood trial,* Ivy. There's no double jeopardy for us. We never went to trial, we were never found innocent. So if you ever leak this shit I could be in a lot of trouble."

"Who would I tell? And you said you didn't do it, so what do you have to hide?"

"I didn't do it. Not what they accused me of anyway."

"What?" Ivy's eyes go wide, wide, wide.

"But I did something else. Would you like to see it?"

She freezes. Her whole body goes stiff. "What do you mean, *see* it?"

"I'll draw it for you, Ivy. You wanted me to draw you?"

I turn into the water and douse myself, then start washing my body and hair. Ivy stands perfectly still—watching, waiting—until I'm done. "I'll take that as a yes?"

"I don't understand," she says.

"I'll draw you and show you why I need to keep secrets."

"Because you draw them nude."

"No," I say. "That's not what I told you, remember?"

"You choke them. You draw yourself choking them."

I smile and walk forward until I'm close enough to take both of her hands and lean into her ear. "That's the PG version, Ivy Rockwell." And then I lean back and look at her. All naked and afraid. Shivering from the cold she hasn't even noticed yet. "So be very sure you want my secrets. Because secrets are dangerous things, and once you know them, you can't *un*know them."

I turn to the door and walk out, dragging her with me by the hand. I point to the front of the bed. "Lie down on your back. Right in the middle. And put your hands above your head."

Ivy looks at the bed, then me, then back at the bed.

"Do it," I say. "Or we're done. You asked for it, Ivy. Now you're gonna get it. And since I came this far, I'm going all the way with you. So get on the bed or get the fuck out."

I fully expect her to walk out because I sound like a class-A dick right now.

But she doesn't. She walks to the bed, still wet, lowers her hands forward onto the white down comforter, crawls to the center, and lies back. Hands above her head.

I walk calmly to the bedside table. My heart is racing with ideas. How far should I go? How much can she take?

I open the drawer and take out the neatly coiled length of bright yellow, double-braided nylon rope and unfasten the end.

"What's that for?" Ivy asks. "You never said anything about rope."

"Live a little, Ivy. Stop asking questions, stop taking so damn much, and just... live a little."

"You're going to tie me up?"

I kneel on the bed and straddle her hips, my cock already hard again when I ease down and rest it on her stomach. And then I say, "Press your palms together and put them out in front of you."

"No," Ivy says.

"Are you sure?" I ask. I'm not mad. I don't care if she says no. I just want to make sure. "Because this is what you have to do if you want me to tell you the whole story."

"Did you rape her or not?"

"I already told you no."

"Did you tie her up?"

"You'll have to give in to find out."

Ivy takes a deep breath, struggling with her decision. Should she give in to me, put her fear aside, even though everything in her body is telling her I'm dangerous? Or should she get up, walk out, and never look back?

Truthfully, I'm not sure which answer is right for her.

She exhales and lowers her arms in front of her. Palms pressed together.

I smile. "I like the double braid because it's soft." I start wrapping it around her wrist, lining each pass up end to end, so it's flat, and elegant, and strong. "And I like the yellow. I have a thing for yellow, Ivy. Which is why I really liked that bikini you were wearing at the pool yesterday afternoon."

"What are you going to do?" Ivy asks, her voice slightly panicked now that she's given me control. I've already got the rope the way I like it and I tuck the loose end underneath, near her wrist to fasten it.

"If you ever get stuck, just FYI, the rope stretches. I don't put it on tight, it would cut off your circulation. So if I ever leave you for some length of time and you become afraid, think I won't come back, or you've had enough—just wriggle around until it loosens. It might take a while, but you're not stuck, Ivy. Got it?"

She swallows hard and nods.

"Good. Because I'm going to leave you right now."

"What? Nolan—"

"Stop," I say. "I'll be back."

I get up before she can say anything else and leave the room.

CHAPTER TWENTY-FOUR

IVY

I hear him in the house. Down the hall. Downstairs. The beeping of something, like he's arming the house alarm. Then silence. Just me, lying here naked, my wrists bound together by soft yellow rope.

He's into something weird. Some bondage thing. He wants to tie me up and hit me with a riding crop. Put those clamp things on my nipples or... whatever. I'm not really sure what kinky guys do. And I haven't read the books everyone has been talking about the past few years.

But Ivy Rockwell, you have to admit, you like it enough to be here.

Right.

A part of me might find it intriguing. In an academic kind of way. I mean, I have to wonder. Why the hell do people like this stuff? I certainly don't feel sexual right now. Lying here on the bed, hands in front of me, chewing my lip as I wait for Nolan to decide to come back.

It's the anticipation, I get it. He's definitely got my mind spinning. But—

"Hey," Nolan says from the bedroom doorway. "Zoning out or what?"

I didn't even hear him come back. "No. I was just getting irritated, actually. For you taking so long."

"Well, no one put you in a corner and called you bad, Ivy. You could've gotten up. Looked out the fucking window or something."

"I know that," I snap. But I... *didn't* know that. Didn't understand it at least. I just stayed here. Where he put me.

"I'm not dominating you, Ivy. I'm not going to ask

you to lick piss up off the floor just to prove to me you're interested. That's not what I'm about."

I wait for it, but he holds it in. He wants me to ask. That *is* what he's about. Control. He's not going to give anything away. I have to come get it. He *is* dominant. He *does* like submission. He just does it in a way I've never heard of before. He's some kind of cutting-edge deviant. And I'm his new project. He's going to use all his magic charms on me and see how far he can get before he has to throw me away and find someone new.

"What *are* you about?" I ask.

He grins a grin that sends a chill through my bare nipples. Like a breeze just passed over my body. He made me react.

"Pleasure, Ivy. I'm about pleasure."

"You want to slap my face while you fuck me."

"Wow." He laughs. "Those are some dirty words coming from the preacher's daughter's mouth."

"Is that what you want?"

"Why do you need to know?"

"Because I matter. You've got me—"

"Ivy," he interrupts, his voice stern. "Relax. Enjoy." And then I see what he's holding in his hands.

"What's that?"

"Paper. And charcoal pencils."

Oh. I forgot. Jesus Christ. I take a deep breath and try to shake off my fear.

"You still want me to draw you?"

"Yes." I have a million little justifications for this want. I don't believe him. I think there's more to it than what he's saying. I think he's sick, that he and his friends raped that girl, and then somehow, some way, the five of them got her killed.

At least I *should* think those things. Nothing Nolan

Delaney has said to me is convincing. And I probably do think them. Do believe them, at least a little bit.

But that's not why I want him to draw me.

I like the way he's looking at me right now. No man has ever looked at me like this before. Nude. Stretched out on his bed. Pretending to be helpless, even though he just told me I'm not helpless.

"Then relax." That grin again. It says a lot. It says he does have secrets. Deep ones. Dark ones. And he's right. Once I know them, I can never unknow them. "I'm gonna pose you, OK?"

Nolan steps forward, kneeling on the bed, and sets the pad of paper and the charcoal pencils down as he crawls forward and wraps his hand around my ankle.

I nearly come undone. By a hand on my ankle. Has anyone ever touched my ankles before? Is it supposed to feel this way?

"Shhh," he says when I jerk my foot away from his touch. "It's not time to be afraid yet, Ivy."

My eyes widen at his words. Yet?

"I just want your foot here." He pushes my foot towards me, making it slide on the smooth cotton comforter, until my knee bends slightly. Then he angles it so that the knee is resting on the opposite thigh. His fingertips flitter up my shin, then slip around to the long muscle of my calf, caressing the soft skin behind my knee.

I gasp. I can't help it.

"It feels nice, right?" His green eyes are bright and his smile is big. "Most men want to lick pussy and bite lips. But they forget about the little dent behind the knee." He dips down to my leg, softly kissing before nipping the inside of my thigh.

I gasp again. But he doesn't pay any attention to me. Just continues to kiss his way up my leg, skipping over my pussy, and resting his lips on my hip bone. "And the hips," he breathes, his breathy words fluttering across my skin. "Defiance is defined as open resistance. But a seductive man knows how to turn resistance into reluctance into acceptance."

I bite my lip as I let all these new feelings flood through me. "Is that what you're doing? Turning my resistance into acceptance?"

He stops his soft touch and kissing to look up at me from beneath his unruly brown hair that falls over his eyes. "What do you think?"

"I think… I think I have no idea who you are, Nolan Delaney."

"I'm Mr. Romantic, Ivy. Didn't you want to meet him?"

I get another chill when he refers to himself in the third person. Is he sick? Is he as dangerous as Claudette said? Was she really just trying to protect me? Is Nolan Delaney some kind of psychopath?

"You should be scared," he says, sitting up and backing away from me until he's at the foot of the bed where he left his paper and pencils.

"Why?" My heart is fluttering now, and not in a good way. I think I've made a mistake. I think I need to get the hell out of here. I think Claudette was right.

"Because when this date is over you're going to know things about me and wish you didn't."

"Is this a date?" I ask. I want to get up. I want him to untie my hands. I want to put clothes on, and get my carry-on case, and walk out of this house.

"It is in my mind." And then all the seductiveness about his actions recede when he picks up the pad of paper, opens it up, and reaches for a pencil.

"Hold still," Nolan says, beginning to sketch before I

even understand we've moved on. "Not perfectly still," he says, looking at me briefly over the top of his paper. "I'll tell you when I need that. I'm going to do your legs first."

It takes a long time for me to get a hold of the fear he caused. And he never talks again as he draws. Every once in a while he moves my legs or positions my arms. He makes me tilt my head way back on the pillow at one point. And he rips off paper after paper after paper. Like he's making mistakes and starting again.

Why? Why did I agree to this? What kind of magic does this man possess that he can talk me, Ivy Rockwell, pastor's daughter and newly deflowered virgin, into posing nude for him?

"Getting tired of sitting still?" Nolan asks when I shift my bottom.

"Yes," I say, my voice hoarse from the long silence.

He rips off another sheet of paper, throwing it down on the floor behind him so I can't see it. His pencil is moving the moment the new sheet appears. "I'm almost done."

"Why do you keep starting over?"

He stops drawing and looks at me, his wild green eyes glazed and zoned. "What?"

"Starting over?" I ask. "Isn't what you're doing?" I swallow hard, uncomfortable with his attention. Even though he's been staring at my naked body for what seems like hours, I don't like the way he looks at me.

"I'm not starting over, Ivy." He chuckles, like that was the most ridiculous thing he's ever heard. "I'm drawing a story."

"What kind of story?" My mouth is dry. I need a drink of water. And even though I am not tied down, I feel like he's holding me captive.

"If I told you then I'd never see that surprised look

on your face when I show you."

I sit up, swinging my legs over the side of the bed. "Maybe I don't want to see your story?"

He stops drawing and watches me. "You're leaving now? After all this?" His hand pans behind him. To the discarded drawings on the floor.

"All what, Nolan? I'm tired, I'm thirsty. I'm cold. I want clothes and I want you to untie my hands." He keeps perfectly still. "Now," I say. "Untie me now."

He sighs, gets to his feet, and walks towards me. "OK. But…"

"But what?" I can't take it anymore. I need to leave.

"But you're gonna miss it."

"Miss *what*?"

"Everything that comes after."

His cock is hard. It hasn't been hard most of this time we've been here. And even though his soft touches in the beginning were very erotic, he hasn't touched me in hours. I'm not turned on. At all.

I'm scared. He scares me.

"After I scare you with these drawings, Ivy Rockwell, I'm going to tell you something no one else knows and make it all better."

"I don't think so, Nolan. I really need to go."

"Stop," he says, taking a firm grip on my arm. "Just sit the fuck back and relax. I have five minutes left. Five minutes and I'll be done."

I don't know if I should force my way out of this situation or just give in and wait him out. Not to see if he's not crazy. This man is definitely crazy. I am convinced Claudette is right.

His kiss on my neck is what makes me wait. His soft lips and words. "Just please," he says. "I've never come this close to spilling my secret before. I've never told anyone what happened that night. And you said you wanted to know. You can't walk out in the middle of the story. It's not fair."

"Life's not fair, Nolan. You're the one who said it."

"I know," he says. Still soft, more erotic, very insistent. "I know that. But this could turn into something good. Just... let me finish."

I give in. He could force me to stay and I don't want to push him. I'll leave as soon as he unties me. I'll make a break for the bathroom, get my phone, call Nora, tell her where I'm at, and then have her call me back saying I'm needed at home. There's an emergency. Something, *anything* to get the hell out of this man's house.

"I don't think your nickname should be Mr. Romantic."

He laughs. Like a great, big, ceiling-echoing laugh. "You got that right."

"What? What do you mean? You said it wasn't ironic."

"It's not, I promise." He takes my bound wrists in his hands and laughs again. "I swear. Just let me finish. No one ever fucking lets me finish. They see what they want to see and then they walk out. Don't walk out, Ivy. I've got something to show you."

I sigh, realize I'm not getting out of here, and give in. "OK, fine. Just hurry up, Nolan. I'm hungry. I want to eat. I want a drink of water. I'm uncomfortable—"

"I'm sorry. It's just this story is longer than most. This is the last drawing, I promise. And then I'll show you. And tell you. And then you can leave if you want."

"You promise?" I ask.

"I promise. But you won't want to leave, Ivy. You won't. If you do, you'll miss it."

"What will I miss?"

"Mr. Romantic, of course." He smiles and points to the bed. "Get back in position. This is the one where I really need to concentrate. It's the most important one."

"Five minutes," I say, scooting back up to the headboard and putting my bound wrists above my head.

"Turn to the side. And close your eyes. Like you're sleeping."

Or dead.

He moves quickly back to his paper and pencil, looking at me, then down at his drawing. His hand making long sweeps on the pad. One hundred percent of his concentration on the image he's creating.

And before I can even count out five minutes in my head, he says, "Done." He rips the final piece of paper off the pad and then bends down to pick up the rest of them, arranging them and sorting them into something only he is aware of.

"You're going to freak out, I already know that. But I just need you to let me tell it from beginning to end before you do that."

CHAPTER TWENTY-FIVE
NOLAN

I'm scaring the fuck out of her. Have been for hours. But I can't stop. Not now. Not with her. I don't why I'm fixated on Ivy Rockwell, but I am.

"First of all," I say, scooting up on the bed with her so our bare shoulders are touching. She's sitting up, leaning back on the headboard, and her hands are in her lap. She's breathing fast and heavy, but that's normal for the level of fear she's experiencing. "It's a fantasy, OK? Just keep that in mind. It's just a fantasy."

"I don't think I need to see it, Nolan. Just untie me."

"Just wait," I say, holding the pieces of paper in my hand so she can't see the first one yet. "It's got a nice beginning. And a nice ending." I wink at her, which elicits a tiny smile. "It's the middle that people have a hard time with."

"So you *have* shown other girls this?"

"You're getting ahead of yourself. Be patient."

I have the stack of drawings doubled over, not creased, just so she can't see the first one until I'm ready.

"Mr. Romantic," I say. "Just keep that in mind, OK?"

"Got it," Ivy says, all her patience gone.

"OK." I unfold the drawings so the first one is visible. "This is us. You and me."

And it is. I always put a lot of detail in the first one. maybe because I'm nervous about the ones that come after. Or maybe I really am just a big ol' romantic at heart.

Ivy is wearing a long dress that reveals her curves. Her large breasts, nipples pressed against the fabric because she has no bra on. My hands are the only thing of me in this picture and they are on her hips. "In my head, the dress is yellow."

"Why yellow?" Ivy says, reaching for the picture so I'll bring it closer.

"I like it. And it matches the rope."

She looks at me with lots of questions but none of them come out of her mouth.

"We're coming home from dinner. We had a nice night. This is our first real date."

"What did we eat?" Ivy asks.

"Who cares?" I laugh. "We're in New England, so let's say lots of expensive seafood."

"Fancy."

"Well," I say, "it's a fantasy, right? Go big or go home."

"What color is your suit?" she asks.

This is going well. I have a glimmer of hope. "Black. And my silk tie is yellow."

"To match the rope," Ivy says.

"Yes."

"I have a bad feeling about this, Nolan."

"Don't give up on me yet, Ivy."

She looks me in the eyes and swallows. "Go on."

I throw that picture off the side of the bed and it floats softly to the floor. "Now we're in the back yard of a huge mansion. We're kissing."

"I can see that."

"It's a good kiss, Ivy." My palm is on her throat, my thumb pressing on her chin, like I'm taking control.

"It's... OK."

"OK? You look like you might come any second."

"Why does my dress look weird?"

"It's wet. I made you walk into the pool and then step out. You're soaking wet."

"Why would I walk into the pool, Nolan?"

"Because I asked you to. And I told you how hard it would make me to see your dress clinging to your body like it is in the picture. Every part of your body outlined by the wet dress. Your nipples hard and peaked. Your mind spinning with anticipation."

She bites her lip. "Keep going."

I toss that drawing aside.

"OK," she says. "What the hell is this?"

"Me, slapping your face. See the spot on your cheek? You have fair skin, Ivy. It won't take much to make it red. Your ass will be the same color."

She shakes her head. "Nope."

"Just wait," I say. "It gets better."

The next picture is me holding her face again, like the first, only this time I'm pushing my thumb inside her mouth. Her eyes are looking up at me. You can't see me in this one either, it's only her. My point of view.

"I'm crying, Nolan. This is sick."

"Your pussy is throbbing, Ivy. Take my word on that. Throbbing. Because my fingers are inside you, pushing inside you. Strumming your clit in those tiny circles you like. If I had more time, I'd have drawn you sucking my thumb like it was my cock. I'd have showed you how turned on you were just thinking about what comes next. You want me to fuck you so bad right now, you're begging."

"I'm not. And I don't."

But her voice is weak. And not with fear. "Just keep an open mind. We're not going to do any of this tonight. You're not wearing the dress."

She inhales deeply as she looks at me.

"Keep going?" I ask.

She shrugs.

I smile. Because I know she's turned on.

"This one skips ahead." She's on her knees now, mouth open, my cock in her mouth. Her makeup is smeared so bad, it hides the mark the slaps are leaving. "What do you think I skipped, Ivy? Tell me, so when this date happens, I know what you want."

Ivy is silent for a long time.

She stares at the drawing, studies it. Either thinking about what I asked her, or trying to plan her escape tonight.

"My dress is gone," she finally says.

"I had to peel it off you because it was wet. We laughed about that and broke the scene."

"Scene?" she asks.

"The... fantasy. It's called a scene, but it's private. I'd never want you to do this in front of anyone. For me and you it will always be private."

"What's next?"

I move on to the next picture, which makes Ivy gasp.

I've got her pushed down on the bed, face first. My hand flat against her hair, her cheek pressed so tight into the covers, most of it can't be seen. "Fucking, of course. My way, which is hard, like I told you."

"You want to hurt me?"

"*No*," I say, more sharply than I should. "I want to play out this scene with you. It doesn't define me, Ivy. Or our relationship. It's just a fantasy."

"Why would I agree to this? Why on earth would I ever agree to this?"

"Because it turns you on." I reach between her legs and finger her pussy. "You're wet just thinking about it. Don't lie, Ivy. You can say no and still admit it turns you on."

"Can I say no?"

"Of course." I'm still playing with her, my fingertip doing a little swirl against her clit that makes her close her eyes for a second. "It's OK to like it. It's playing. It's sexual fun, that's all. I don't do this every day. No one I've ever talked to does this every day. It's an understanding. It's set up ahead of time so everyone knows the rules."

"What are the rules?" she asks. "What exactly are you asking me to participate in?"

"Fantasy…" I hesitate. Unable to make myself say it out loud.

"Fantasy what?"

"Rape."

She goes stiff and silent.

"Fantasy being the important word here, Ivy. You're going to agree to it. So it's not rape. You're going to agree ahead of time. We're going to have rules, and boundaries, and limits. And when this happens, we're going to do it exactly how I've planned it. That's why I need to know what you want me to do in between the pages. Fill in the blanks, so to speak."

She shakes her head. "You're sick."

"And yet you're still turned on." I play with her a little more. "Get up and walk out if you're not interested. But I'm not done with the story yet."

She remains silent. Just staring at the drawing as I continue to stimulate her.

"Should I continue? And don't just nod, Ivy. Say something. Make a decision."

"Fine," she whispers. "I want to see how it ends."

"Oh." I laugh. "We're not at the end yet." The next picture is me on top of her. My cock halfway inside her pussy. My silk tie in her mouth, tears streaming down her face. Hands tied together in front of her, just the way they are now.

"I'm crying again?"

"You're coming all over my cock, Ivy. Those are not crying tears. You're begging me to keep going."

She takes the picture and throws it aside. "What's this?"

"This is after." She's sleeping, a half smile on her face with her unbound hands tucked between her legs. I'm behind her, spooning her, but propped up on one elbow so I can tuck a stray hair behind her ear. "We're happy," I say. "We planned it all perfectly and it was fantastic. The best sex we've ever had. And in the next moment I kiss your head and lie down, pulling you close so I can fall asleep with you."

Silence. I want her to say something. Anything. But she stays silent, just looking at the final drawing.

Finally, just as I'm about to go crazy waiting, she says, "Where did you learn to draw like this?"

"Self-taught. I might've missed my calling. But there's no money in art, so I own clubs."

"How many girls have you done this with?"

"Ten, maybe. Fifteen?"

"Jesus Christ."

"Ivy," I say sternly. "Do you really want to play a game like this with an amateur? I haven't done it in years. A long time. Because I can't trust people. But I want to trust you."

"Why?" She laughs. "Do you know that the whole time I've been sitting here I've been thinking how to escape? I've pictured you killing me, throwing my body over the side of a boat, never to be heard of again. I've made an escape plan. I've had whole conversations in my head of what I will tell my father when this gets out. I've—"

"But you're still here." I play with her clit again and a

whole new wave of wetness coats my finger. "You're still here because it turns you on."

"I'm still here because I'm as sick as you."

"Ivy," I say, leaning forward to whisper in her ear. "It's just a fantasy."

"If we're not doing it tonight"—she looks up at me— "then why am I here?"

"To negotiate. That's why I like you, Ivy. You said that yesterday. You're a negotiator. If there's something off limits in these pictures, then say so and we'll negotiate it."

"I think I'm here because I'm inexperienced. I think you want to take advantage of me. I think I'm an easy target."

"You're smart to think that. It's all true. But that's not why I like you, Ivy. I want you. *You.* Not because you're innocent, but because you're smart. You'll be able to tell the difference between the fantasy and the reality. That's why you're here."

She's silent.

"And I want to fuck you. Not like this," I say, tossing the last drawing aside. "Just a good, old fashioned, semi-vanilla, hard fuck."

CHAPTER TWENTY-SIX

IVY

Semi-vanilla, hard fuck. What the hell does that even mean? I'm so out of my league. So, so, so out of my league. Nora was right, guys like Nolan are not for me. He's way too much.

"Nolan—"

"Ivy." He's got his hand under my waist, lowering me down the bed, positioning himself over the top of me, his knees on either side of my hips. "Just enjoy it."

But I don't know which part of this I'm supposed to enjoy. Having my hands tied? Being a nude model for his sick fantasies? Or the fact that he will be fucking me again, no matter what?

"Do you want me to stop?"

"Yes," I say, closing my eyes to keep him out.

He leans down and kisses me on the lips. It's so soft and so tender. "Ivy."

"What?" I can barely speak. I have no idea what's happening.

"If you don't like the terms then *renegotiate*."

I open my eyes and look at him. His face is hovering less than an inch from mine.

"It's fluid, Ivy. Changes can be made at any time. *Any* time. You can say yes and then say no. You can say no and then say yes." He smiles. Because Nolan Delaney wants me to stop saying no and start saying yes. "We can stop right now and go to the races. They started without us. We can go the club and have a nice dinner. We can walk on the beach if you want. Buy ice cream cones and stop at a bar and get a drink."

I picture this alternate reality afternoon in my head. Putting our clothes back on and going over to the track. That would be exciting. I've never been to Del Mar. We'd make bets and cheer. Talk about work. Maybe I'll tell him my plan for the Hundred Palms Resort. After the races we'll watch the sunset and hold hands. And come back here and all the awkwardness would be back.

We'd be thinking about this moment when I said no.

He'd be wondering if I'll always say no or if this was a one-time rejection.

I'll make an excuse and a car will come or he'll drive me himself. Take me to the airport where I will get on his jet, or some jet, or book my own ticket. We'll say goodbye. Maybe pretend we'll stay friends on Facebook. And I'll never see him again.

It's what I want, right? Escape?

But the word *renegotiate* changes things. I'm pretty sure what he likes to do in the bedroom is way over my head. And I'm pretty sure he wasn't kidding when he drew the red mark on my face from his slap. Why would he kid about that?

But he's asking me to give him limits.

So… Not a rapist.

"I don't think I'll like the slap."

"No?" he asks. "You've never tried it, obviously. Would you like me to explain it? Why some girls like it?"

I nod. Because I just don't understand.

Off in the distance I hear a bugle. Nolan turns his head and looks out the window where down below people are living their lives, wholly unaware of what is happening up in this bedroom, high above them on the hill.

"You know when you're watching a horse race?" he says, looking back down at me. "And they're coming down the home stretch. Each horse jockeying for position, going all out for the final furlong, just trying get to the finish line first. People are fucking screaming. The bettors who think they're going to win a trifecta, or the owners who are hoping for a little bit of money to keep their stable going, or the claimers who want to buy that winner and change their luck.

"But the horses are excited too, Ivy. And the jockey has a crop in his hand. He's reaching back to smack his horse on the ass or wave it in front of his face, give him one more reason to try harder. Driving him home. They don't use the crop in the beginning of the race. It's only a signal, Ivy. A way to harness the excitement the horse feels, his energy—or lack thereof at this point in the race. A way to focus the horse on the win."

He stops talking as I picture this in my head.

"That smack on the ass—or the face—is only a signal, Ivy. To focus you on the sex and the way we're going to come together. That's all. The winning horse could give a fuck about that spanking he's getting at the end. He doesn't even feel it. He's so pumped up on adrenaline, that smack is the last thing on his mind. And when I'm fucking you, Ivy, and I reach down and smack your face, you'll only feel what you want to feel. If you're scared, I did it wrong. If you're not turned on, then I did it wrong. If you don't want me to do it again later, then I did it wrong. Do you understand me?"

I nod, unable to speak.

"Do you want me to untie you?" he asks. "Or would you like to renegotiate? Because I *really do* want to fuck you right now. And if you want to fuck me too but have limits you need to make clear, then now is the time to do that."

"I don't want to be hit. Not right now."

Nolan smiles and a small laugh escapes. "I'm not going to hit you right now, Ivy. Don't be crazy."

"You're the one who's crazy," I say. "And don't *laugh* at me. I have no idea what's happening."

"You should trust me."

"Why? You just asked if you could rape me."

His head is shaking no. "That's not what I asked you. I asked if you'd like to participate in a fantasy with me."

"You fantasize about rape?" I cannot believe he's saying this shit.

"No," he says. "*No*. You're not listening. I want to feel the struggle but have permission at the same time, Ivy. It's really not that uncommon. And it should feel good for both of us, or I'm doing it wrong. It's not something you do on the fly. It's something that's set up. I told you that."

"I just don't know."

"Then tell me to untie you and let's just go to dinner. How hard is that? Just say it and it's done."

But I'm silent. Because I don't want it to be *done*. I want more of him. I'm just not sure how much more. Or in what way.

"Can I touch you?" he asks. "Like this?" His fingertips start caressing small circles around my nipple. His touch is so light and gentle I close my eyes, feeling exhausted at the pleasure of that small caress. "You need to answer me, Ivy. Or I'll stop and make this final decision for both of us."

"Yes," I say. "Yes, you can touch me."

He pinches my nipple so hard, I squeak. But in the next instant, that soft swirling of his fingertip is back.

"It's a give and take, Ivy. Everything we do from here on out is a give and take. You give, I take. I give, you take. That's how you come to terms. You understand this. You're a businesswoman. You know that negotiation is an art. Just like those pictures I just drew. It's all part of the negotiations. I've laid out the contract and the next step is for you to agree to the terms or ask for something else."

"I just don't know what I want."

"I know you want this, Ivy." His fingers lightly trace the length of my ribcage, round the bone of my hip, and slip back between my legs.

I have to squeeze my eyes closed, that's how good it feels.

"You like that?"

"Yes," I say. "I do."

"Can I keep going?"

I should say no. But I don't. "Yes," comes out and in that instant I realize what I'm doing. I'm giving in to his request. It's not happening tonight, but that's what my yes means. I'm going to do this. I'm going to let him do all those things he put in the drawings.

His finger pushes inside me and my back arches just as his lips cover my nipple and begin to suck. He nibbles, then bites. I suck in air through my teeth just as his mouth claims mine.

We kiss. His tongue pushing into me, his lips soft, then hard. He bites my lip, bites my tongue, and then he's soft again. Caressing me, and whispering things like, "You'll love it, Ivy. Or we won't do it," between the nips and the tender touches.

This isn't even kissing. Not even close. He's making love to my mouth with his words, and his promises, and his control.

His finger pumps me hard, then harder, making my knees draw up towards my chest. One strong hand pushes them down, then opens them up wide, so he can position himself on top of me.

His hard cock is between my legs, both hands in my hair, fisting and pulling until I open my eyes and see him smile.

"Are you ready to try something new?"

I nod and say, "Yes," because I know he won't keep going unless I am explicit in my consent. And I don't want him to stop. Not yet. I can say no. He said I'm allowed to say no at any time. "Yes," I say again as he watches me.

He enters me. I'm so wet and ready for him, there is none of the painful friction of yesterday. He fills me up easily, pushing inside me so far, I gasp.

But his mouth is back on my mouth. Telling me all the things I need to hear. "You'll love it," he says. "I'm going to make you come so hard, you'll scream."

I'm whispering, "Yes," over and over again as his rhythm picks up. His hips pressing against me, my bound hands trapped between us, pushing him back.

"I love that, Ivy. I love that your hands are tied. That you feel helpless. Just remember," he says, leaning down into my ear. "You can tell me no."

"I'm saying yes."

One hand goes to my throat, pressing against my windpipe. My eyes fly open to watch his face as he watches mine. The pressure increases and I struggle a little. My hands fisted up, tied together, pushing him back, and back. But he presses on. Kissing me still. He never stops kissing me as he thrusts harder, and harder, and harder.

I am screaming in his mouth. He is biting my lip and then my neck. The pressure on my throat eases and I take in a long breath of air, just as it increases again.

He pounds me. My legs are unable to stay still. They come up to my chest, only giving him better access. He moans into my scream and the choking continues, pressing as I squirm and writhe.

"Come," Nolan says between the light touches of his lips on mine. "Come, Ivy. I need you to come first or everything will be ruined. I'll ruin you if you don't come.

And I can't ruin you. I haven't even fucked you in the ass yet."

Just as he says the word ass, his fingers are there. Pushing inside me, filling me up. It hurts, but then... it feels good. It feels so fucking good my head spins and the climax is there. Building up, and up, and up until... *I am out of control.* I am moaning, and screaming, and begging him to never, ever stop this moment.

He's laughing as he pulls out and comes on my breasts. I force my eyes open just as the warm gush of semen streams out. And I watch him pump the tip of his thick hard cock as he scoots up my body and places it in my mouth.

I suck him. I lick him and seal my lips around his head as he continues to pump his hips for a few more seconds before letting out a long breath and falling off to the side.

His arms wrap me up, positioning me on my side and pulling my back into his chest. "Holy fuck," he says, breathing heavy from the exertion.

I feel like I will never get enough air in my lungs. My whole body shuts down as I gasp for air, and understanding, and stillness.

But then I just give in and enjoy it. I meld against him. His heart is beating as fast as mine. I can feel it against my back. His hand comes up to my breast, but he doesn't squeeze. He places it flat. Like he's searching for the beat of my heart too. So we can feel each other in this moment. Feel the excitement we created and the aftermath of calm.

"I could get used to this, Miss Rockwell. I could do this every night."

I push away all my hesitation from earlier. All the fear, and the talk, and the negotiations.

And I just enjoy it as we fall asleep, wrapped tightly around each other.

CHAPTER TWENTY-SEVEN

NOLAN

A buzzing phone wakes me and I sit up in bed, wondering what time it is. Ivy is still asleep, her face awash in yellow-orange light from the setting sun that makes her glow.

I get up and look around for my shorts and find them in the bathroom. The buzzing has stopped but another buzz tells me there's a voicemail. I pull the phone out of my pocket, tab it, recognizing Claudette's number.

"Nolan," her message says. "Where is that girl? Did you take her home? Where is she? This is bad news. I need to talk to you now. *Now*, Nolan. I'm not joking."

I end the message and go back into the bedroom. Ivy didn't wake up so I go out into the hallway, walk along the catwalk that overlooks the living room, and hop down the stairs two at a time.

I grab a water from the fridge and I'm just about to call Claudette back when the doorbell rings. When I get to the foyer I can see Claudette through the glass doors, standing on the step, hands on hips, looking very pissed off.

I open it and say, "Jesus Christ, Claudette. I was just going to call you. No need—"

"Is she here?" Claudette cuts me off.

"Yeah, why?"

Claudette pushes past me, ignoring my question. "Where?"

"Upstairs. And keep your fucking voice down, she's sleeping."

Claudette shoots daggers at me with her eyes. "You

189

fucked her."

"What the fuck do you want? And why the hell did you follow me here?"

"I need to tell you something. But I don't want her to hear. Let's go into the kitchen."

She doesn't give me a chance to object or agree, just walks off to the kitchen. I follow, helpless to derail her when she's in a mood like this.

The kitchen is open to the living room, so it only offers a little bit of privacy. "What?" I ask her.

"What do you know about this girl? Ivy Rockwell? How did we get her résumé?"

"Corporate sent it. Why?" My sister is agitated. Which is not uncommon. She's about as high-strung as those horses down on the racetrack. Her hair is blonde, but not naturally. And it's short and has a soft curl that that makes it look bouncy. How the two of us are related is beyond me. My hair is dark, my eyes green. And even though she dyes her hair, it's not really dark, so the blonde looks good on her. Her eyes are blue though. My mother's eyes, I suppose, though they are more gray than blue.

"Well, he's fucking with you then."

"Why?"

"Do you know who Ivy Rockwell's father is?"

"Some pastor up in New England. *Why?*"

"Because he's a little bit more than that, Nolan. He was on the board at Brown."

"So?" I'm not following. And my sister likes to make her points in dramatic ways that I have no patience for. "Just tell me what the fuck is going on."

"He was on the board when you were expelled, Nolan."

"Hmm. Is that weird?"

"Don't you think it's weird?" Her eyes are wide in

surprise. "I mean this girl shows up practically uninvited, with a fake résumé, and now we find out her father was on the board when you were kicked out?"

The five of us weren't technically expelled. We were 'asked to leave' by the administration with the understanding we could return if we were found not guilty. None of us thought it would take two years to clear things up. And by that time, college was nothing but a dead end in the rearview mirror.

"Did you forget Amy, Nolan? The girl who tried to sue you six months ago?"

"Shit." Amy was a manager at one of my clubs. She and I had a similar affair. Not the fantasy stuff. We never got that far. But the whole, *I'll fuck you before I hire you* thing. We did fuck. And then I hired her and fired her all in the span of a few months. She was totally incompetent. We didn't do anything while she was actually working for me, but we did before. And after. Which is why she tried to claim sexual harassment.

But Match did some digging for me and found out she was an outspoken advocate for the girl who accused us of rape. Some blogger who wrote the most vile things about us online. I don't know what Match said to her, but the sexual harassment threat disappeared a lot more quietly than it appeared, and I never heard from her again.

"I think this Ivy girl is in on it."

"In on what?"

"Trying to take you down. You know I was convinced that you were the reason the whole thing blew up."

I *was* the reason. But I never told anyone. Match came and called his friend. And then we were told to shut the fuck up and not say a word, not even to each other.

So she doesn't know what I did that night. No one

does. Just me and that girl. And she's dead.

I sigh and lean against the counter. "For what purpose though? I don't get it."

"Trying to milk us for money, Nolan. How stupid are you?"

I squint my eyes at my sister. "Don't call me stupid. I don't need a college degree to understand your paranoid reasoning, Claudette. I've gotten to know Ivy. She's not like that."

"You've gotten to know her? In twenty-four hours?"

"It's more like thirty-six. And yeah. I think I know her better than you."

"She's trying to trap you. And by the way, Travis confessed that you made him call me and lie about another girl saying she was pregnant. I hope you're using protection with this one. Or I'll bet a thousand dollars she ends up pregnant with your child and sues you for support."

"I always use protection," I huff. But it isn't true. Ivy and I fucked last night with no protection. I pulled out today. Besides, Ivy was the one who tried to warn me she wasn't on birth control. I was the one who did it anyway. "That girl wasn't pregnant. And Ivy wouldn't do something like that. She's a nice girl." Far too nice for me, and not because I don't want her. I do. She's just a little out of my league.

"She needs to leave. You need to stop seeing her."

"No," I say. "No. I like her. And as long as she keeps accepting my invitations, I'm not gonna kick her aside."

And… she likes the way I fuck. That's not easy to come by. She's in for the fantasy, I know it. It's only a matter of time before we set that shit up. And holy fuck—I cannot wait.

"You're going to get hurt, Nolan. I mean it. There's

something fishy about her. Something's off."

"There's something off about you too, Claudette." She recoils and puts her hand over her heart like I offended her. "But you don't see me kicking you to the curb like trash."

"I'm just saying—"

But my sister's words are cut off by my buzzing phone in my hand. I look down and smile. "Look, it's Corporate." I tab the accept button and say, "Wassup, asshole? I've been trying to get a hold of you since yesterday morning."

"Yeah, I just got home, man. Sorry about that. Some emergency meeting with a big hush, hush contract. Fuckers are trying to drive me crazy. Now what do ya need?"

"You know that girl you sent?"

"Which girl, Nolan? I've got like a hundred clients right now."

"Ivy Rockwell? New England? Just graduated from Brown?"

"No, don't recall. And why the fuck would I send you a recent college grad?" He practically snorts. "What kind of amateur do you think I am?"

"Wait," I say.

"What?" Claudette says. "What's he saying?"

"You didn't send her? Are you sure? Ivy Rockwell? Her résumé said she got her MBA while she was still doing undergrad?"

"Yeah, right!" Corporate laughs. "Brown would never give up the extra years of tuition money. I've never heard of Ivy Rocks-her-face, Nolan. Is this what you wanted to talk to me about? Because I thought it was gonna be about that little deal we're cooking up for Match."

"That's a no, by the way. I'm not in on that. That girl looks wild. You know Oliver, he'd never go for that. But anyway, fuck that shit. I need to know how the hell Ivy Rockwell got her résumé on my desk and how the hell the jet was sent to pick her up, if you didn't schedule it."

"I didn't schedule it. And you know what? I'm kinda pissed about that. I needed the fucking jet today and I got a *sorry, not sorry* message from scheduling saying you've got it tied up in San Diego. What the fuck is wrong with you? You don't schedule the jet for a forty-five-minute ride. Do you have any idea how much that costs? No probably not. That silver spoon is so deep down your throat—"

"Would you shut up for a minute?" I say. "This is serious. I have Ivy Rockwell here. In my fucking Del Mar house. Claudette says her résumé was fake and her father was a Brown board member, just like that last bitch who weaseled her way into my life."

"I don't know what you're talking about, brother. I never sent her. Can I have the jet now? I've got scheduling on the other line. That's the real reason I called. I need to take a trip and I can't fly commercial."

"Yeah, sure—"

"Thanks, man. Good luck with the girl. But if I were you, I'd get her the fuck out of there before you're behind bars again."

Corporate hangs up on me and I'm left standing there trying to figure this all out.

"What did he say?" Claudette asks.

"He says he didn't send her. Has no clue who she is."

"I told you, Nolan. I fucking told you! She's up to something. I don't know what her game is, but she's not going to win. Get rid of her."

And then Claudette walks out of the kitchen and a few seconds later the front door slams.

I follow, but stop in the living room trying to wrap my head around what just happened. If Corporate didn't send Ivy, then who did?

"So…" Ivy says from above.

I look up and find her on the catwalk. Fully dressed in her shorts and t-shirt. Correction, my shorts and t-shirt. The ones I gave her this morning.

She walks to the stairs and descends slowly, her hand sliding down the banister as she walks. She's dragging her little carry-on case behind her. "I take it the honeymoon is over."

"How did you get to my resort, Ivy?"

"Your jet."

"How the fuck did you get on the jet?"

"An invitation. Hand-delivered. I heard everything you guys said. I heard your bitchy sister say that stuff about me. And you know what?"

She's mad. Very mad.

"What?"

"I'm going to solve all your problems and just go."

"I just said Corporate could take the jet. So I can't—"

"I don't need your jet," she seethes. "I've already called an Uber to pick me up and I'll buy a plane ticket when I get to the airport. I'm not trying to get pregnant with your baby, Nolan. How stupid does a girl have to be to get pregnant with Mr. Romantic's baby? I'm not interested in your money, or your fancy house, or that jet, or your *job*." She practically spits the words out. "And I'm especially not interested in that *fantasy* of yours."

When she gets to the bottom of the stairs she snaps the handle up on her little carry-on suitcase, hikes her purse over her shoulder, and says, "Good day, sir," as she walks out my front door.

CHAPTER TWENTY-EIGHT

IVY

"Just take a deep breath," Nora says. "And tell me what happened."

What happened was I got in that Uber car and hauled myself all the way down the coast to the San Diego airport where I arrived after the last flight of the day and had to spend the night on the concourse because the Motel 6 was all booked up and I didn't have an extra two hundred and twenty dollars for the Hilton after I paid for my one-way ticket home.

And the worst part was that all I kept thinking about was the jet and how comfortable it was to sleep in that bed and order drinks at a bar with a real bartender.

Stupid jet.

"Ivy," Nora says, shaking me by the shoulder. "Why are you crying?"

What am I supposed to say? Nolan Delaney took my virginity, played some kinky artist game with me, and then asked me to participate in a fantasy rape scene? Oh, and by the way, I didn't get the job. Even though I had really great ideas! Really, *really* great ideas!

"Ivy?" Nora says again. "Do you need a cup of tea?"

"Yes," I sniffle. "I'm damaged, Nora. I swear to God."

"What happened? Was he rude?"

"Tea?" I squeak. I want the tea, but what I really need right now is not to have to explain myself.

"OK. Just sit here and calm down. I'll be right back."

We live in a townhouse, so the kitchen is on the second floor and the bedrooms are on floors one and

197

three. I have the bottom, since this is technically Nora's place and I only pay rent. She has the master bedroom with the rooftop terrace.

Nora runs up the stairs to the kitchen to get my tea started and I sit on my bed, still wearing Nolan Delaney's clothes, and... and... I can't even say it...

But I can smell him. His manly scent is all over these clothes. All over my body. And I know that makes me a freak, but I can smell him and it just makes me want to cry harder.

Calm down, calm down. Nora is going to come downstairs with my tea and start demanding details. And I'm not telling her anything. No one will ever know about this weekend and horrible....

I stop crying.

I take deep breaths and try to think of something else.

Like that stupid Mr. Corporate. Nolan followed me out of the house, saying, "We'll figure it out," and, "I don't think you did anything wrong." But then stupid Claudette came back and called me a lying whore from the comfort of her ugly Mercedes. And that I was only after Nolan's money. And that I probably wasn't on birth control.

I'll probably get pregnant from the one time he came inside me and then she will be proven right!

I want to die.

And then Nolan said, "Shut up, Claudette! Go home!"

But she said, "No. I'm not letting you make more embarrassing mistakes and this tramp is..." Well, I don't remember. By that time, I was walking down the hill, in what I thought was the direction of the main road. But it wasn't and then the Uber driver charged me extra because I wasn't at the right address.

And Nolan and I had a big fight in the middle of the

street and people turned on their lights and the cops came!

I can't believe this.

So I just got in the Uber car and said, "Drive!" And he said, "Where, lady?" And then I had to calm down and be all rational and explain. "The airport," and, "Could you please hurry?"

It was all very dramatic.

I sigh, feeling a little better now that I ran it all through my head. I'm still not telling Nora. I can't tell her what happened this weekend. She will want all the details about losing my virginity and what he did, and what I did, and how it was. And that will lead to the next day and the posing nude for him, and his offer.

That fucking offer.

And the worst part is… I can totally picture that yellow dress in my head.

"I'm sick."

"Oh, honey," Nora says from my bedroom door, my tea in hand. "I'm sorry. Is that why you're crying? Did you get the shits while you were there? Did you drink that water they have? It does that sometimes."

"I think that happens in Mexico," I whine. "But yes," I have to say something to account for how upset I am. "Yes, I totally got the shits and I had to borrow these clothes!"

I cry again. Wail into my pillow. Because I'd rather pretend I shit my pants in front of a hot guy instead of what really happened.

"I need to go home and see my parents," I say. "I need to decompress."

"Decompress from what?" Nora asks.

And I really do need to tell her something. So I opt for half the truth. "I didn't get the job."

"Oh, Ivy," she says "I'm sorry, honey. But you knew

that, right? You knew you weren't going to get the job."

"I know, but it's worse. They said they never asked me to come. And they had a copy of my résumé that wasn't mine. That's why I got invited in the first place. It was just some big old mistake!"

"Well, that's weird. How do they explain that?"

"They didn't. They just sent me home."

"Hmmm," Nora says.

"So I'm going to go home for a few days and cry about it." I sniffle. Then wipe my hand across my face.

"OK," Nora says, sitting down on my bed and hugging me. "That's a good idea. A few days away will do you good."

"Yeah." I get up and open my little carry-on. It's filled with business clothes and right on top is the revealing black bathing suit that someone who is not me put inside my suitcase.

I realize it must've been Nolan and want to cry all over again.

Suck it up, Ivy.

I do. I suck it up. I throw my interview clothes into my closet and pack some shorts and tanks, and then slam it shut and fish through my purse for my keys.

"When will you be back?"

"I don't know. A few days, maybe?"

"OK," Nora says. "OK, if that's what you need."

I nod. "I need to be with my family. I'll call you later, OK?"

Nora pouts her lip and hugs me again. "Drive safe," she says. "And if you need to have another cry, just pull over and get it all out."

"OK," I say. "I will. Don't worry about me. Really. I'm OK."

"Oh, and I didn't want to tell you, but I have an

interview in New York on Wednesday. A huge PR firm. I'm leaving tomorrow night so I can miss traffic and then go shopping for a new outfit before. So I'll be gone anyway. It's good you're going home. I don't want you here alone."

I feel like a complete loser. "I'm so jealous."

"Oh, Ivy," she says, sad again. "I'm sorry it didn't work out."

But I wave her off and force myself to smile. "Congratulations, Nora. You deserve a good job. Really. I'm so happy for you."

She squeezes my arm and says, "You too, sweetie. The right one will come along, don't worry."

That was *the right job,* I think as I walk out of the house and over to my car. I beep the lock open and then throw my carry-on into the back seat and get in. My ideas were so great. And Nolan never even got to hear them.

I pull away from the curb and start making my way back home to Bishop, Massachusetts.

But the only thing I see in my head is that yellow dress he promised me. And the date. The date and the fantasy. And his smell makes it all worse.

But by the time I drive the hour and a half to my parents' house, nestled at the end of a winding road in the middle of the Bishop School for Girls campus, I'm all cried out and just need to sleep.

I greet my parents like nothing is wrong, but then make a hasty excuse to escape to my old bedroom for a shower and a nap, and stillness.

That damn dress. That dangerous offer. And that dark man.

Those are the only things I think about.

I even dream about him. And to my horror, when I wake up, there's a pool of wetness between my legs.

I came just from the memory of what Mr. Romantic was promising.

CHAPTER TWENTY-NINE

NOLAN

"Yeah?"

"Pax," I say.

"Who is this and how did you get this number?"

"Don't be a dick, asshole. Match gave it to me."

There's a long silence on the other end of the phone as Mr. Mysterious works out who's calling.

"Nolan," he deadpans.

"Paxton," I say back.

He lets out a long breath. "I hope it's not bad news."

"It's not." *Not yet,* I think.

"I hope you're not gonna sell my house. I still want it back when I'm done."

"Dude, it's not about you."

"Then why the fuck are you calling me?"

Man, this guy. I swear. He's got no people skills at all. How the fuck he ever got into Brown, I will never understand. "I hear you can find dirt on people."

"Who told you that?"

"Jesus Christ." I scrub a hand down my face and try to be patient with the guy. "I know you, Pax. Mr. Mysterious, remember? All those good times in court ten years ago? It's *Nolan.*"

"Don't patronize me, Romantic. I know who the fuck you are. What I don't know is why the fuck you're calling me on this phone and who the fuck gave you permission to do so."

"Match, asshole. I got your number from Match."

"What do you want, Nolan?"

"I... don't know. I mean... I don't *know.* Something

feels off, man. I met this girl—"

"Wait. You're calling me about a girl? I don't give out my secret love advice."

I decide to ignore him. I think there's a ninety-nine percent chance he's fucking with me anyway. So I just move on. "Something is wrong, man. I can feel it. It's the past, Pax. I just know someone is *on to us*."

"Hm," he says. "Where are you?"

"Del Mar house."

"I'll be there in three hours. I've got blood on my hands at the moment. So I'm gonna need a shower."

The call ends and I just stare at the screen. He could be serious about the blood. Or not. It's hard to tell with him. He's my last resort though. Perfect is off on vacation somewhere and Corporate is working some job, I guess. Match lives in Colorado, so he's too far away. Mysterious is the only one close enough to talk to in person. He's up in LA doing… whatever the fuck he does. I really have no idea what he does. But I do know he'll help if he can. He won't leave me hanging.

Because something is *wrong*.

It's not just Ivy and the fact that no one knows how she got invited to my resort. How her folder with that fake résumé got delivered to my desk. How our motherfucking *jet* was scheduled to pick her up. But that's most of it.

The other part is her father. And normally I'd chalk that up to coincidence—she did come from Brown, and her father is some do-gooder pastor who heads up a private school that probably sends all its graduates to Ivy League universities. So it's not that unusual that he'd be on their board at some point in his career.

But the last girl—that last girl in San Diego I fucked about six months back—that's where all the coincidences fall apart. I remember something she said once. I just can't recall what it was. I only remember the feeling it gave me. It shook me up for some reason.

We were drunk, sitting out on the sand in front of the Pacific Beach bike path, eating tacos we got from the little Mexican place across from the club a few blocks down. It was like two in the morning and the beach was almost empty.

And she said... fuck. What did she say? I can't recall. I just remember having this *feeling*. This feeling of warning bells, and red flags, and lighted signs flashing *danger, danger, danger—stop talking*.

And I did. We stopped talking and we fucked.

That was the first time. And I hired her the next day. Forgetting all about our drunken conversation and all the reasons she made me uncomfortable.

Even when she tried to lie about being pregnant, I still shook it off. It wasn't the first time some girl pulled that shit on me.

But how does Ivy fit into this? She has to fit, I just know it. She has to fit. Someone fucking *hacked our jet*. Someone got that file with her résumé to me. Someone sent her an invitation to interview. Someone—pretending to be Corporate—told me she was coming and to expect her.

Who?

That's why I need Mysterious.

He's got a reputation these days. Hell, now that I think about it, he's always had that reputation. He comes from Hollywood money, I know that much. He's some bastard child from some big-time movie star. But he didn't grow up in Hollywood. He comes from old Kentucky money on his mother's side. A true blue-blood family who made their fortune in bluegrass thoroughbreds.

Which is why he has a thing for the track, I guess.

And even though Kentucky isn't deep South, it's South enough. They do justice a little differently in the South.

It came in handy back in college and from the hints Match has been dropping over the years, it might still come in handy.

Might. I'm not sure yet. Maybe I'm just being paranoid? But maybe not. But there's one thing the five of us Misters learned from our little run-in with the law.

It pays to be paranoid.

If Ivy is involved, I'm positive she's unaware. That girl just doesn't have it in her. She doesn't. I can tell. She's innocent—was innocent before I got my dick inside her—and she's sweet.

But she might be in danger. She might be caught up in something bigger than herself and she might be in danger. And even though she walked out of here and we had a huge fight in the middle of the street a few blocks down—a big enough scene that neighbors called the cops, which I handled—Ivy got in some Uber car and left. She might be in danger and I might be the reason why.

I let her get away because I know where to find her. I looked her up a little more thoroughly this time and it wasn't hard to find everything I need to know in order to make contact again. Which I will be doing as soon as I talk to Mysterious.

So I'm gonna make contact again. For her own protection.

I try to convince myself of that but… that's not the only reason.

She's into the fantasy. She just doesn't know it yet.

That is the only thing that makes me smile right now. Picturing her in that yellow dress as we start the date. Picturing me taking it off her as we begin the scene.

Picturing her writhing underneath me as we fuck.

Yeah, that shit is happening. She just doesn't know it yet.

I look inside at the discarded drawings and go pick them up. Arranging them in order of how things will go down.

I got her likeness pretty good. I've always been good at art. Always had a thing for drawing the female form. Always been a planner. And what better way to plan a night of taboo sex than to imagine it in my head and draw it out to make it real?

No. I'm not done with Ivy Rockwell yet. She's in for a surprise if she thinks she can just walk out and I'll forget about what we talked about. If she thinks I'll just forget and move on without putting on my A-game. If she thinks she won't be getting the fuck of her life the next time I see her, she's in for a surprise.

A very big surprise.

CHAPTER THIRTY

IVY

I lie in bed just thinking about him. Nolan Delaney, the infamous Mr. Romantic. The media always used that word in front of his name. Infamous. It implies a lot of very bad things. None of the other Misters were called infamous. And even though most of the details about what happened that night never became public, Mr. Romantic was the one everybody talked about.

Why?

Why, Ivy?

"Yeah." I sigh. "I know why."

Somehow, some way, Nolan Delaney was the one responsible for what happened that night when those five guys were back in college. That was the rumor. The police found something of Nolan's in that frat house. Some kind of evidence. Something powerful enough to charge five very rich boys, from five very rich families, with rape.

A familiar voice drifts up from downstairs and I wonder what time it is. I lean over and look at the clock on my bedside table. Almost dinnertime.

My parents are very traditional. We have Sunday dinner. I don't, not anymore. Not since I left home for college, except for the rare occasions I'm home on Sunday evenings. Like tonight. But all growing up my mother has put on a Sunday dinner. And my father, because he's the dean of the school, would invite various people to have dinner with us. Mostly students, but sometimes important church members.

But the voice downstairs is not a student. It's Richard.

My father loved Richard. And I'm pretty sure that my

mother started planning our wedding the first time I brought him home and he insisted on sleeping in the guest room.

As if I was ever going to let him sleep in my bed. But my mom loved it. Ate it up.

Why is he here?

I check the mirror, horrified that I look as wrung-out as I feel. I drag a brush through my hair and pinch my cheeks to get some color.

OK. Time to get back to real life. Dinner with parents and ex-boyfriend, agenda task number one.

I walk down the stairs of my parent's historic four-square brick colonial, remembering the high ceilings and amazing view I was looking at yesterday at Nolan's house.

It feels like a dream. I lost my virginity to Nolan Delaney.

How did that happen?

Get it together, Ivy. Put on the public face and smile.

And that's how I walk into the dining room.

"There she is!" my father exclaims, getting up to take my hand and walk me into the living room where everyone gathers when guests are over. "Did you have a nice sleep, princess?" He leans down to kiss me on the head.

"I did. Hi, Richard."

Boring Richard smiles at me.

"Do you feel better, honey?" my mother asks.

"Much. I just needed some sleep."

"I heard you were on a job interview this weekend," Boring Richard says.

"You were?" my parents exclaim together.

"How did it go?" my father asks.

"Yes, Ivy," Richard says. "How did it go?"

Hmmm. Something is up with him. "What are you doing here, Richard?" I change the subject.

"Got a call from Nora this morning. Said you were coming here and I should check up on you."

My father gives me a weird look. But it's my mother who asks the obvious question. "Is everything all right, Ivy?"

I open my mouth to say yes, but Boring Richard beats me to it. "No," he says. "Nora said she was interviewing with someone we all know."

"Who?" my father asks.

"Richard, it's not important."

"She came home crying." And then Richard turns to my father. "Do you remember Nolan Delaney?"

My father snorts. "How could I forget that scoundrel?"

"Richard," I warn in a stern voice.

"Well, he invited Ivy to interview for a position in California and—"

"You're moving to California?" my mother exclaims, dramatic hand over heart in shock.

"Mom—"

"She didn't get the job," Richard says.

"You're wrong, Richard. I did get the job."

He squints his eyes at me. "Nora said—"

"Nora doesn't know." I turn to my parents, who are sitting their matching plush chairs, facing me. "I told her I didn't get the job. The one I was interviewing for. But I did get an offer for something else."

Richard does not believe me, but I don't care.

"Yep," I say, pulling out my huge good-pastor's-daughter smile. "I'm moving to California."

Screw Richard. It's not his story to tell. So I'm going to tell my own story.

"You're going to work for Nolan Delaney?" my father says. "That awful boy who—"

"They were innocent, Dad. Everyone knows that." Everyone does not know that, and my father is about to object when I continue. "And yes. I am. I'm going to gather all my stuff and move away. It's about time. I need a change anyway."

"How will you afford it, Ivy?" my mother asks.

I can't afford it. I spent a lot of money on the flight home. Money I really don't have after tanning out at the pool of our townhouse community all summer, hoping against hope that a job would come through. But I will do anything to start somewhere fresh right now.

I don't know why I'm lying, but I just don't want to have this conversation. Especially in front of Richard. "I don't have all the details worked out, Mom. But I'm gonna go through with it. What's for dinner?"

The change of subject works, because my mother jumps up saying something about mashing the potatoes and then we'll eat.

I smile at Richard, who has a full-on scowl on his face now. His familiar cologne makes me wrinkle my nose.

"Well," my father huffs. "This is quite a surprise, Ivy."

"A good one though, Dad."

"I don't like that boy. There's something bad about him."

Yeah, I think. *His sexual appetite.* "That was ten years ago. He's not that kid anymore."

"So you met him?" The question comes from my dad, but I'm looking at Richard, daring him to contradict my lie about the job.

"Yes. He's very nice, actually." And when I say it out loud I realize it's true. "He took me to dinner and I saw the resort. It's nice, but he really needs a lot of help marketing it. And that's where I come in. He hired two other men to run the place, but he asked me to be a private contractor for the marketing. So it's not a permanent job. But I'll be fine," I interject before my father can comment about that. "It's a great opportunity."

This really isn't a lie, I decide. Nolan did offer me a contract position. We just never had a chance to get back to business. I might still be able to remedy that if I put together a good proposal. We can forget all about the weekend and start fresh. Forget all about his insane offer to have a fantasy rape date with him. Forget all about his amazing house overlooking the racetrack.

"Well, princess, if you think it's a good idea, I'll support you. But I have to tell you that I was partially responsible for his expulsion. Are you sure you want to work for a man you have that connection with?"

"He's probably using you, Ivy," Richard says.

"For what?" I ask. But it's a legitimate question. Why me? I've asked myself that so many times. And now that I'm back home, why do I want to go back?

"Revenge, I'd imagine," Richard says.

"No," I say. "And I'm not going to discuss it." I tilt my chin up and smile. "My mind is made up."

"Dinner is ready!" my mother calls.

My father rubs his hands together and pops up out of his chair like he can't wait to get to the table, and then rushes to the dining room to help my mom.

Richard grabs my arm and leans into my ear before I can follow. "Nora called me. Told me all about this, Ivy. She said you were up to something."

I will kill her if she mentioned my plan to lose my virginity to Nolan. Kill. Her.

"And she asked me to check on him using the database at work. I had to call in a favor to get this info—"

213

"What info?"

"You have something in common with a girl he hired and fired several months back."

"What?" I'm so annoyed that he's here.

"Both your fathers were on the board of Brown when he got expelled. And she was an outspoken advocate for the girl they—"

"They didn't do it. Why is everyone conveniently forgetting that fact?"

"How do you know?"

"He wasn't found guilty, that's how. You're a lawyer, you know what that means."

"He never went to trial because that poor victim was killed. It does not mean he was innocent. You're the one who's innocent, Ivy. And naive. I've seen the evidence. I went into the office today and it would make you sick to know what they had on him. I've seen it all and you've seen nothing. You wouldn't know the difference between a predator and a peacock if they were standing right in front of you. He's setting you up for something. He called you in for that interview with some kind of sick revenge plan in mind. Just like he did with that last girl. I did some digging and she tried to file a sexual harassment complaint and he shut her down. He's going to do the same thing to you, Ivy. He's going to ruin your life to get even with your father for that expulsion."

I shake my head and huff out some air of disgust. But I gather myself and straighten my spine as I lean into his ear and whisper, "I'm not as innocent as you think, Richard. And thanks for the vote of confidence in my marketing abilities. You know what I'm capable of and yet you are standing here insulting me, my intelligence, and my sensibility. So you can take your advice and shove it up your ass. And if you bring this up again tonight, I will ask you to leave and tell my father that you tried to pressure me into fucking you and that's why we broke up."

And then I pat him on the chest and walk off.

Richard excuses himself as my father sets the table, claiming he has to get back to Boston for an early day tomorrow. I smile and make a big deal about missing him as he squints his eyes in fury at me.

But I get my way. I get rid of the ex-boyfriend, have a lovely Sunday meal with my parents, and find some clarity about this whole Nolan Delaney experience.

I'm going to get that job. Even if it only lasts two weeks, I'm going to show Nolan Delaney what I'm made of and he's going to stop seeing me as innocent.

When I'm done, no one will call me naive again.

****

After dinner I help my mom with the dishes and then go upstairs, still exhausted even though I slept all day.

The first thing I notice when I get to my childhood room is my buzzing phone. It stops buzzing by the time I pick it up and that's when I notice thing number two.

I have seven missed calls from an area code in California.

Nolan has been calling all evening.

I smile. Because he's chasing *me* now, probably regretting letting his sister say all those awful things about me. Or maybe he really does want my help with the resort marketing? At any rate, when the phone buzzes again, I answer with a cocky, "I knew you'd call again."

"I'll be in Providence on Wednesday. Make sure you clear your schedule. We left a lot of things unfinished."

The call ends.

And that's when I know—am one hundred percent

sure—that Nolan Delaney has no professional interest in me at all.

He still wants me to help him live out his sick fantasy.

CHAPTER THIRTY-ONE

NOLAN

Claudette comes bursting into my office, making the door bang into the stopper, pissed off as all hell. It's written all over her face.

"What's this I hear? You're taking a long weekend? Since when? We're opening soon and you're—"

"I'm very aware," I say, cutting her off. "It's *my* resort, Claudette. So I'm very aware of what's on the agenda this week. But I don't need your permission to take a few days off. I'm driving to San Diego, getting on a plane, and going to Martha's Vineyard for a few days. The resort will be fine."

Claudette cocks a hip and one hand goes to rest there. Ever since our last encounter out in Del Mar she's been weird. Asking me all kinds of questions. Where am I going? Who was I with? Did I hear from "that Rockwell girl?"

I have not heard from that Rockwell girl. Not since I called her on Sunday and told her I'd be in town tonight. I half expected her to call me back and flat out say, *Don't bother. I'm not interested.* And she didn't, so I'm taking that as a good sign. I also half expected her to call the police and have them serve me with a restraining order.

But what I did not expect was an envelope, Overnight Express, delivered to me here at the resort on Tuesday afternoon, which stated...

I have to put a hand to my mouth because Claudette is still ranting about what the fuck ever and I can't help but smile.

Which stated... her qualifications for becoming my

personal marketing assistant.

It's cute, actually. It even had a stack of colorful graphs and pie charts. A sneak peek, she called it in the letter, of what she was capable of.

She definitely has balls.

And while I'm impressed with her first attempt at a real-life business proposal—especially after the man she's proposing it to told her he practically wanted to hold her down on the bed with a hand over her throat—the only business I'm interested in is the one where I rip the wet yellow dress down the middle while she stands in front of me shivering from the cold.

"You're not listening to me."

"You're right," I tell Claudette as I look over my schedule on my laptop. Everything is clear. The guests we had last weekend are gone now, Bram and Daniel are both working on their individual assignments, Claudette is here. "Look, I hire people to work for me, Claudette. People like Bram and Daniel, each of whom are getting paid a shitload of fucking money to do it. And you—"

"Don't," Claudette warns, pointing her polished nail at me. "Don't you include me in your list of employees, Nolan. I'm a partner."

"A very minor one, Claudette. I told you that when you offered me money. I didn't need your money—"

"You did," she snaps.

"It was nice to have the money, I'm not going to deny it. But I've been funding my businesses for a decade with no help from your side of the family."

"It was your choice to be estranged from our father."

"Was it, Claudette? Was it? No school was going to touch me after the charges were filed. Sitting around doing nothing for two years was preferable to starting my own business?"

"That's not what he meant."

"When he cut me out of the will when I said I wasn't going back to school, I got the gist of what he meant, Claudette. So it was nice to have you on board with me. Nice, but nothing else. I don't need another mother."

Claudette's lips press together. She hates it when I bring up my mother. "No," she snarls. "I don't suppose you do. You had one all growing up."

"And you had a father. So don't blame that on me. It wasn't my fault you stayed with him."

"She didn't want me."

"Well, *he* didn't want *me*." I laugh. "Same fucking shit." I slap the laptop closed and get up, tucking it under my arm. "I've gotta pack. So," I say, walking towards the door and sidestepping her attempt to grab me by my shirt. I grab her wrist instead, holding it tight. "Don't," I warn in a deep voice. "Don't fucking start with me again, Claudette. I'm serious. If you get crazy, I will buy your ass out of this venture and wash my hands."

"That's what you want, don't you?" The familiar shrillness of her voice is back. I've been wondering how long she'd last in this facade she puts on for the public. Claudette has always been high-strung. Like the goddamned thoroughbreds out at Del Mar. Temperamental, and spoiled, and demanding.

It's her way or the highway. That's practically her motto. We were as estranged as me and my father for years before she showed up six months ago acting all apologetic. And while I was suspicious, it was nice. It was nice to think that she might've calmed down over the years.

But I was wrong. She's not any calmer now than she was back when we were kids.

"Every day you show me that you haven't changed, Claudette, makes me want to walk away again. So be careful, sister. I'm not gonna put up with your meddling. Stay the fuck out of my personal life."

"Or what?" she snaps.

"Or I'll remove you from it myself."

I let go of her wrist and push her out of my way, walking into the outer offices towards the stairs.

She follows, screaming. "Don't do that, Nolan!"

Typical temper tantrum.

"Nolan, stop!" She runs at me, throwing herself into me, so we both collide with the railing of the stairs.

I look down and see the front desk girls looking up, surprised expressions on their faces.

I turn back to Claudette and seethe as I grab her by the shirt. "Lower your fucking voice. You will not start a scene here in front of my employees."

She gasps and makes a lot of noise, so I let go and just walk down the stairs, doing my best to calm myself as I shoot the girls at the desk a warning look. "Get back to work," I say as I pass them and make my way into the lobby.

"Nolan!" Claudette yells, following. "You promised me!"

Jesus Christ, here it comes. A full-on tantrum. I'm done with her.

I just keep walking as she screams, "I'm going to tell everyone what you did that night! Because you promised me!"

She's the one who promised. I never promised her anything. She's the one who needed to agree to my stipulations. She's the one who said she'd never do this again. She's the one who broke our agreement today. And she is the one who will pay the price.

I push through the lobby doors that lead to the pool, her yelling still echoing out behind me. A minute later she's outside too, but I'm already walking back to the private residence area, and when I reach my bungalow, I go inside and lock the door.

She pounds on it, screaming the entire time I'm packing.

I want to fucking kill her right now. I want to get rid of her so bad.

When I'm packed, I call the valet to bring my car, grab my bags, and walk back out. Claudette is still yelling. I try my best to ignore her as I make my way back into the main lobby, but she is not easy to ignore when she's having one of her meltdowns.

We're just passing the front desk when she grabs my shirt, trying to make me stop. I push her and she goes reeling backwards in an exaggerated way, falling down on her ass.

Her makeup is all smeared down her face from her fake tears and I go hot all over. "You're fucking fired," I say, my anger boiling over. "You better be gone when I get back on Sunday, because you're fucking fired."

"Don't do this again, Nolan!" she yells, making the biggest scene possible. "Don't do this!"

But I just walk out. My Carrera is waiting, so I throw my bag on the passenger seat, get in, and drive away.

She's not going to ruin this day for me. No goddamned way.

My phone rings again, but this time it's not Claudette. It's Mysterious. I tab the accept button on the car navigations system.

"Yeah?"

"Where are you?"

"On my way to San Diego. But I'm heading to Boston once I get there. You have something for me?"

"In person," Pax says.

"I'll be at the house on Martha's Vineyard, but I've got plans tonight, Pax. Plans that require privacy and seclusion."

"I'll call when I get in and we'll set it up."

CHAPTER THIRTY-TWO

IVY

Wednesday. It's finally Wednesday.

I got the delivery receipt for the package I sent Nolan yesterday, so he got it. And he knows what I'm after tonight. But then the doorbell rang a few minutes ago. I didn't expect a hand-delivered package back.

I look at the white box tied with a yellow satin ribbon and my heart beats wildly. What is in here?

Open it, Ivy. I'm begging myself to open it. But I'm scared too. Because I know what's in there.

I untie the ribbon and it falls away in a soft puddle of fabric. Then I lift off the lid and pull the yellow tissue paper back.

The dress.

I hold it up and take it in, then hang it on the top of my bedroom door so I can see it properly. It only has one strap, and the satin is the same color as the ribbon on the box. Soft, smooth, like silk, as my fingers pick it up and let it drop, fascinated by the weight, and the sheen, and the way I get wet between my legs as I picture myself wearing it.

I go back to the box and find a silver envelope. The same kind of silver envelope that the first invitation came in. It's thick.

I open the unsealed flap and pull out a folded handwritten letter on the most beautiful silver paper I've ever seen.

Dear Ivy,

Welcome to the preparation phase of our fantasy date. Please read everything carefully.

I will make advances tonight and you will reciprocate. I will become rough and you will say no. NOT STOP. If you say STOP, the fantasy ends. That is your safe word.

But you can, and should, say no. Say no like you mean it. Say no often and loud. Scream no, Ivy. My dick is getting hard right now just thinking about it.

The first time you say no, the real fantasy starts. You should be afraid. You should wonder if you're crazy. You should second-guess yourself the entire time... until it's over. And then you should not feel guilt or shame because you loved it.

You will enjoy this or we will STOP. You are the one in control even when you feel like you're completely helpless.

One word to make it STOP, Ivy. Just one word. Don't be afraid to say it. I will expect *you to say it if I do something wrong. If I gag you, and I will—I like the gag—you will cross your fingers to signal STOP. Don't forget that. You will cross your fingers to signal STOP.*

There's a man waiting outside. Don't worry, he will be there no matter how long it takes for you to make up your mind. We discussed what will happen tonight last weekend. You saw the pictures and I've gifted you the most important one at the bottom of the box.

Read the enclosed card. Check the stipulation boxes, sign it, seal it inside the envelope, and then open your front door and present it to the man waiting in the silver car.

Prepare yourself, Ivy. This will be a night we will never forget.

Nolan

And then I read the card.

Here is what you can expect:

Rough play, including but not limited to slapping, biting, spanking, and choking.

Fantasy rape, forcing you out of your comfort zone. You will be held down if you struggle. You will be chased if you run. You will be fucked hard and bruising and/or swelling of certain areas of your body should be expected.

Severe temperature changes including, but not limited to, extreme cold and heat in the form of water and hot wax.

Bondage of the wrists, as demonstrated last weekend.

Aftercare as demonstrated last weekend and by the included graphic image.

Do not wear a bra, but do wear the panties and shoes delivered in the box.

You will not be burned, punched, caned, cut, or strangled, Ivy. None of what I do to you tonight is in anger. None of what I do tonight will leave a scar. Everything I do to you tonight is for our pleasure.

Nolan Delaney

I go looking for his drawing, finding it underneath yet another layer of yellow tissue paper. It's the one where we're lying in bed, spent and exhausted, Nolan kissing me on the head.

I read the stipulations again.

Do I want this?

My fingers dip down between my legs and find the pool of wetness.

I think that answers my question.

I quickly put a checkbox next to each line and then sign the bottom of the card, put it back inside the envelope, and seal it up.

When I open my front door a man inside an expensive-looking silver car gets out and walks towards me. I hand him the card. He nods his head, wordlessly, and then I go back inside.

I said yes.

My heart is beating so fast.

Not only did I say yes, I didn't even think twice.

I'm sick.

I don't care.

I've thought a lot about what he said last weekend. A lot. How he explained it. How he drew it all out. And it didn't really look that bad. In fact, when I break each picture down in my head, it's not that weird. Lots of people like rough sex. I Googled it. Lots of women fantasize about being held down. Forced. Lots of men want to be the aggressor. And a rape fantasy is a way to do that in a safe way.

Safe. I say the word in my head. Nolan laid out everything in the letter and the card. Every little detail. How to make him stop. What he will do. There will be no surprises.

Well, maybe one. When will he come pick me up? Soon? It's already four thirty. I imagine a date starts at seven? Eight? Just enough time for me to say yes and get ready, I realize. Just enough time to be excited but not enough time to change my mind. Nolan has to be on his way. Unless he's already here?

I bite my lip and smile.

I have no idea how I will feel at the end of the night, but hopefully I'll have a smile on my face. And just picturing him doing those things he drew last weekend makes me want to masturbate.

But I don't have time.

I don't have time to do anything but prepare myself for my fantasy date with Mr. Romantic.

CHAPTER THIRTY-THREE

NOLAN

When I land at Boston Logan I find my driver and head over to the municipal airport to make the last leg of my journey before picking up Ivy.

The entire ride to Providence my head is filled with visions of tonight. What she'll look like in that dress. How long it'll take her to say the first no. How many times I'll make her come before we're done.

When we land in Providence, I thank the pilot and get in the waiting Panamera—what can I say, I have a thing for Porsches—and enjoy the drive over to Ivy's side of town.

College Hill is way too close to Brown for my comfort level and the only good things about being back in this neighborhood are Ivy and the amazing Colonial architecture. I've missed the East Coast. I like the west. I was born there. And I like the South because it reminds me of my mother. But I spent most of my years up here in New England. It was home during all my formative years.

And they chased me away.

Ivy's house is a stately light gray colonial townhouse with authentic white trim. I already know it isn't hers, but belongs to her roommate. Ivy might've come from privilege but she doesn't come from money.

I like that, I think, as I pull in front and take a deep breath to calm my nerves.

What if she says stop? What if I set all this up and she says stop?

What if I get to the door and she's changed her mind?

I will sulk away like a chastised dog. I will probably never try this again with anyone.

"You won't know until you get your sorry ass out of the car, Romantic." I say the words, but in my head it's Mac talking. He was always the calm one. The rational one. The logical one. Mr. Perfect comes by his name honestly.

Unlike me.

I get out and walk up to the low wrought-iron gate, let myself in, and then walk to the front door filled with equal parts excitement, dread, and curiosity.

The door opens before I can knock and suddenly my face is stinging with a slap.

I just stare at my date. Her hand is still raised, her expression is one of surprise, and her dress—holy fucking shit, her dress—hugs her curves like it's painted on.

"Why did you hit me?" I ask, kinda stunned.

"Oh, my God." Ivy starts laughing so hard, she doubles over.

"What's so funny?"

"I'm so sorry! I just figured… oh, my God. I can't believe I hit you! I really hit you!"

She's laughing so hard I start to laugh too. "Ivy?" I say. "What's going on?"

"I'm sorry," she says, waving a hand in front of her face to stop her laughing. "I'm sorry. It's just, I was thinking that I might want to do that to you later, but I won't be able to because we'll be in the fantasy. And even if I did, you wouldn't understand what it meant. You'd think it was part of the scene."

I just blink at her.

"Shit, your whole cheek is bright red. And my hand is stinging!"

I reach for the hand that slapped me, place it against my cheek. The heat of the slap doubles as we come skin to skin. And then I hold her palm up to my lips and kiss away the sting. "I get the point."

"I'm sorry," she says through the constant smile.

I don't know how I expected this date to start, but this certainly wasn't it. "Don't be. I get it. I will probably scare you a little tonight. And this is a good way to get your point across. *You*," I say, stressing the word, "are the one in control. Even when you feel out of control."

She nods and then takes a deep breath. "I don't know what I'm doing. I don't know why I'm doing this. But I'm going to do it anyway." And then she bites her lip. "People will think I'm crazy."

"No one's gonna know. This night is a series of private moments between us, and *only* us. No one will know unless you tell them. OK?"

She nods, becomes shy again, and then says, "OK."

"Are you ready?"

"When do I say no?"

It's my turn to laugh. "Well, I was thinking we'd have dinner first?"

"Dinner?" She looks surprised.

"It's a date. Our first real date. Did you already eat? We can do something else. Get dessert or go for a walk in town. Although, I have to say, walking around this neighborhood brings up all kinds of bad memories."

"A walk?"

"If you want. If you're not hungry—"

"No, I'm hungry. I just didn't expect…"

I cock my head to the side and grin at her. "Didn't expect… what?"

"Romance."

I laugh almost as hard as she did when she slapped me. "My name is Mr. Romantic, Ivy. Give me a little credit."

"I thought it was ironic?"

"Not tonight. Tonight you get all of it if you want. The romance. The fantasy. Even the truth if you're still interested."

"The truth?" Her smile drops. "About... that night?"

I shrug. "If you still want to know. I'll share. It's the least I can do considering what will happen after."

She looks very uncertain. Does she still want to know? Will it scare her off? Will she see it through my eyes? Or the eyes of my presumed victim?

"That sounds... perfect. I do want to know. I don't know what to think about you right now, but I'd like to learn more."

I lean into her, pushing her body back, until she almost trips over the threshold. Until we are inside her foyer and I have her pressed against the coat closet. "Good," I whisper in her ear, my lips dragging down her neck before I bite her shoulder. "Good. Because I'm about to show you everything, Ivy. All the secrets," I say, taking her hand in mine and placing it over my heart, "in here." I kiss her on the lips and her mouth is soft, and sweet, and tastes like peaches. "Are you ready for that?"

She sighs into my mouth and says, "Let me get my purse."

CHAPTER THIRTY-FOUR

IVY

I'm breathless as I grab my envelope clutch from the side table. Nolan is staring at me when I turn back, looking like a wolf who wants to eat a rabbit.

I have been thinking about how this night will go all afternoon. Thinking, and overthinking, and wrestling with cold feet and hot desire for what he's offering.

But now that he's here I can't help but feel a little thrill. He's dressed in a very nicely tailored black suit with a yellow silk tie that matches my dress to perfection. And now that the slap has released some of my pent-up apprehension, I realize I want this more than anything else in my entire life.

More than my first pony, which I bought with my own money. I worked in the school kitchen for two years to afford that pony so I could take lessons on my own horse like the other girls at school. But by the time I got her, I was almost too big.

More than I wanted the free-ride scholarship to Brown, which was the only way my father could afford to send me there, even with his tuition discount as a board member.

More than graduating Brown with honors. Not just part of the top twenty percent of my class, but in the top five.

I want Mr. Romantic, everything he's offering tonight, more than anything. So I'm going to trust him to keep me safe and make me happy.

Nolan is smiling so big, I have to suck in a breath. "What?"

"I'm just happy you agreed."

"I'm trusting you for one night, Nolan. Just one night. Please," I say. "Please don't disappoint me."

He extends his hand and when I take it, he pulls me close again, and says. "I won't, I promise. But when I tell you the truth about what happened ten years ago, please do me the same favor."

I nod, swallowing hard. What does that mean? What did he do? Will I be able to go through with this night after I know the truth?

"Are you ready?"

I nod, unsure, yet completely sure at the same time. "Yes. Let's go."

We walk to his car and he opens my door, taking my hand to help me get in, and then closes me up and walks to his side.

Nolan slides into the butter-soft leather seat and starts the engine. It purrs like a sports car, but it's a classy sedan, the Porsche logo on the steering wheel telling me all I need to know about his taste in cars.

"So," Nolan says, once we are on the road and headed towards the river. "Do you like seafood?"

"I'm from New England." I laugh.

"Small talk, right? I don't want you to feel weird about the silence that seems to have taken over in the last few moments. Anyway, I got us a reservation at Waterman Grille. Even got them to give us a semi-private table near the river."

"Do you plan on starting our fantasy in the restaurant?"

"You're the one who gets say go, Ivy." And then he winks. "Or no, as it may be. The second you say no and I'm doing something rough, we start. So if you tell me to stop playing with your pussy under the table, you'll regret it later."

"Oh, my God. What am I doing?"

"You're about to have the most sexually explicit night of your life. Would you like me to tell you how I'll start it?"

Do I? "No," I say, just as Nolan pulls into the parking lot. "I want to be surprised."

"Good girl," he says. When he gets out, I wait. I know he has manners and I'm right. He walks around and gets my door, taking my hand to help me out.

His arm slips down to my waist and he grips my hip. I am so ready for this night to begin.

We wait a moment to be seated, and when we're finally at our table, I have to look at the river for a few moments before the sun slips away and it disappears from view.

Nolan orders us wine and as soon as the server leaves, his attention turns back to me. "It was a weird night."

I realize with a start that he is talking about the past.

"Perfect took her out on a date but he didn't like her. That's what he told me later that night. After I... well, I'll get to that—Perfect actually took her home. Dropped her off at her dorm and came back to the house. I lived in back. We had this little carriage house back then for the fraternity. After the bad publicity, the Greek association shut that carriage house down. It's too bad, too. It was nice. And private. But I guess that's what they didn't like about it. That I had the whole carriage house to myself. And I made good use of that privacy."

Nolan stops, his attention only on me, as the server talks about the bottle of wine he chose and pours some into our glasses.

"Go on," I say, taking a sip of my wine once we're alone again.

"But she came back to the house too."

"On her own?" I never heard this.

"Yeah. She came to my carriage house because I was in the middle of a fight with my date for the night."

"What were you fighting about?"

"The fantasy."

"Oh," I say. "So you've been doing this a long time?"

He shrugs. "I wouldn't call what I was doing back then quite the same thing I'm about to do with you tonight. I meant it when I said you do not want an amateur to run this sort of thing. It takes time and experience to understand what it means to you, as a man, and the woman, as well. Since she will be very emotional afterward."

"Did you do a fantasy with that girl?'

"No," Nolan says, like I should know this already. "No. Never fucked her at all."

"Then how did it all get twisted up into so many... lies?"

"I was trying the fantasy out on my date. The drawings, Ivy."

"Ohhh," I say. "Oh. So you drew her something like what you drew me?"

He shakes his head. "I drew something a little more graphic."

"What?"

"Gang rape."

The words are tossed around in my head as I take in his answer. "Wow. Did you ever live that fantasy?"

"No. But I thought about it enough to draw that picture and show it to my date that night to see what she'd say."

"You asked her if she'd... do *that* with you?" Gang rape fantasy. I stare at my hands for a moment to try to understand. "What happened?"

"Not surprisingly, my date walked out. I followed her, trying to explain myself." Nolan turns his head to stare at the darkening river and then gives me a sidelong look. "She was not convinced… but…"

"And then what?" I can see he needs prodding. I can see he's ashamed. I can see he has struggled with this many, many times over the years. In fact, I might see more than he intends to show. It's possible that the infamous Mr. Romantic isn't as self-assured as he pretends to be.

"I walked the date to her car, apologizing and telling her it was OK. And when I got back to my carriage house I realized I had left the door open. My drawings were inside and so was that girl. My would-be accuser."

"Did you make her the same offer?"

"No." Nolan laughs. "No, I wasn't that stupid. She pointed to the drawings and said, 'What's this?'"

"And you told her?"

"I just said a fantasy, Ivy. There was no *Fifty Shades of Fucked Up* back then to ease people into the taboo."

"Do you think people who participate in what you do are fucked up?"

"Do you?"

I nod, silently. "Yeah, I do."

"But you're still here."

I nod again. "I'm still here. So I guess we have that in common."

He relaxes as the server comes to take our order. I don't even pretend to pay attention to what he orders us, just roll all this new information around in my head.

"She gave me a blow job, but I didn't fuck her. And I didn't force her. In fact, by that time, she and I had been drinking for about an hour. Shots, not beer. Two at a time, so we were pretty buzzed. And then she made me an offer.

Make the girl in that gang rape drawing look like her so she could fantasize about it later and she'd blow me."

"And you said yes."

"When I should've said no. How many times I've gone back to that one moment and wished I had said no."

"So how did all your friends get involved in her accusations?"

He shrugs again. "I wouldn't know. I honestly— swearing on my life and the life of my mother, Ivy Rockwell—I have no clue what everyone else was doing that night. I assume she left my carriage house and went into the main house where she bumped into Mysterious, Corporate, and Match. But I only assume that because they also admitted to coming into contact with her. We don't know each other's story."

"You're kidding."

"No," he says. "Match took over once the cops came and told us what was happening. He was only eighteen, just a freshman. And all of a sudden he took the rest of us into the back yard, into my carriage house, and said, enunciating each word so they were perfectly clear, 'I. Will. Handle. This. No one says anything to anyone, not even each other. I have a guy.'"

"Who?"

"I don't know who he was. Not even now. Match called him Five. But I never got a real name. This Five guy showed up, took over, and the next thing we knew, we had lawyers, we were in some house in Connecticut, and we just stayed there until they charged us, booked us, and then got released on bail. We all talked on the phone, but I didn't see any of the other Misters in person again until after the charges were dropped two years later."

"Wow." I try to imagine it all. "Wow," is all I can say after I do that. "Do you think any of your other friends did anything with her?"

Nolan shrugs. "No clue."

CHAPTER THIRTY-FIVE

NOLAN

"So," Ivy says, then stops because the servers come with our food. We wait, nod and say thank you. But I can tell Ivy has something to say about what I just told her.

"Finish your thought," I say, ignoring the food. "If you've got something to say about it, now is the time."

She pouts her lips a little bit and it's makes me want to lean over this table and bite them. Right here, in front of the whole restaurant. "So it's all your fault. It was your drawing. That's what got you all arrested."

"Yup," I say. "It was all my fault."

"At least it looks that way. We can't know. Not really. Not unless we get everyone's story."

"I like the way you say *we* in that sentence, Miss Rockwell."

She blushes, then smiles. "Well, I guess I'm invested in you at this point. I'm taking a risk, Mr. Delaney. I'm trusting you tonight."

"And I appreciate that. I do."

"Are you looking forward to it? What we'll do tonight."

"More than you can imagine."

"Why?"

"Why?" I laugh. "Seriously? You're beautiful, smart, and even though you have less than one week of sexual experience, you're wild, Ivy. I can tell. And I'd be lying if I said I wasn't feeling a little possessive of you at this point. I got you first and I'd like to think you're mine because of it."

"Yours?" She squints her eyes at me.

241

"Mine."

"Hmm." And then she notices the food on the table. Sea bass with toasted barley. "This looks delicious."

"You look delicious," I say. "If I didn't think you'd need your strength tonight I'd make us skip dinner. But you will."

This makes her take a deep breath. "Tell me what you're going to do."

"No." And I smile when I say it. "It's not fun if you know what's coming."

She takes a bit of her food and then sips some wine. Clearly she has something more to say about that comment, but she's not sure how to say it. "You want me to feel afraid." It's not a question.

"No, not exactly. I want to feel you struggle and I want it to be as real as we can possibly make it. Because what I really want is that moment when you give in." Fuck. I'm getting hard just thinking about it. "When you realize you want me. When you realize that it feels good. When you realize," I say, lowering my voice and leaning closer to her, "that you're going to come and you don't want to. You don't want to admit that you like it, but you can't stop it from happening. No matter what I do to you tonight, you're going to love it. You're going to feel good. And you're going to wish it would never end."

"I think you have a lot of confidence for a man who knows almost nothing about me. I could stay stop instead."

I lean back in my chair and nod. "You could. But I don't think you will."

"Why not?"

"Because you wouldn't be here if you weren't turned on by the thought of my fantasy, Ivy. Because my fantasy is now *your* fantasy. I'm sure you have never thought about a fantasy like this before I made my offer. But I'm equally sure that you can't stop thinking about it now."

"I might still say stop, Nolan."

"Understood."

She picks at her food for a few minutes, silent, just enjoying the taste and the atmosphere. I force myself to eat as well, but only because I know I'll need it just as much as she will. And when the server comes asking about dessert, we both smile and stare at each other across the table.

Because she's in.

Deep.

"We've already got plans for dessert," I say. "The check is fine."

"You never said where we were going," Ivy says once we on the highway heading south.

"No, I never did."

"Is… is the fantasy starting now?" She sounds nervous.

"Have you said no to my advances yet?" I ask, taking my eyes off the road for a second before returning them to the lines of the highway.

"No."

"Then it hasn't started. This is still the date, Ivy. So relax. Enjoy it. Do you like my car?"

"Um." Ivy takes a look around her, like she's just now noticing things. "You have a thing for fast cars."

"I do. I like this one. It's a rental, but I have one just like it in San Diego."

"You have a lot of money, I take it. And by a lot, I mean, God money."

I almost laugh. "Yeah. You're just figuring that out?"

"I don't know. I saw the house and the resort. But you have a lot more than most. I don't think about money much. Beyond needing it for things. And I really did want that job." She grabs her little envelope purse that I sent her with the dress and shoes, and pulls out her iPad. "I have a presentation—"

My laugh stops her cold.

"What?"

"You came here tonight, knowing what we're going to be doing, with a *presentation*?"

"I have graphs, Nolan. I have good ideas. And solid projections."

I place my hand over hers to stop her from opening the cover of the iPad. "Put it away."

"But I want you to know what my ideas are."

I can tell by the tone in her voice it's true, so I make my voice soft. "You'll still have time to impress me afterward."

"No," she says quickly. "You said once we fucked then there's no possibility of me being hired by you."

"Well, nothing is set in stone."

"Except the word stop," she says in a small voice.

"That goes without saying."

"I'm just making sure."

"Do you want to stop before we start? You can, you know. I'll take you home."

"I just want to know where we're going."

"You're going to see right now. So be patient."

"We're at the airport?" Her voice actually quivers. "Why are we at the airport?"

"Why do people usually go to an airport?"

"You're taking me somewhere?"

"I thought that was understood?"

"But... but you never said anything about getting on a plane for this."

I just smile.

"Nolan?"

"Ivy." I turn onto the access road and follow it around to the helipad. "Relax. We're going to Martha's Vineyard. I'm taking you on my helicopter."

"You have a helicopter? Here? How the hell do you have that here when you live two thousand miles away?"

My phone buzzes in my pants and I reach in and check the screen, then tab accept. "Talk to me."

"I'm here," Mysterious says. "Where are you?"

"Can this wait until..." I check the dash clock and calculate how much time I'll need with Ivy. I don't want to rush it, so I say, "Early AM? I got you a ride. Be at the helipad in Middletown and I'll send it back for you."

"It's your money, Delaney. Not mine. So if you want to finish whatever it is you're doing while I charge you by the half hour, be my guest."

"Your way with words makes me miss you, Pax. Makes me wonder why the fuck I haven't talked to you in years."

But the call ends.

"Who was that?" Ivy asks again. "Someone else is coming?"

"We'll be done by then. I won't let him come until we're done."

"So he's going to see me there? Nolan—"

"Ivy," I say in a low growl. "*Shut. Up.*"

She's stunned silent. Which was the whole point of starting the fantasy early.

"Paxton Vance does not give one fuck about you, take my word on that. So whether he sees you there or not, he won't care. He's coming with information I need.

But if you think I'm not in control of this night, say stop now and I'll put your ass in a cab and send you home."

When I look over at Ivy her mouth is hanging open like she's about to say something. But then she closes it.

"Good girl," I mutter, pulling the car up to the helipad. "Now keep your mouth shut until I tell you to open it for my cock."

I don't look at her this time. Just exit the car and slam the door. Waving to the crew, who wave back. I walk around to Ivy's side, open her door, grab her arm, and yank her out.

Still, she says nothing.

I almost sigh, that's how fucking spectacular this night is going to be if she plays along. I look back at the crew, who have all disappeared, just as I ordered them to, and drag her over to the helicopter, out of their sight, even if they do disobey orders

Ivy stumbles once, then twice, but I don't turn back, just pull the door open and point. "Get the fuck in and keep quiet. If you scream, no one will hear. But I will, and it will really *piss me off.*"

Ivy is conflicted. Her chest is rising and falling so fast, I think she might pass out.

"Ivy," I bark, leaning down into her ear as I grab her hair and yank. I slip a hand between her legs and begin to rub small circles over her clit through her panties. "You're lucky you didn't wear a bra. That makes me happy. But your resistance doesn't. So get the fuck in the helicopter and I won't hurt you."

She stares at her feet for a moment and then, in the smallest voice I could possibly imagine, she says, "No."

I push her face first onto the helicopter seat, holding her head down as I pull her dress up to give me a good look at her ass. I smack it. Hard.

Ivy gasps, then tries to get up, but my hand pushes down harder on the side of her head as my other hand gets busy between her legs. "You can't wait to come, can you, Ivy? You dirty fucking whore. Do you want me to make you come right here? In the middle of the airport? Or do you want to get in like a good girl?"

She's panting now. Her breathing is seriously disturbing. "I'll get in," she says.

I ease up on her head, pull her dress down, and point to the seat. She climbs in, which is not easy in those stiletto shoes I sent her in the fantasy box. But she manages and before she can even look at me, I grab the handcuffs hanging on the door and fasten them to her wrists. There's a long chain attached to them, with a clip on the other end, which I secure under the seat, pulling it tight, so she has to lean over.

Then I close her door and walk over to my side, get in, and power up the engine. "I hope you don't get motion-sick, Miss Rockwell. Because if you do"—I look at her and find her wide eyes filled with fear—"I'll make you lick it up before you get out."

The rotors above pick up speed and then the deafening roar of the blades fills the cockpit, making any more talking useless.

Good. I'm glad.

She needs this time to get herself together. Because as soon as we get out on Martha's Vineyard, she will have a choice to make.

Stop.

Or keep going.

CHAPTER THIRTY-SIX

IVY

I feel like I might hyperventilate so I concentrate on taking in long draws of air to calm my racing heart.

Why are you doing this?

What if this is real and not a fantasy?

What if he hurts me?

All these questions run through my mind as we take off, nothing but the rhythmic sound of the rotors to fill my head and drown out my concerns.

I can stop it at any time.

But can I really? Will he really stop? I can't know unless I use the safe word. And if I use the safe word and he does stop, then we can never try again. The trust will be broken and I will forever be certain that he will stop. And isn't the whole point of the fantasy to feel like he won't stop? To let him overpower me, to make me give in, to struggle, be taken, and love every minute of it?

If we finish what we started and come out the other end smiling will it be worth it?

Yes, I decide. Yes. Because like it or not, I'm thoroughly turned on. I want him to do this. I want him to do it the way he promised. I want to feel safe, even when I don't feel safe. I want him to prove to me that he's not what people think and I want to submit to his fantasy because it's my fantasy too.

Martha's Vineyard comes much too quick. My body is just starting to come to terms with what I'm doing when the helicopter descends, wobbles a bit, and then touches down. Nolan doesn't turn it off, instead he reaches between my legs, uncuffs me, and pulls me up to a sitting position.

"Don't speak to the man out on the helipad, do you understand me?"

His eyes are darting back and forth between mine. I think he's nervous too and that makes me feel a little better.

I nod and say, "I won't."

His smile is very small, almost undetectable in the dim lights of the cockpit. But it's there. "OK," he says, still staring at me. "Stay put and I'll help you out. We don't want this guy to get any funny ideas about what he might be witnessing, right?" He pulls my hair when he says *right*.

I swallow hard and nod. "Understood."

Nolan gets out, speaks to the man standing just off to my left, and points off in the distance. That phone conversation was about sending the helicopter back for his friend. They must be discussing it.

And then the other pilot nods and they walk towards the helicopter together. Nolan comes to my side and offers me his hand. I accept it and step down as his hand immediately wraps around my waist and firmly grabs my hip.

He leans into my ear and hisses, "Don't scream or struggle or I'll make you pay when we get inside."

I nod again, remain silent, and stare at the house lit up before us. It's... massive. I have seen Nora's family mansion and this makes her place look like a playhouse. We are in the back, a large pool directly in front of us, surrounded by high hedges and gardens. It's something out of a magazine, the luxury almost too much to be real.

A fantasy, I realize.

"Where are we?" I ask once the helicopter has left and the *whomp, whomp, whomp* of the blades is fading away. My gaze wanders to the second floor where the windows and balcony are lit up with candles.

Nolan reaches up for my hair, pulling it so hard my head falls back. "Family compound, Ivy. We are miles from the nearest house. No one will hear you when you scream."

"I thought you wanted me to be quiet?"

"It doesn't matter anymore."

Now what? What do I do now? I have to decide one way or another. I can change my mind later, but I'd rather not let it go too far if I'm not comfortable.

We walk up to the pool before I can decide and he places his hands on my shoulders and pushes, signaling that I should get on my knees. I hesitate and his hand comes down hard on my ass, making it sting.

Not hard enough to make me cry out. But just hard enough to make me want more.

I feel the flood of warmth between my legs and take deep breaths again.

Am I more disturbed about what he's going to do? Or how it might make me feel?

"Ivy," he growls. "Get on your fucking knees before I lose my patience."

He's playing a part, Ivy. He's playing a part.

Does he want me to play the part back?

Duh.

I hang my head a little to try to hide my smile. Because yes, this is the whole point of the fantasy. We play the parts perfectly and it all feels real. If I let him do everything he wants, that's not a rape fantasy. That's just submission.

He doesn't want submission, I realize. He wants a struggle. A fight. He wants me to resist him so he can overpower me.

I try to run but he grabs my upper arm and twists it behind my back. "Try that again and I'll make you suck my cock so hard—"

I try again, writhing and ducking as he reaches for me. I get a few paces this time, but Nolan tackles me onto the soft lawn. We land together with a thump, his body pressing down on mine, my face turning sideways to be able to breathe. His mouth is in my ear. "I'm going to make you pay for that."

He lifts up his body and flips me over so I have to look at him.

The anger on his face makes me gasp. "You fucking bitch," he growls as his hands wrap my wrists together. I look down at the rope—yellow, soft, doubled-braided—and recognize it. Once my wrists are bound he stand up, yanks me to my feet by my hair, and pushes me so I have to walk forward. I stop at the pool's edge, but he pushes me again and I fall over the side and into the water. I am unable to swim for the surface because of my bound hands. I struggle, then panic, as I sink. But I realize that my feet can touch the bottom. I have one shoe left, the other floating by as I stand, trying to maintain my balance as the waves of the pool splash into my face when I break through the water.

I gasp for air. My lungs feel like they can't get enough, my throat burning with the effort.

Nolan is standing over me on the side of the pool. I see his leather shoes first, then lift my head up and take in his legs in the perfectly tailored suit. I stop at the yellow silk tie and remind myself what this is.

A fantasy.

"Walk," he commands. He's pointing to the other end of the pool where steps lead the way out of the water.

My head and neck are exposed to the cool sea air, but the rest of my body is under the heated water.

"How deep is it?" I ask, eyeing the middle of the pool

that I must cross.

"It doesn't matter, Ivy. You're going to walk or I'll let you freeze to death out here all night long. I'll tie you to the steps and let you freeze."

I turn away from him, but in that moment he's kneeling down and he's got a hold of my hair again. "Don't fuck with me, bitch," he says. "I'm deadly serious."

I pull away and reach for his leg, trying to pull him in with me. He swings his hand, barely missing my head with a closed fist, and I panic.

He said no punching!

I struggle again, make him lose his grip, and then scoot away to the center of the pool where it suddenly becomes deep and I go under. I kick my other shoe off and tread water, my tied hands in front of me, desperately trying to paddle.

"Do what you're told, Ivy, and you'll make it through this night. Wander off the path I've set for you and bad things will happen."

Is that a warning?

I spit out some water and struggle my way across the pool until I'm on the opposite side of him, but my feet can touch again.

"Walk to the end of the pool and get out," Nolan barks, his shout echoing off the walls of the monstrous mansion.

I keep my eyes on him as I walk. He follows me on the other side, step for step. And when I get to the end of the pool safely I climb the steps. The cold air hits me immediately, making my nipples peak and the tight silky dress cling to my body. He's waiting for me, just a few paces off, when I exit, dragging water with me that pools at my feet as I stand on the cold concrete.

I begin to shiver uncontrollably and Nolan smiles.

"You're as pretty as a picture, Miss Rockwell."

The first picture, I realize. I'm the image in the first picture he drew. Standing in the drenched dress, nipples pressing against the fabric, everything clinging and wet.

He walks towards me, reaching between my legs to rub my clit in small, slow circles. I press against his chest, wanting to be warm so badly. Want to hate the way this makes me feel so badly.

But it all feels… *good.*

"Are you cold?" he croons in my ear.

I nod. The only heat I feel is between my legs. But then his lips come up to mine, just a flutter of warmth. I almost lunge for him, that's how bad I want more contact. I want his heat, and his kiss, and his mouth. I want his arms around me, shielding me from the frigid night air. His palm is suddenly on my throat, his thumb pressing on my chin, so even if I wanted to pull away, I can't.

I don't want to pull away.

"I'm going to take off the dress and make it worse."

I practically convulse with his words, that's how much my body is trembling. He peels the single shoulder strap down my arm until my breasts are exposed, the air hitting my nipples and making them bunch up into hard pebbles.

Nolan continues, his warm hands pulling the fabric down my body until my hips are exposed. And then he drops to one knee and brings the garment to the ground as his hands reach up to my ass and he buries his face in my pussy. He licks my panties, the panties he told me to wear, and then he fists them with both hands and rips them apart.

A squeal of fright escapes through my chattering teeth, but his hands are there again, his warm hands that feel like fire against my freezing skin.

When he stands up and leans into my neck, his soft breath caresses me into a lull. I press against him again, desperate for his arms to wrap me up. Desperate for his touch. "We forgot to laugh," I say, when his mouth kisses mine.

"What?" he asks.

"We broke the scene when you peeled off the dress, remember?"

"It's not a scene, you stupid cunt."

I hiccup a sob as I begin to cry, the cold and the name-calling too much. His hands come up to my head and press. This time, it's soft. Nolan looks me in the eyes, his dancing, mine frightened. And he says, "Pretty as a picture. Your tears are as pretty as a picture. And I will take you this night the way I planned. Kicking and screaming. Your nails digging into my flesh as you fight me off. Your pussy throbbing the entire time."

What does that mean? I want to scream it. Is he playing with me? Or is he serious?

But before I can ask, Nolan takes off his suit coat and places it over my shoulders. I sob harder from the relief. The way this one simple act can make everything better.

"Let's go," he says. "Your mouth has a date with my cock."

CHAPTER THIRTY-SEVEN

NOLAN

She whimpers as I drag her into the house. It's almost dark in here, but not quite. Just enough light to see what's necessary. Not nearly enough light to expose us. I push her towards the stairs and say, "Climb, Ivy," when she hesitates. "Climb or I'll drag you up the stairs by your hair and that's not nearly as fun as watching your ass in front of me."

I'm preparing myself for her eventual stop. I imagine what it will take to get her to say that word. How far I will have to push her. How much she will be willing to endure to get to that point.

And, of course, what I'll do after she says it.

"Bend over," I say, when she's a few steps shy of the top.

Ivy stops climbing, but she doesn't bend over.

I whip the jacket off her shoulders and throw it over the banister. Her head turns to watch it fall to the ground thirty feet below.

"You're going next, Ivy, if you don't bend the fuck over."

A squeal escapes her chattering teeth, but she leans forward, places her bound hands on the top step, and then presses her head to the floor next to them.

"Your pussy looks delicious," I say, rubbing her ass with my palm. I stick a finger inside her as another plays with her clit. "I'm going to make you come right now. Before we even get started. Because I want to know how much you love it."

She draws in a deep breath and in the same moment

257

my hand slaps down on her ass cheek so hard, it echoes off the high ceilings.

"Ow," she sobs.

I rub her ass, feeling the heat my hand created radiating over her skin. And then I play with her again. Softly this time.

She looks over her shoulder as I unzip my pants. "Nolan—"

"Quiet," I whisper. She's crying, as she should be.

"Nolan, please st—"

I wait for it. She almost says it. And then she looks back at me again, like it was a mistake. I smile and slap her ass again, making her sob quietly as I pull my cock and balls through my open zipper.

"You're a filthy whore, aren't you? You want to pretend like you hate this, Ivy? You want to pretend you didn't come to my resort to be fucked hard? That you didn't want to open your legs for me the minute you realized who I was?" I grab her hair and pull her head back so I can look down at her eyes. Her back is arched, her eye makeup streaked down her cheeks.

I kiss her mouth and she resists, but my other hand leaves her pussy and wraps around her throat. I feel her swallow. I imagine my dick in there in a few minutes. The way I will force her muscles to tighten around my head, how I will choke her with my come.

And then I ease up and go soft.

My lips barely touch hers. She parts for me and breathes heavy into my mouth for a moment. I kiss her again, my hand tightening on her throat. But I let go of her hair and she stays in place. Perfectly posed, eyes looking straight into mine as I play with her pussy again.

"I know you want me, Ivy. No matter how many times you say no."

"I don't," she says. And then she spits on my face.

I grab her hair and yank her head back, and then I spit right into her open mouth. She closes it, struggles to push me backwards, but I lean forward and cover her cold body with mine.

She stops suddenly. Her freezing and trembling body holds absolutely still.

"Are you cold?"

"Yes," she says. "I'm c-c-cold," she stutters. "Let me put clothes on, please, Nolan. Let me get warm."

"There's only one way you'll get warm tonight, Ivy. And you're going to have to work for it. Now spread your legs so I can fuck your ass."

She looks back at me with a horrified face. And shakes her head. "No. Please. No. I don't want to. I swear to God, I don't want to, Nolan. Please don't—"

I smack her ass so hard, she wails. "Hold still," I yell. "Or it will hurt and I won't let you blame me for your mistakes. Hold *still*."

She obeys, her limbs still trembling from the cold and her adrenaline. I reach down to her knees and spread her legs open, then push her face down onto the hardwood floors. "Keep it right here, Ivy. Press your face into the floor and don't move or this won't go easy. It's up to you. Let me do it right and you'll enjoy it. But make me fuck up—" I yank her head back by her hair again, and press my mouth to hers to whisper, "And it will be all your fault."

I let go of her hair and she lets her head fall down to her chest, then rests it back on the floor.

"Such a good, good girl." I step down two steps until my face is even with her wide legs and then I lower myself to her spread-open pussy.

The first lick is delicious. She tastes sweet and ready.

And the way she begins to moan as I lick and suck has me tugging on my cock.

I lick her asshole while pushing my finger inside at the same time. She moves forward, trying to escape the pain.

"Shh," I say. "Keep still." I reach into my pants pocket and pull out a small tube of lube, uncapping it with my teeth.

She moans as I squirt it on her puckered ass, and then leave it on the stairs, uncapped.

My fingers slip around her open legs, pushing in and out of her ass, in small strokes. When she keeps still I push it all the way in.

Her whole body bucks back, almost setting me off-balance.

"Quiet," I whisper. "Be still, Ivy," I say softly. More softly than I should. But I want my cock inside her. I want to feel her ass squeeze me when she comes. I want to hear her moan when she realizes it feels good. It feels spectacular, and she wants me to keep going.

I stick two fingers inside her pussy, pumping harder and harder as her bound hands, thrust forward and resting on the hard floor, open and close into fists as she desperately reaches for something to hold onto.

My cock is in her ass and she's screaming before she can think too hard about it. I grab her tits as her back crashes into my chest, her arms wild as she tries to elbow me in the ribs. She can't reach, not with her hands tied. I know this, so I ignore it, and go back to making her feel good.

Fingers on her clit. My teeth biting her earlobe as I hold her close. She's crying and even though I shouldn't love that... I love that.

"Be still. The hard part is over. Now just bend over,

Ivy. Rest your head on the floor, and let me make you come."

"I'm not going to come. You're a sick, sick monster, Nolan Delaney. I won't, I won't I won't..."

She's still muttering it. *I won't, I won't, I won't* over and over again, but the words lose their meaning when she goes limp and I pump in and out, very, very slowly.

I play with her clit the entire time. And her protests turn into something else. Turn into moans, into grunts, into begging.

"Does it feel good now?" I ask.

"No," she says through her moan.

And then there's this moment when we both laugh. I bite my lip to make it stop and I'm grateful that she can't see my smile.

"There," she says.

"There what?" I ask, continuing to pleasure her in every way I can think of.

"The laugh we missed from earlier," she says.

"Don't get your hopes up, whore," I growl, thrusting hard and smacking her on the ass. "You have no idea what's coming next."

CHAPTER THIRTY-EIGHT
IVY

OK. I'm convinced. I heard him laugh. This really is just a fantasy. We're playing, I like it. And even though he took me by surprise with the anal, I like that too. It did hurt, I won't lie. But it feels so good now.

His hips slap against my ass, the sound enough to pull me back into the moment. I was afraid, I admit it. But that laugh puts me at ease like no words ever will.

Nolan yanks on my hair, making me look at him as he fucks me from behind. "There should be only one thing on your mind, Ivy. How this will end."

Is that code? Didn't he say the ending is the best part?

"And not the ending you're expecting," he clarifies. Just like he's reading my mind. "You think you deserve the hearts and flowers, Ivy? You think I'm going to fuck you like this and then... what? Just say, *Kidding?*"

His hand is gripping my left hip tightly one moment, and the next... a crack sounds off in the room and my face is stinging from his slap.

I can't breathe.

"You have one job right now, Miss Rockwell. *One.* Be in this moment with me or I'll drag you into it." He reaches down to grab my throat, his thumb and fingers gripping either side of my jaw so hard, I cry out. "Do you understand me?"

I nod.

He spits in my face, rubs it over my lips, and then slaps me. "Talk, bitch!"

"Yes," I say, trying not to cry. Telling myself over and over again, *It's a fantasy. It's a fantasy. I'm going to love the end.*

263

I will love how it ends. "Yes," I manage, just as he's about to slap me again. "Yes. I understand."

He lets go of my face and the hard pumping slows. He eases in and out several times before leaning over my back and resting his chest on me. We are skin on skin. His breathing isn't nearly as labored as mine.

Every part of my body is shaking but I'm no longer cold. My legs tremble from exertion. My arms can't even hold me up anymore, and when he rests more of his weight against me, I just collapse on the floor.

He fucks me in the ass so slow, I want to close my eyes and forget this fantasy. Just enjoy it. Enjoy everything about what he's doing.

"You've been bad, Ivy. You laughed at me. So I'm not going to let you come. But I will let you decide what I should do next. What is the one thing you're probably hoping I *won't* do?"

I can think of many things I've seen in porn that have disgusted me, but before I can articulate them, his fingers find their way into my mouth, forcing it open. "Should I choke you with my hand before I choke you with my cock?"

I shake my head, the gag reflex taking over. I can't stop it, and a pool of saliva drools out of my mouth as he pinches my nose closed. I gag again. And while I'm busy recovering and figuring out how to breathe with a hand in my mouth, he stands up, his cock slipping out of my ass as he pulls me with him, an arm hooked under mine, and walks us down a long hallway.

There are so many doors up here I can't make sense of them. The mansion from the outside looked massive, but from the inside it looks like a puzzle. A maze. A place to get lost and never come back. Is that why he brought me here? So I will give in to him and lose myself?

We stop at the end of the hall, near another set of stairs that go both up and down, and he twists the handle and opens the door.

There are candles everywhere. In every corner they are alight, atop tall pillars, atop the pretty white mantel over the fireplace—even in the chandelier.

Nolan pushes me forward, making me trip and fall to my knees onto a soft sheepskin rug. He slams the door closed and then I hear the tell-tale click of it being locked from the inside. "Just in case you get any funny ideas about leaving early tonight, Ivy."

My heart races. Why does he have to say these things? Just when I'm certain this is nothing but the fantasy we discussed, I get this. Either deliberate attempts to keep me frightened or a promise that things are about to go very wrong.

I might be the only one here living the fantasy tonight. He could be totally serious about what he doing.

No, I say in my head. No. He laughed. I heard it.

He's mocking you, Ivy. Tell him to stop. Now! Before it goes too far and you can't even press charges because you agreed to it!

No. No, he can't be that man. Nolan cannot be that man that everyone says he is.

You haven't even known this man a week, Ivy Rockwell. You're as stupid as he is sick.

"Do you like the candles?"

I look up at him as he looms over me. He's slowly unbuttoning his shirt. My wrists are burning from the rope. It's soft, but it's rubbing and they are red and will be inflamed tomorrow.

You're not going to live until tomorrow.

"Yes," I say.

"Well, that's just about the only romantic thing I've planned for you tonight. The rest can go easy or hard.

Depending on how you like it. Do you like it hard, Ivy?"

"Jesus Christ," I say. "How am I supposed to answer that, Nolan?"

"Truthfully," he says, extending his hand. I take it, gripping it in both of mine, the rope sliding along my skin, the friction making the burning sensation even worse.

"I'll tell you," I say, squaring my shoulders. "I'll tell you if you untie me. I don't want to be tied anymore."

"You're not the one in control tonight, remember? I am. I get to tell you what to do, not the other way around. And if you hate the rope, you can bet I'm gonna leave you tied up even longer now."

He grabs me by both arms and hauls me over to the bed, throwing me down on the soft down comforter face first. Then his hips have me pinned, but I buck my body at just the right time, in just the right way, and he falls to the side. I get a foot up and kick him in the chest, giving me even more space. And then I'm off the bed, running towards the open bathroom door. If I can just get in there and lock it. If I can just—

He grabs my ankle and I go down hard onto the rug. And then he's dragging me by my foot as I kick and yell and—*panic.*

The word is there. My tongue is pressing against my teeth, that *sssss* sound even coming from my mouth, but then he goes still.

I stop. I don't say it, I just go still and wait. I'm sobbing, tears are running down my face. I'm breathing so hard I can't stop the hyperventilation this time.

His next touch is soft. Just one moment of softness. A single fingertip slides up my calf and stops in the dent of my knee. Then his lips are there. Reminding me of what this is.

I won't say it. I won't.

He grabs my foot and drags me back to the bed the instant he realizes I gave in again. "I'm going to tie your legs open for that little stunt, Miss Rockwell. And then I'm going to fuck you sore."

I don't know what to do at this point. Cry? What good is crying? Tell him no? That will only make him try harder. Let him do what he wants? That feels like defeat.

Tell him to stop?

That feels like a mistake.

The yellow rope is around my ankles before I even reach that conclusion. He ties one leg to the footboard, then pulls my other one open, looking at my pussy as he walks to the other bedpost.

"Now you can't move."

But that's not true. He didn't tie my hands down. They are still bound together, so not much use. But they are not tied to the headboard. Yet.

"Do you know why I left your hands free?"

I have a feeling, but I stay silent.

Nolan leans down and kisses me on the lips as he unfastens his pants and pulls out his cock.

"So I can give you a better blow job?" I say.

He shakes his head and smiles. "So you can fight back. Maybe you'll get in a good punch. Right here, Ivy. Right where you slapped me earlier this evening."

I'm terrified again. How can my feelings be so all over the place? "It's fantasy, it's fantasy, it's fantasy." I whisper it like a chant.

"You think so?" Nolan asks, climbing on top of me and settling down on my hips. He leans forward, making his long, hard cock rest on my bare stomach. He grabs my wrists and flings them over my head, pressing them painfully against the headboard.

I don't struggle. I want to close my eyes and make it

stop. But I'm too chicken shit to even say the word.

"Do you really think you got here by accident, Ivy Rockwell?"

"What?" My eyes fly open.

"You're perfect, right? A *virgin*," he whispers. "When I claimed you. Did you really think I didn't know? Please." He laughs. "You're so trusting. So innocent. So repressed. I knew you'd buy into the lie. Fuck you in the shower, make you come, talk you up with all that drawing business. Most girls don't want me to demonstrate, but I did a passable job, don't you think?"

"What?"

"You didn't really think this was just a fantasy, did you?" He *tsks* his tongue and places one hand on the side of my head. My hair is wet, and not from the pool. I am burning up and sweat is pouring down my back. "So, so sweet," he croons, dipping his face down to mine. He licks my lips and I recoil.

"What?"

"It's real, Ivy. It's real and you agreed to it. I've got it in writing. I've got—"

I spit on him. "Fuck you, fuck you, fuck you, fuck you—"

He places a hand over my mouth and nose and says, "*Sshhhh*, Ivy." And then he slaps my face so hard, the sting takes a second to catch up.

I buck my back, trying to throw him off me, but his hand is back over my nose and mouth, holding tight until I really *can't breathe*. I'm in the full throes of a panic when he lets go and I start gasping for air.

"Just think of all the pretty pictures we're making, Miss Rockwell." Nolan kisses me on the mouth and I lose it.

"Goddamn it!" I yell, my bound fists pummeling into

his chest. I reach for the tie and yank, taking control of him for once.

"Goddamn it!" I scream. "Goddamn it! Goddamn it! *What is real?* I can't fucking *tell!*"

But my outburst only lasts a second and then he's got his silk tie wrapped around my face, painfully tight against the corners of my mouth.

Nolan cocks his head the way he does when he's amused, as he ties the knot at the side of my head.

"That's the point," he says, grinning like a madman.

CHAPTER THIRTY- NINE

NOLAN

I've got her right where she needs to be. Confused. Conflicted. And terrified.

She mumbles something from behind her gag, that sounds like, "Nolan," but I just shake my head and *tsk* my tongue. "I gave you a chance to be good, Ivy. I trusted you, and you ran. Now you have to trust me. It's out of your control. This whole night has spiraled out of your control. You need to accept that and give in."

She starts crying. Real tears. I watch her fingers for her signal as her fists tighten then open, splayed against my chest, trying to push me off her. But I stay right where I am and wait for her to calm down.

Why am I doing this? Why the fuck am I doing this to her? Especially her. Ivy Rockwell, Jesus fucking Christ. Why do I need this?

"Are you going to be good?" I ask.

"No," comes out pretty clear from behind her gag.

My crooked grin makes her eyes widen. Her breathing is labored and her legs are kicking up. Harmlessly, but she's still trying. I lean down and kiss her ear, whispering, "I like it when you fight. So keep fighting. It only makes me harder."

She stills. Staring into my eyes. "Nolan—"

"Shhh," I say. "I can't understand you with the gag."

A tear runs down her cheek and I know she's very close to saying her safe word. But she's not there yet. "Do you think…" I say, pausing for a moment to let the silence speak. "Do you think that *word* will help you now, Ivy? Do you really think I'll stop if you cross your fingers?" My

271

yellow silk tie is wet from her saliva and her gasp sends drool down her chin. "I won't, Ivy. We're here, in this together now. You're mine, just like I said. You're mine and you're not going to put a stop to anything. I don't want your legs tied, I want them open and thrashing when I take you. But you're being bad. So here's what's going to happen. I'm going to untie your feet and you're going to lie here and let me fuck you. And when I tell you to, you're gonna come all over my dick. Do you understand me?"

Ivy's eyes are wide and filled with fear. I'm still waiting for her to try the safe word. Waiting for her to cross her fingers.

But she doesn't do either of those things. She simply nods her head.

"Good girl," I say, scooting down the bed to her feet. I untie the rope from the post, leaving it on her ankle. She watches me like I am her whole universe when I slip my shirt off and pump my dick through my open zipper. I move to her other foot and untie that one from the post too.

I expect a fight, but she remains still. Like she's too scared to move.

"I'm a little disappointed you're giving in already."

She mumbles something through her gag and even though it's hard to hear, I know what she said. *Fantasy. It's a fantasy.*

"It's not a fantasy, Ivy. This is one hundred percent real. And you're going to be so turned on, you're gonna come back for more when I let you go home. You're gonna think about this night with your fingers in your pussy. You're gonna get off to this night, over and over, and over again."

Ivy shakes her head no.

"No?" I ask, positioning myself between her legs, and

then crawl my way up the bed with her body underneath me. My cock dragging along her stomach, aching to be inside her. "Let's see about that."

I drag the gag down her chin and she immediately starts crying and gasping for air. I don't give her time to regroup, just grab a fistful of hair and shove my cock towards her mouth. "If you bite me, Ivy. I'll bite you back."

She's frowning.

"Do you understand?"

"I'm never going to give you the satisfaction you're looking for."

"You have no idea what I'm looking for, Miss Rockwell. So just open your mouth and suck my cock the way you did last weekend."

She hesitates. I wait for it. And just when I know for sure she's gonna try that safe word out, she opens her mouth.

I lean down and kiss her mouth, saying, "You're a quick learner," as she cries. I pull back and ease my hips forward until the tip of my cock is on her tongue. Her wrists are still tied together, and they press against my thigh, but she doesn't try to punch me, even though I practically asked her to a few minutes ago.

"Open wider, Ivy. My cock won't fit and I wasn't joking about that bite threat. If you know what's good for you, you'll take my cock like a champ."

She gags as soon as my dick presses against her soft palate, but I rise up and scoot her whole body forward so her head is hanging off the side of the bed. Her throat opens up and it's so fucking beautiful, I get up and stand facing her hanging head, and shove my cock inside her warm mouth.

Her tied hands are immediately pushing, pressing on

my lower stomach, desperate to make me step back. I watch her fingers carefully, but she is either too busy dealing with being choked by my cock, or she likes it.

I pump a few times and then lean over her body and play with her pussy. Ivy gasps for air during this reprieve, and then she moans.

"I told you," I say. "I told you you'd like it. You won't be able to help yourself, Ivy."

I push another finger inside her, pumping her with the same rhythm she's sucking me. I want to eat her out so bad, but that comes later. So I push my hips into her head instead. Her hands reach for my balls. I have a moment of worry that she will grab those fuckers and never let go, but she doesn't. She cups them between her palms. Gently.

Yes. *Finally.*

I pull my cock out of her mouth and my fingers out of her pussy at the same time. The little moan tells me all I need to know. She's ready. I bend down and kiss her upside-down mouth, my tongue sweeping over hers. She kisses me back, her fingertips gripping my hair.

"You like it, don't you?"

She doesn't answer.

But she doesn't have to. I am back on the bed, pushing her legs open, my giant cock positioned and ready when she opens her eyes and stares into mine.

"What?" I lean down, her breasts pressing against my chest, and take her head in my hands as my cock slips inside her. "What?" I ask again. She's so fucking wet, there is no groan of pain. Just her back bucking up, her heavy panting coming out loud, and then her eyes close again.

I begin moving inside her. Slowly. And each movement she makes matches mine. Her knees come up to my shoulders, giving me even more access. She whimpers as I push deeper, her fisted hands pressing on my chest, but only because I know she can't help it.

Her head falls back over the side of the bed again, exposing her throat. Her lips press together like she wants to say, "Mmmmm," but her mind is blown and sounds do not exist.

I kiss her as I fuck her. I mumble everything she needs to hear in her mouth.

"Fuck yes," I say, unable to take my eyes off her face. I pump my hips hard, making her little mouth open, a squeal escaping into my mouth. "You like it, don't you?"

"Mmm," she says this time.

"Yeah," I say. "Fuck yeah, you like it hard, Ivy? You want me to pound my dick into you until you come?"

Her mouth opens but no words come out. I thrust and slip a finger inside. She sucks on it for a moment, but the intensity of what the other parts of me are doing make it impossible for her to keep it up.

So I just kiss her as we fuck. Over and over and over. Until I know she's so close, all I have to do is talk her into it.

"You dirty whore," I whisper. She moans back in response. "You sweet, filthy, dirty slut. Goddamn it, Ivy. Come or I swear to God, I'll keep you here forever. I'll never stop until you come."

Her whole body seizes up. Perfectly still. I thrust so hard, her hands come up and almost knock me out. I grab her hair and pump my hips. Her nearly helpless hands, not so helpless anymore as she digs her nails into my shoulder. All I can see is her reluctant passion and her exposed throat as she arches her body and explodes.

I switch gears, slowing down so she can moan out her release. I kiss her mouth so I can capture those sounds, just keep kissing her mouth until she stills. And then I pull out and come all over her tits.

We lie there, sucking in air like we've never tasted anything as good as oxygen. Spent, and tired, and satisfied. I flop back on the bed, tugging her body into me. She tucks her bound hands into my chest when I swing a leg over her thigh and hold her down. Mine. She's fucking mine and this seals the deal.

I stare out the window as her breathing evens out. The blackness out there, just like the blackness in here. And then Ivy sighs and presses her head into my neck, ready for sleep.

"How many times?" I ask.

"What?" she mumbles.

"How many times did you think I'd really rape you tonight?"

"Not now—"

"*Answer me*," I urge softly. "I want to know if you thought this was real or not. I want to know how deep that trust went. I want to know if you thought I'd really do that."

"Nolan—" she whimpers, opening her eyes.

I sweep her sweat-soaked hair aside and tuck it behind her ear. Her make-up is smeared all over her face. Dried saliva on the line of her jaw. There's a red blotch where I slapped her that last time. "Tell me, Ivy. I need to know."

And I do need to know. Because I can't... I can't be with someone who thinks I'd really hurt them. I can't outrun this reputation. I can't outrun the past. What that fucking girl turned me into. I can't go back, I can't change it, I can't even change *me*. Because there's nothing to change.

"There's nothing to change, Ivy."

She squints her eyes at me. She has no idea what I'm

talking about.

"I didn't do anything *wrong*," I say. I don't even know where this is coming from. It just pisses me off so bad. "I drew something. People draw things. People make slasher movies and never get accused of the shit they said I did. People write books, and poems, and songs and never get accused of being the fictional person in their art. But I did. Why?"

Ivy's bound hands come up to my cheeks. She spreads her hands apart as far as she can and places her palms on either side of my jaw. "I'm sorry."

"For what?" I ask. My voice is loud enough to echo off the high ceilings. "For letting that lying bitch change my whole life? For all the fucked-up things they said about me? Still say about me? I sat in that interrogation room, Ivy. For hours. And I had to listen to them say the vilest things about me. My lawyers were there, so they heard it too. And I couldn't say a word. Not one word. *Just shut the fuck up, Nolan.* That's all I kept telling myself in that room. Every time I turned on the TV there I was. The police weren't allowed to release the details of the evidence. The judge blocked it after my lawyers filed a motion for a gag order. But they hinted, Ivy. They hinted that I was one sick motherfucker."

"I'm sorry," Ivy says again. "I knew you would stop if I told you to. I had just the right amount of fear and uncertainty—"

"I *am* one sick motherfucker." I shake my head and roll off of her.

I'm crossing the room, reaching for the lock on the door when Ivy says, "Don't walk away, Nolan. Don't walk out, not now."

"Do you know why I do this?" I say, not even able to look at her.

"Tell me," Ivy says.

"*No*," I say, turning to look at her in the bed. "I'm asking you to tell me why. Why the fuck do I do this?"

She sits up on the bed and swings her legs over the side. Her hands are still bound. Her wrists are red and raw from the yellow rope. "Fuck," I say, walking back to her and reaching for them. I begin unwinding the yellow rope, trying my best not to look her in the eyes.

"I agreed to it."

"Why?" I ask, looking at her. "Why the fuck did you agree to it?"

"It was exciting."

I can't breathe.

"But that's not why you do it, is it?"

I can only shrug. "I don't know. I really don't. I don't know why, after all that shit that happened to me, why the fuck I'd be fixated on this stupid fucking fantasy."

"Maybe you're just trying to prove something to yourself, Nolan. Prove that you'd *never* have done something like that."

"It was just a drawing. A spur-of-the-moment drawing. Would I like to do a gang bang one day?" I laugh. "Maybe back then. Maybe that's just something twenty-year-old guys think about? We think a lot of fucked-up shit when we're twenty. But no. I didn't really want to do it. It was just... a fantasy. A drawing. And the next thing I know I'm on TV. I'm being pulled in for interrogation. And my friends are looking at me like I'm guilty. And I'm looking at them like *they're* guilty. And I still don't fucking know, Ivy. What the fuck they did to her that night that made her lie about me."

"Maybe she lied about all of you?"

"But why?"

"I don't know, Nolan." Ivy is pouting her lips at me.

Sad. I've made her sad.

"Do you have any idea how badly she fucked me up? She ruined my fucking life. And you know what?"

Ivy stands up and put her arms around my waist, pushing herself into my chest. Her body is chilled and I reach for a robe on a nearby chair. The robe I was going to wrap her in once the play was over. I place it over her shoulders and Ivy presses her cheek into my hot skin.

"What?" she asks. "Tell me."

"I hate myself for bringing you here. For asking you to do this with me. I fucking hate myself. Every time I find something good, I break it. And now look, I did this to you and I hate myself for it. That stupid lying bitch did this to me. She turned me into this fucked-up piece of shit. She made me become Mr. Romantic. Why? Why did I let her ruin my life?"

"Your life is pretty good, Nolan," Ivy says. "Even if she did ruin it for a little while, you got back up and made something of yourself."

"A club owner?" I laugh. "Really? This is all I've got to look forward to? I don't need the money, Ivy. I've got money. I've got family houses, like this one. More than I need. It's not about the money. Do you know what I was going to school for?"

Ivy tips her head up and looks at me. "Was it art?"

I laugh. "I guess it's obvious at this point."

"And your father?"

"He wanted me to be an artist. He was so pissed off when I didn't go back. He was so pissed off when I went into business. He cut me out of the will, stopped talking to me. Hoping his grudge would convince me to go back."

"But you didn't."

"Obviously."

"And you regret it, don't you? Is that why you bought

that land in the desert? To make something beautiful out of the ugliness? I mean, I haven't seen your clubs, and I'm sure they're nice. But a resort implies a very different level of clientele. And talk about a challenge. Borrego Springs is not a guaranteed win, is it?"

"I don't know, really. I'm just…" I look down at Ivy. God, she is so pretty. And sweet. "I'm just looking for something *good*. The land was cheap. No one wanted it. And I could relate to that, you know? I could relate to the feeling of being… discarded. I don't want to spend my life thinking about stocking the bar with alcohol, or DJ's, or all the other shit that goes with running clubs. I want more, Ivy. It might be wrong to want more, but there it is. I want more. I want this resort to work. I need this fucking resort to *work*."

CHAPTER FORTY

IVY

God, he is so broken right now. I don't like it. I hate it, in fact. He is a good person. "I was a little scared, Nolan. But every time I got to that point, you were there with something reassuring. The pretty picture stuff. The laugh. Kissing me behind the knee. I knew it was a fantasy. Even when I didn't. I trusted you to just be... so goddamned good at what you do that I let myself believe. I believed in *you*, Mr. Romantic."

Nolan shakes his head, but I get a small smile.

"And," I say, "you're in luck. Because I told you earlier. I have a great plan for Hundred Palms Resort. I'm here to save you from certain doom."

"Is that right?" He smiles bigger this time.

"Yes. I have my presentation all geared up and ready—aww, I think I left my purse in your car." I get a small laugh out of him for that remark and it lifts my spirits. I can't stand to see him this way. I never once thought about how his past might affect the way he acts now. Not really. I made lots of assumptions. Made lots of accusations, in fact. But it never even entered my mind that he'd be repressing pent-up anger and sadness over what he lost that night. Not just his life, but his sense of self.

"Want me to fly back and get it?" Nolan asks.

"Are we done here tonight?"

"Do you want to be done?"

"Um, no. I can see there's something going on in the bathroom, Mr. Romantic. I want whatever all that is for."

Nolan takes my hand and leads me towards the

bathroom. There's soft flickering light making shadows on the walls, and when we enter, the sight takes my breath away.

"You did this?"

"Do you like it?"

I love it. The entire room is filled with candles. And there's a balcony on the far end, also filled with candles. This is what I saw from outside on the helipad.

"I made that pilot come in here and set it all up before he met us out in back. He was pretty pissed about it."

"Are we taking a bath?"

Nolan walks over to the tub and checks the water. It's still steaming. There are pink rose petals floating on top of the water and scattered in between are small ivy leaves.

"God, you really are romantic."

"Well, I have more plans for this than meets the eye." He drops his pants and takes off his thoroughly wrinkled dress shirt, throwing it on the ground.

I can't stop my grin, so I step forward and dip a toe into the water. "It's hot!" But it feels wonderful after all we did tonight. I step all the way in and the memory of the cold pool water disappears into the thick steam. "Are you coming in?" I ask.

Nolan nods, then gets in behind me and sits down, hissing from the heat. "Sit, Ivy. This is where I make it all better."

I sit and lean back. His strong hands massage my shoulders as I relax and let the heat overtake me. My body is exhausted, but in a very good way. Nolan leans back and I lean with him. He hikes my leg over his, spreading my legs open so he can reach down and begin to stroke me softly. He doesn't enter me. I'm glad, too. Just strokes lightly so that the familiar throbbing is back between my legs.

Mr. Romantic: A Mister Standalone

"I'm sorry," he says. "But I can't let this go to waste."

"What—Ahhh!"

The hot wax is dripping down my breast. It makes it to the tip of my nipple, then merges with the water and hardens.

"It's your turn, Ivy. Just relax and enjoy it."

I close my eyes and let him do whatever he wants. Which, it turns out, is everything I want too. The wax is hot and erotic. His fingers are gentle and perfect. I come three times in the tub. One as he plays with the candles. Once when he sits me on the ledge of the tub and licks my pussy like he's starving. And once when I suck him off and swallow everything he has to offer.

Later, when we're clean and tired in all the right ways, aching in all the right places, and relaxed enough to start thinking of sleep, he leads me out of this room and takes me through this maze of a house and into another one.

Fresh sheets on the bed, fresh candles ready to be lit, pink rose petals scattered all over the floor, and the softest silk lingerie.

That seals the deal for me.

I watch him fall asleep, my body tugged up tight against his, like he's afraid I'll walk out in the middle of the night.

I'm in love. I might not be the most experienced woman, but I know what I'll be missing if Mr. Romantic ever gets away.

Everything.

I'll be missing everything.

CHAPTER FORTY-ONE

NOLAN

The helicopter jolts me from sleep and I'm up and looking for pants before the sound fades. Mysterious. *Fuck*, I think, searching the other room for my clothes. I forgot all about him.

I pull the pants up and forget the shirt, just hop down the steps to the back of the house. By the time I get to the family room, Pax is coming through the massive double glass doors.

"Thanks for picking up, you asshole," Pax says. "I thought you were dead or something. I should've figured you were getting your dick sucked."

"Hey." I point at him. "Ivy is here, so shut the fuck up. And I left my phone in my pants." Which I fish out right now to prove my point. Pax has called fifteen times, no voicemail.

"Yeah, well, about Ivy," Pax says. "This is some fucked-up shit and I'm sorry I have to be the one to break it to you."

"What are you talking about?"

"Everything, man. Your sister—"

"What? What's Claudette have to do with anything?"

Pax ignores me, just walks over to the bar, reaches under the counter, pulls out a tumbler, then finds the most expensive bottle of Scotch on the top shelf and pours himself at least four fingers. He gulps a healthy dose and then says, "Ahh. I really fucking like working out of this house. You rich assholes have everything here."

"What? You've never even been here before." But as soon as the words come out of my mouth, I know I'm wrong.

"I do business out of here all the time, dumbass."

"This is not your house, Mysterious. Where do you get off doing business here?"

"Hey," Pax says with a shrug. "What's yours is mine and what's mine is mine. That goes for all the other Mister Assholes who dragged me down with them ten years ago. Just think of it as my way of getting even."

"I didn't drag you into anything."

"The hell you didn't. I know that bitch blew you that night. I saw it. I see everything, Nolan," he says, tapping his head with his glass. "So fuck off. Your family never uses this house anyway."

"That's not the fucking point, Pax. You don't just use other people's shit."

"When your name is Paxton Vance you do. Now, do you want to hear the total fucking shitstorm I just dug up about your sister? Or do you want me to slap down a Benjamin to pay for the drink and swim back to the mainland?"

Somehow when Pax says it, swimming from Martha's Vineyard to the mainland doesn't sound ridiculous. I have no doubt in my mind that if I told him to leave, he'd jump off the fucking dock and disappear. Not die, mind you. Just disappear. I have a feeling the Atlantic Ocean couldn't kill Paxton Vance even if it was trying.

"Just get on with it," I say, waving my hand in a rolling motion.

"Well…" he starts, then gulps the rest of his drink and slams the glass down on the bar as he breathes out the burn. "Your sister is psycho. Your girlfriend is her target. And I hate to be the one to tell you this, even though I think you're a total dick. But your dad is dying."

I just stare at him. "What?"

"Your sister—"

"Fuck my sister, Pax! My father?"

"Cancer, dude." Pax shrugs and it even comes off as genuine. "And I got a hold of his will—"

"How?"

"Would you just shut the fuck up? I'm not telling you *how*. Trade secrets, asshole." He scowls at me and then continues. "Anyway. That will you thought you were cut out of?"

"Yeah?" My heart is racing.

"Not so, my soon-to-be billionaire friend. Your sister was the one cut out. Turns out your old man was quite the cheater before you were born. Claudette isn't your sister. Well, she is, I guess. At least half. She was cut out several years ago. You were added back the day your father was diagnosed. He's not doing well. They expect him to die any day."

I just stand there, stunned. Pax grabs another glass and pours me a drink. I take it and gulp. "What the fuck?" I ask him, grimacing from the whiskey.

"Well, I'll try to piece it together as best I can. But bear with me, I just got all this tonight."

I am suddenly disgusted at the thought of Paxton digging through my family history.

"Listen, I know you don't like me, but I'm straight with you, right? I've always been straight with you guys. So what I'm gonna say needs to be taken at face value and then we gotta get your girlfriend out of here so—"

He's interrupted by the doorbell. "Who the fuck is that?" I ask.

Pax has a huge gun out and he's pointing it in every direction at once, morphing into some Navy SEAL clearing a building on the spot. "Here," he says, whipping another gun out of his jacket. He tosses it to me. I catch it, because it's a fucking gun and no sane person throws one at you. "Keep it close. This shit is going down now." And then he waves the gun at the hallway and says, "Answer the door."

CHAPTER FORTY-TWO

IVY

The mattress sinks down as Nolan gets back in bed. "What was that all about?" I ask sleepily.

He grabs my hands and is wrapping them in rope before I can even open my eyes. "What are you doing?" I smile, try to turn, and take a punch to the head.

My vision blurs and then everything goes black as a hood is placed over my head and a cord of rope ties it around my neck. "Nolan!" I scream. "What the fuck? Stop! *Stop!*"

He doesn't stop. He hits me again, and again. I am shocked beyond belief. And then the words I was so successful in keeping at bay tonight as we had our fantasy pop into my head.

He really *is* a rapist. And I'm the dumbest girl on earth.

I kick and land it somewhere, his chest or his back. He goes flying and I scramble in what I think is the opposite direction. I fall off the bed, hit my head, but keep going. I'm crawling across the floor when he grabs my ankle and pulls. I twist my body, kick him once, and land it squarely on what I think is his jaw.

He roars in anger and pain and this is when I realize... I'm not being attacked by Nolan.

A heavy body rests on mine. I gasp for breath as a hand cups my mouth on the other side of the hood. I breathe in the foul-smelling chemical and everything just disappears...

CHAPTER FORTY-THREE

NOLAN

"It's the cops." I can see them the second the glass-front doors come into view as I turn a corner. Pax is approaching from off to the left, so he can't see them, but I can see him.

"Shit," Pax says. "OK, play it cool. We don't know why they're here, so let's figure that out first. Just..."

"I know what to do."

And I do. We've been here before, right? I know all the loopholes. I know exactly what to say. And what not to say.

I walk up to the door and pull it open. "Is there a problem?" I ask. There is most definitely a problem. Six patrol cars are in my driveway with lights flashing. More sheriff deputies are on my doorstep than I can count offhand.

"Sorry to disturb you this late, Mr. Delaney. But we're looking for Ivy Rockwell. Is she here with you?"

"How did you get through my gate?"

"Um..." The deputy looks nervous, but another officer is there to save him.

"The gate was open, sir."

"The gate was not open. I didn't come here tonight using a road, so the gate was not open."

"Is Ivy Rockwell here, Mr. Delaney?" the first guy repeats. "We got an anonymous tip to check on her house tonight and found her door wide open. We went inside and found this letter signed by you." The deputy holds up the letter I wrote Ivy and placed in the box I had her dress delivered in.

"Close the door, Nolan," Pax says from off to my left. He's got his gun ready, pointed up towards the ceiling, and he's hidden from view by the hallway. My gun is in my hand, hidden behind my back. They will shoot me if they see it. I know this for a fact. They will fucking shoot me if they see it. "Close. The. Door."

I tap the door and it swings closed with a smart *click*.

"You don't want to do this, Delaney," the deputy says through the glass. "You don't want us to come back with a warrant."

He's wrong. I do want to do this. And if they have to leave and come back with a warrant I can get a hold of the situation. Because everything happening right now is a little bit too familiar.

"Step away," Pax says. "Get out of their line of sight."

I turn the lock on the door first. Not that it will stop them. But if they break the glass, there will be a fantastic alarm and security companies will be notified. They are all yelling at me from outside now, but I don't care. I back away.

"What the fuck?" I ask Pax once I'm in the hallway with him. "Why the fuck are they here?"

"What are they going to find, Nolan? What kind of shit went down tonight?"

He's not asking me if I killed her or anything. He's asking what kind of kink I was up to. "Her shoes are in the pool. Her clothes are outside, panties are ripped down the middle, out there as well. There's lube on the stairs, which we can't retrieve without the cops seeing, since it's a straight-line view. There's rope in one of the bedrooms. She's... got some marks on her wrists. Maybe her face, but I think those are gone by now. I didn't come inside her."

"I tell you what, Romantic. You sure as fuck don't

make life easy."

"It was planned, Pax."

"I figured that out, asshole. I'm not accusing you. But we should wake her up and get her to come down and talk to them. Outside," he stresses. "They cannot come in the house without a warrant. Otherwise we're gonna be on the news tomorrow."

"But who knew she was here?"

"Your sister?"

"No," I say, as we walk to the other end of the house so we can take the back stairs instead of the main ones in the foyer. "I haven't told her shit."

"She has people following you, Nolan. I've been on your case for one day and I know this."

I say nothing. Fucking Claudette has gone off the deep end.

The path back to the bedroom Ivy and I were sleeping in is complicated. This whole fucking house is complicated. More than twenty thousand square feet and filled with bedrooms, storerooms, garages, offices, and even two separate guest houses outside. By the time we reach the right hallway, I'm relieved. "Ivy?" I say, walking into the bedroom. "Ivy?" I call again, looking in the bathroom. "Where the fuck are you—"

And that's when I see what's on the bed.

Pax crossed the room and snatches it up just as I'm about to.

"What the fuck?" I ask him. "How the hell did that get in here?"

But Pax is stunned silent. And I can't blame him. I know this little piece of history he's holding. I know because the cops showed it to me once when I was being questioned.

I just didn't know it was *his*. His little part in the whole

Mister Browns rape case.

"What the fuck is going on?" Pax asks. "Is your little girlfriend part of this?"

"No, fuck that. She's here—" But my words trail off as I step around the other side of the bed and see blood on the floor.

"*Someone* is here," Pax says. "Someone who knows very intimate things about what we did that night."

"They took Ivy," I say.

"Nolan, they can't get off this island. They can't even get over to the main part of the island. There's cops out front. No one is getting past them. I didn't see a boat at the dock when I flew in. So she's still here. In this house somewhere. Where would she be?"

"Fuck me. This place is huge, Pax. There's so many places."

"Choose two," Pax says, pointing his gun at me and then himself. "And we'll each take one."

"The attic and... the basement, I guess. The fucking attic is six thousand square feet. The basement probably the same. But she could be anywhere. We have fifteen bedrooms. Hell, she could be in a bathroom. We have twenty of those."

"Well, we're not going to find her just standing here, so let's go." Pax takes off, disappears into the hallway, then peeks his head back in a few seconds later. "How the fuck do I get to the attic?"

Ivy.

That's the only word on my mind as we run through the hallways. I point to another set of stairs, Pax going up, taking them three at a time, and I hop down until I'm in the main room of the basement.

Everything is lit up. Everything is on. The TVs in various rooms. The lights above the pool table. The surround sound is blasting something from the media room. The doors leading out to the pool are wide open and the sea wind is blowing the curtains like ribbons.

"Ivy," I call. "Ivy, can you hear me?"

But she can't. She can't hear anything because of the music, and the movie, and the wind. I walk over to the master control for the surround sound and turn it off. There is still the sound of the TVs, so I enter each room, one by one, gun ready, and turn them off too.

And when I get through them all, I realize something. She's not here.

CHAPTER FORTY-FOUR
IVY

I wake up lying on a cold concrete floor. My eyes flutter as I try to open them, but all I see is a fuzzy glare. My head is splitting with a headache and everything is silent.

There is no one here.

"Help," I say, my voice hoarse. "Help," I try again, a little louder.

But then a black shadow moves in one corner and someone walks towards me wearing a ski mask and bulky clothing.

"Why are you doing this?"

A photograph floats down to the ground in front of me. I can't even focus yet, so it takes time for me to get a good look at it. To realize what it is.

Nolan and me. Outside near the pool. He's ripping my panties off and I'm just standing there, letting him. Someone has written Rape Me over the top of the photo.

I look up at the masked person and shake my head. "That's not what happened."

My captor says nothing. Just walks slowly towards me.

I panic and start thrashing. My hands are tied behind my back, and every time I twist, my raw skin screams for me to stop. I manage to get into a sitting position, but only because a hand reaches down and grabs me by my hair and pulls me up.

The person leans down and a familiar smell permeates the air.

A sickly smell that tells me exactly who this person is.

I wait for words to explain why this is happening, but none come. I am dragged across the floor until I'm at the entrance to a bedroom. The figure points to the bed inside, lit only by a small lamp of a bedside table.

I shake my head and say, "No."

I am slapped and kicked and pushed until I am absolutely on that bed, lying down, in my pretty lingerie as my feet are tied to a bedpost.

Where am I? Where is this place? There's no windows, just this bed and just this one light.

I struggle to free my hands and realize I'm tied up with the same rope Nolan used. His words come back to me. *If you ever get stuck the rope stretches. Just wriggle around until it loosens. It might take a while, but you're not stuck.*

I struggle some more and realize he was right. The rope *is* stretchy. I'm not stuck. And I'm not going to let this happen either. I get one burning wrist through one loop and the whole rope becomes loose. My hands are flying behind my back as my legs are tied tighter.

And then the black ski mask faces me. I know before he takes off the mask who he is.

Richard.

He kneels on the bed and then straddles my waist, gripping my breasts firmly. "Is this how you like it, Ivy? Is this why you never let me fuck you? I'm not abusive enough?" His smile, mixed in with that sick cologne, makes my stomach turn. "Well, if this is what you need, I'm happy to accommodate you."

I reach for the bedside lamp and swing it against his head. He goes reeling to the side, falling off the bed, and I'm already trying to untie the knots at my ankles. I mess up so many times as Richard comes to his senses on the floor next to the bed. My heart is racing so fast. My breathing is nothing but panic.

I get one leg free just as he stands back up and lunges for me. I kick him in the chest with the heel of my foot and he goes down again, this time shaking his head like I stunned him. Blood is pouring down his temple as I scramble back to the other side of the bed. But I'm still prisoner. I'm held in place by the one length of rope. I scream when he gets to his feet again. "Nolan!" I scream. "Nolan!" I don't know where I'm at, or if he's even close by. But I know that there is no way I can get my foot untied before Richard gets to me.

"He's coming," I say, still frantically trying to get the last knot out of the rope. "He's coming. And… and… his friend is coming too. The bad one. You know that bad one. Mr. Mysterious," I spit.

"You're gonna let them all fuck you, aren't you, Ivy? You stupid little whore." He slaps my face so hard, I almost black out. "This is what you're been holding out for? A gang rape from the most infamous rapists in the country? Well"—he laughs—"I'm sorry to disappoint you with just little old me tonight. But I'm sure you'll still love it."

From some far off place I hear Nolan's voice. Richard stops everything. Goes completely still.

"Ivy!" Nolan is yelling. "Ivy, Ivy, Ivy!"

"Here!" I scream.

And then Richard's hand is over my mouth and the cold blade of a knife is pressed to my throat.

"Scream nice and loud for your boyfriend, Ivy. Nice and loud now."

CHAPTER FORTY-FIVE

NOLAN

"Nolan!"

Ivy is screaming. It's faint, like she's far away. But she *is* here. Where? I've checked every room. *Where?*

"Ivy!" I yell. "Pax," I yell again. I start searching the basement again. Where the fuck can she be? All the doors to each room are open. She's not in any of them. "Pax!" I yell again. And then I take out my phone and text him.

Basement. Now.

"Ivy!" I yell.

I hear her respond. "Here!"

But where? Why the fuck can't I find her?

"Think, Nolan. Think, think, think."

Boots crash down the stairs and Pax comes rushing into the basement, gun drawn, pointing it at every open door and every dark corner before he stops and looks at me. "Where? Who the hell is messing with us?"

"I can hear her." We stop and listen, but there's no more calling from Ivy. "Fuck!" I grab my hair and shake my head. I know what that silence means. "I've checked every fucking room. It's like she's stuck inside the walls or—wait. I know where she is. The safe room."

"What safe room?"

"The house was built with a panic room, Pax. It's on the far side of the media room."

I take off running, Pax following me, and enter the media room. The movie is still playing without sound. Some slasher movie. A bigger-than-life girl is screaming her silent scream as we walk past and I open a door that appears to lead to a mechanical room. But when we step

301

around the giant furnace, there's another door.

"What's the code?" Pax demands. "We need the fucking code, Nolan."

I know the code. I know the code. I know the code.

I know I know the code. It's been the same since I was a little kid and we first bought this house.

You are a target, Nolan.

My father's words in my head.

I make you a target. So if anything ever happens, you run in here and you lock yourself inside.

"What's the fucking code?" Pax yells.

A scream comes from inside. Clear as fucking day because it's on the little speaker near the keypad used for two-way communication.

A broken, crackling voice comes out of the speaker next. "The code was changed tonight, Mr. Romantic. You don't know the code."

I take the butt of my gun and smash the cameras. One above the door, one behind me, one to the left.

Pax catches on quickly and finds more, each one is smashed.

I pull him close to me and whisper, "There's a master code. And I do know it. No one else on this fucking planet knows it, because I was the one who set it. So whoever this is, they got a code from one of two people. Claudette or my father."

"Your bitch of a sister is behind this, I know it. I'm gonna fucking kill her when I get inside there."

"She's not here, Pax. She sent someone else to do this. And we can make plans for that later. Right now we've only got one chance to save Ivy. We bust in and kill whoever it is on the other side of that door."

CHAPTER FORTY-SIX

IVY

The next thing I know an alarm is screaming. I cover my ears as Richard gets off me, throwing the knife down on the floor as he reaches for a gun.

My fingers are instantly back on the rope around my ankle, but another blow to the head knocks me over, right off the bed, so most of me is on the floor, but my one ankle is still tied to the damn post.

And then... shouting. Voices yelling. Nolan, and someone else, and Richard. Guns are going off, and a bullet hits the concrete wall just off to my left.

I sit up as best as I can and reach for my ankle as the men yell threats and shoot at each other.

There's a loud thumping of feet above my head somewhere. People are here. Many, many people. A whole army of people from the sound of it.

"Ivy!" Nolan yells. "Get down!"

But I'm so close. I'm so close. Just one more knot and—I'm free!

Richard is suddenly next to me, pulling me up by my hair again. I grab his balls and pull so hard, I get a sick, sick feeling in my stomach. His gun goes off and a sharp pain shoots through my body.

I scream, but he falls, and I fall, and then I ignore the pain and scoot under the bed. I crawl for my life as a warm pool of blood puddles underneath me.

CHAPTER FORTY-SEVEN

NOLAN

The guy shoots straight. I'll give him that. The bullets are flying. Pax has disappeared. Hit, or waiting, or hell, maybe he thinks my girlfriend isn't worth dying for.

I think she's worth dying for.

Ivy screams, and when I peek my head out from behind the corner, I see the man fall just as another shot goes off. This time Ivy's scream is serious. It's a scream of severe pain and I know she's been shot. More bullets fly at me as I make a break for the bed. Ivy's fingertips are reaching out from under the bed, and I pull her out, sliding her along the smooth concrete floor, and then jump up on the bed and I don't even bother thinking twice.

I shoot that motherfucker in the head.

A second later there's cops everywhere. Not just deputies, but men in tactical gear. Rifles longer than my arm pointing at me. Red laser dots dancing on everything in the room.

You will always be a target, Nolan. Don't ever let them get you.

But I'm not their target tonight.

So I drop my gun and slide down on the floor next to Ivy. She's bleeding and she's crying, but she's still alive. And that's the only thing that matters.

CHAPTER FORTY-EIGHT

IVY

Nolan's bright green eyes are the first thing I see when I wake up. The hospital room is cold and the air smells funny. But he's there and that's all I care about.

"Hey," he says, brushing some hair away from my eyes. "How you feeling?" He looks tired. And he's wearing dress pants and a t-shirt that says *Property of Massachusetts State Police* on the front.

"What happened?" I ask, trying to sit up as Nolan urges me to lie back. "Where's Richard?"

"*Richard?* You knew him?"

"He was my ex-boyfriend. The boring one."

Nolan's smile lights up my whole life and when he laughs, I laugh with him. Just before I start to cry.

"Hey," he says, slipping into bed with me. His arm slides under my back, gently, so he doesn't disturb my sling. "It's OK. You're OK. They removed the bullet and stitched your arm all up. You're fine, Ivy. You're gonna be fine."

"He was going to rape me, Nolan. He was—"

"Shhh," Nolan says. "Stop. It's over. OK?" He looks me in the eyes and then kisses me softly on my lips. "All that stuff is over now."

And then he lies back with me, rests his head on my pillow and places his hand over my heart.

"We're gonna start fresh, Ivy Rockwell. So just relax. I've got this."

CHAPTER FORTY-NINE

NOLAN

"So..." Match says. "Big doin's, huh?"

"You're next, asshole."

"Nah, not me. I'm fine just the way I am. You and Perfect can keep your newly domesticated lives. I'm just fine with the way things are."

"Never mind that shit," Perfect says. "We have a problem."

"A big problem," Mysterious says as he cleans his gun on Perfect's dining room table. "A very big fucking problem."

Ivy and Ellie are out shopping. We're here on official Mister business, but the girls don't know that. Ivy's arm is healing nicely. She might need another surgery or two to remove bone shards if they become a problem, but she's OK. She's good. We're both good.

"Where the fuck is Corporate?" Match says. "He's late. Why is he fucking late?"

"I told you he wasn't gonna show. He's got some big deal going on. Said he'll read the Cliff's Notes when he gets back."

"Well, that's fucked up," Match says. "If you're a target, then we're all targets."

"Where the fuck is Claudette?" Mysterious asks, never taking his eyes off the gun.

"I dunno," I say, frustrated. "I've had people looking for her since she missed the funeral."

My father died. Just two days after all that shit went down at the Martha's Vineyard house. We hadn't been close for years and even though it would make a nice story to say we patched things up in the end, we didn't. He was in a coma by the time I got to the hospital in San Diego. I've been to more hospitals in the last two weeks than I have in my whole life.

But it didn't matter that we didn't get to talk. I know now. I know why my mother ended up divorcing him. I know why Claudette was never welcome at our house in Florida. I know why my father kept her with him.

I don't know why she was cut out of the will and I was put back in. That is still part of the mystery. But it makes sense that she attached herself to my hip these past six months. Why she offered up some of her own money to get that resort started. She was cut out of the will and wanted back in. She was playing the good big sister part to make that happen. But she was doing more than that. She was setting me up. How she came up with Ivy to make that happen though? That is also still a mystery. But I know—I feel it in my gut—I know she set me up with Ivy. I know it was her who forged Ivy's résumé. Sent that invitation. How many people know about the silver envelopes we use? Not many. People connected with the old case. They know. And Claudette certainly qualifies as one of them. I fucking know it was Claudette who put all the events of the past few weeks into motion.

But why?

She's a devious fucking cunt, that's why. And I have no doubt that her mother was the same kind of woman. I know my father wasn't perfect, but he was not a psychopath.

Claudette is.

I was waiting for her to show her face at the funeral, and when she didn't come, I knew. She's on some kind of revenge vendetta. She won't get one penny of my father's money. Not one penny. But hey, if she wants to fight that shit, I'm ready. I'm waiting. I'm gonna take her down from the inside out.

She wasn't at the MV house. In fact, there was not one shred of evidence that could link her back to Ivy's ex-boring-boyfriend. But we all know it was her.

There are very few people who have access to schedule the jet. Claudette is one of them. The only one connected to me.

"I still don't understand what Boring Richard had to do with this," I say.

"Did you ask Ivy?" Match says.

"She had some kind of argument with him when she went home for dinner the Sunday before all this happened."

"About what?"

"Me, I guess. He looked me up. Told Ivy I was a deviant or something. Told her to stay away from me."

"But why?" Match asks again.

"How should I know, Oliver? I don't see the connection."

"I do," Perfect says. "Or at least I'm starting to. People are coming back. Allen came back into my life the same day Ellie popped into it. And somehow Allen and that Ellen Abraham woman were connected too. I don't know how, but I know they were. Same thing with you, Romantic. You find a girl; your sister goes nuts. Now what we don't know is what part Claudette played in those events ten years ago. Where does she fit in? Because I already know where Allen fits in. Too bad Boring Richard is dead. We could've put some pressure on him to give up the answers we still need. I should try and find Ellen Abraham. See if she might talk."

"Yeah," Mysterious says, snapping his gun back together with satisfying clicks. "And Boring Richard left me a present on the bed up in Nolan's house. So that's another clue that he's connected to all this somehow." He looks up at me and I see it. I see just how dangerous Mysterious really is. He's out for blood over that little gift. And I don't know how he managed it, but Mysterious picked up every piece of damning evidence left out at the MV house. The cops never saw any evidence of what Ivy and I were doing that night. He got his own reminder of the past safely tucked out of sight too.

Got to hand it to him. When Mysterious takes a job, he's not fucking around.

"Well," Match says, "we're just gonna have to take care of business. That's what my old man always told me. He always said, 'Oliver, my boy, when the shit hits the fan, you just turn that fucker around.'"

"Your father's a regular poet," Mysterious says.

"Maybe nothing's happening?" I say. "Not the way we think it is. I mean, we don't have anything to go on. We just have your old vendetta with Allen, Perfect. And my sister is a crazy cunt. Maybe that's all there is to it?"

"It's not," Mysterious says, stashing his gun in his pants. "You can't overlook the fact that Mac had some weird woman fucking with Ellie at work at the same time Allen was fucking with him. And now we have two examples. Because Boring Richard was fucking with you at the same time as Claudette. Why was he looking you up?"

"He told Ivy her roommate told him to. But she asked her roommate after, and she said that never happened."

"Yup," Mysterious says as he looks inside a duffle bag. "What we have here is a classic tag-team operation happening, my friends. One operative distracts while the other takes care of business. And if anything else happens, I'm gonna do exactly what Old Man Match said. Turn that shit back on them. And they do not want to be my target. Whoever the fuck *they* are."

"Someone needs to get a hold of Corporate and make sure everything's cool with him," I say.

"I'll handle him," Match says. "We have a business deal going, so he's gonna show up for that in a few days for sure."

"All right," Perfect says, peeking through the curtains of his front room. "The girls are back, so just..." He stops and looks at Mysterious. "Dude, get rid of the guns." Mysterious has another one out, all ready to start cleaning it when Perfect says this.

Mysterious grunts, but he stashes it back into the pack he brought with him, hikes it over his shoulder, and walks out the front door.

"Jesus Christ," Perfect says. "He's gonna kill someone."

And then Match and Perfect both look at me. Because even though Mysterious has killer written all over him, I'm the one who pulled the trigger this time.

"Maybe someone has it coming," Match says, shrugging his shoulders and sliding his shades down his face. He turns and leaves it at that. Following Mysterious out the door.

Perfect and I watch Ivy and Ellie talk to them for a few seconds before they both get into Match's Hummer and drive off.

Maybe someone does, I think as I watch them go.

Maybe all that shit we've put up with for the past ten years is about to come back around. Only maybe this time, it's not the Misters who have to stand in front of the fan while people throw shit.

Maybe it's someone else's turn.

NOLAN

"Just be nice," Ivy says as she straightens my tie outside her parents' house.

"Hey," I say, "they don't call me Mr. Nice for nothing."

"They don't call you Mr. Nice *at all*, Nolan. Now stop." She shoots me a sideways grin as the word comes out. We haven't had another rape fantasy. And I'm not saying we'll never do it again, but I'm over it. It was fun, but it was a stressful fucking night. And every time I think about yellow rope, I see Ivy's foot, tied to that bedpost as the guns went off and that sick fuck, Boring Richard, shot her.

I don't need to prove I'm innocent to Ivy. She knows.

I don't need to prove anything to anyone, I decide. Fuck them all.

The front door opens and the Reverend William Rockwell stands there looking very much like a pastor's daughter's father.

Well, except him, I guess.

"Come in!" Sophia, Ivy's mother, calls. Ivy slips past her father and leaves us there together. On the front stoop. He doesn't invite me in, so I shift my feet a little, wondering why I'm letting this conservative dinosaur make me nervous.

"You're not good enough for her," my father-in-law says.

I nod, pressing my lips together. "Yes, sir," I say. "I know that."

"And you eloped, so you're *never* going to be good

315

enough for her."

I nod again. "I know. I don't deserve her. Not one bit. And I'm going to spend the rest of my life thanking God for letting such a smart and beautiful woman be my wife." I have apologized profusely on the phone and email for weeks about the elopement. "We're already planning a real wedding, Mr. Rockwell. So we can make it official in your eyes."

He's never going to forgive me. Especially after I tell him she's pregnant.

"Hmmph," Rockwell says, stepping aside. "If you keep kissing ass like this, Delaney, then we might even like each other in about twenty years. Come in."

I step into his house and immediately feel at home. Ivy is everything my life was missing these past ten years.

And together we are building the best motherfucking resort the Southern California desert has ever seen. Ivy's marketing plan was a whole lot more than free rooms to pique interest in the San Diego corporate community. It was cooking class weekends with our professional chef. It was golf lesson weekends with our new resident pro. It was dark-sky stargazing with guest astronomers. It's a place for parties, and weddings, and anniversaries and corporate events.

In fact, my new career looks almost nothing like my old one. I might not have ever gotten that art degree, but I got something much better instead.

And it was just what I needed.

A beautiful new life with my beautiful new wife, Mrs. Romantic.

End of Book Shit

Welcome to the End of Book Shit (fondly called the EOBS in my little pond), the place where I get to say anything I want and readers have to listen. ;) Just kidding. I bet most people don't even bother reading these.

OK, so like most of my stories this one started out based in fact. If you read the Rock EOBS you know that I got a lot of the original premise from real life and if you read the Social Media series, you might've suspected I based it off something that really happened as well.

The Mister series is loosely based off another real event. All the characters are made up in my imagination. The settings are made up, the scenes---all fiction. But the basic premise—a group of guys get accused of something and suddenly their lives are turned upside down because the court of public opinion pronounces them guilty—is real.

My premise takes place ten years after the "big event" that changed their lives. And my questions are valid ones I think. What happens to people who endure social outrage on a vast scale? People who might not just get national attention, but global attention? How do they go on when the dust settles?

Well, this my version of how that scenario might play out. Mr. Perfect made pretty good use of his ten years between then and now, but Mr. Romantic? He's not so sympathetic. And the way it affected him is definitely not sympathetic.

But I feel for this guy. I always want to believe people are innocent. I root for people to be found not guilty. Not to get off. Not to avoid justice. But because I want them to be unequivocally innocent and I want that to be a final judgment in a court of law. I want to believe that people are good.

I have a master's degree in forensic toxicology. If you don't know what that is, it's basically drug testing. Biological analysis to determine what, if any, chemicals are inside the body of victims and perpetrators. And in my last semester we had to take an ethics class to prepare us for expert testimony in the courtroom. The one thing they hammered home in this class is pretty much the only thing that stuck with me. (I'm not a forensic toxicologist, right? I'm a writer. So I didn't do much in this field to make it stick). But that one thing was this – "It is far more ethical to let the guilty go free than it is to persecute the innocent."

I still believe that. While it sucks when a criminal gets off, it literally makes me sick to my stomach to think of an innocent person sitting in prison for something they didn't do.

So I like to believe that everyone is innocent unless there's a good reason not to.

Sadly, I'm a bad judge of guilt and innocence. Remember Laci Peterson? That pregnant lady who went missing just before Christmas in 2002? I wanted her husband to be innocent so bad. Not because I have some weird fixation with would-be murders. But because I want to believe that no man is capable of killing their pregnant wife and dumping her body in the ocean.

I was genuinely distraught when it became clear he was guilty. Lost my faith in humanity.

So when another high-profile case came on the news not long afterward I decided I wasn't going to invest my opinion again. I got burned with Laci Peterson's animal of a husband. I'm out of the guilt or innocence business.

But you know... you hear the news. You hear the evidence. You see the completely fucked up reaction of the media, hell almost the entire nation trying to lynch the people accused before they get to trial. And you form an opinion.

I had an opinion, I just told myself I didn't. I wasn't going to invest in these things anymore. I always lose. They are always guilty. So when the details of this case came out and it was found they were innocent—well, I got some of my faith back.

Not everyone is a monster. Sometimes people are set up. It absolutely happens. And for whatever reason, this case was one of them.

So when I started plotting the backstory for Mr. Perfect in February 2016 I decided I wanted it to be about a case like that. Ten years earlier a group of friends are accused of a terrible crime and maybe they did it, maybe they didn't, but they got off because the witness died.

Now this is not exactly how the real-life case went. And believe me, that one is pretty interesting. But the book isn't about that case. This isn't their story. It's just a story. One that could happen to anyone.

But then I started looking up what happened to these people after the case was over and that's where the backstory really came to life. That's when I knew it was what happened after that mattered.

No one gave a fuck about them after. No one cared that their lives were disrupted or that they had to find a way forward. No one cared about what they lost. No one even cared why they were accused in the first place.

This was my story. What did the public outcry do to these people? How did that experience of unjustified persecution change them?

This book is a look at five men, ten years later, and how one lie changed who they were forever. That's it. It's not a thinly veiled commentary on anything happening right now in the news and it's not a statement about how people are treated by society and the media if they find themselves wrapped up in something bigger than themselves.

It's not about any of that. It's just about these five fictional guys trying to come to terms with how one night turned into a nightmare.

Mr. Perfect did pretty well. We're all kind of proud of his reaction. He wanted to make the world a better place. Mr. Romantic? Well, not so much. He's a cynical asshole with a rape fantasy fetish. Maybe he was this guy before the lie, maybe he wasn't. Maybe that lie changed him for the better? He will never know because he can't see his alternate reality where that night never happened.

I try to write unlikable antiheroes. I think I do a pretty good job. But I also try and give you a reason to root for them as they find redemption.

Mr. Romantic isn't as dark as some of my characters. James Fenici is dark. Merc is dark. Hell, I think Ford is probably darker than Mr. Romantic. So that's why there's no trigger warning in my blurb. This isn't a dark book and if you think it is, you missed the point. All Mr. Romantic wants is an answer. Why? Why was he a target? Why did people lie about him? Why does he have to live with a stigma for the rest of his life over something he never did?

And it turns out, that's all each of the Misters want. Why?

Well, if you read the whole series you're gonna see why. Mr. Corporate will have his own demons to deal with. Mr. Mysterious will have you questioning everything. And Mr. Match will get that final answer, no matter what he has to do.

Stick with me, I've got a story to tell. And I promise you, it's something you've never read before.

If you'd like to hang out with me on Facebook I have a private fan group called Shrike Bikes. Just ask to join and someone will approve you as soon as they see it. I am in that group chatting with the fans every single day and we have a lot of giveaways and fun stuff going all the time. Especially around release days. I usually do a takeover and give away all kinds of stuff related to the new release, so come on by and say hi.

If you enjoyed this book please consider leaving me a review where you purchased it. I'm still indie. And the success of each and every book I put out depends on readers like you leaving their thoughts and opinions about the story in a review.

Thank you for reading, thank you for reviewing, and I'll see you in the next book.

Julie
JA Huss

About the Author

JA Huss is the New York Times and USA Today bestselling author of more than twenty romances. She likes stories about family, loyalty, and extraordinary characters who struggle with basic human emotions while dealing with bigger than life problems. JA loves writing heroes who make you swoon, heroines who makes you jealous, and the perfect Happily Ever After ending.

You can chat with her on Facebook, Twitter, and her kick-ass romance blog, New Adult Addiction. If you're interested in getting your hands on an advanced release copy of her upcoming books, sneak peek teasers, or information on her upcoming personal appearances, you can join her newsletter list and get those details delivered right to your inbox.

JA Huss lives on a dirt road in Colorado thirty minutes from the nearest post office. So if she owes you a package from a giveaway, expect it to take forever. She has a small farm with two donkeys named Paris & Nicole, a ringneck parakeet named Bird, and a pack of dogs. She also has two grown children who have never read any of her books and do not plan on ever doing so. They do, however, plan on using her credit cards forever.

JA collects guns and likes to read science fiction and books that make her think. JA Huss used to write homeschool science textbooks under the name Simple Schooling and after publishing more than 200 of those, she ran out of shit to say. She started writing the I Am Just

Junco science fiction series in 2012, but has since found the meaning of life writing erotic stories about antihero men that readers love to love.

JA has an undergraduate degree in equine science and fully planned on becoming a veterinarian until she heard what kind of hours they keep, so she decided to go to grad school and got a master's degree in Forensic Toxicology. Before she was a full-time writer she was smelling hog farms for the state of Colorado.

Even though JA is known to be testy and somewhat of a bitch, she loves her #fans dearly and if you want to talk to her, join her_Facebook fan group where she posts daily bullshit about bullshit.

If you think she's kidding about this crazy autobiography, you don't know her very well.

You can find all her books on Amazon, Barnes & Noble, iTunes, and KOBO.

Made in the USA
Middletown, DE
04 April 2017